MISTS OF AFFLICTION

BOOK TWO OF

THE KEYSTONE ISLANDS SERIES

CHAPTER 1: NO STRINGS ATTACHED

Donovan tapped the transparent glass of his underground lab's observation room. A map of Earth filled the whole wall.

"You're not looking for the Phantom Queen again, are you?" his wife, Inara, asked as she maneuvered videos to a different wall.

Although she looked 30 years his younger, their life experiences amounted to the same age. The real Inara was born only two years after him. A few months ago, Donovan succeeded in uploading her consciousness and her memories into a younger, healthier body.

"She's going to make headlines sooner or later." Donovan's fingers swiped across the glass, spinning the globe in search of news. "She and the activists made so much noise in Cantera Bay before this all happened. Why the sudden change in tactics? What are they doing?"

Inara rolled her eyes and turned back to her work. Donovan didn't blame her. Every day since his ship sank to the bottom of the ocean, and the Activists teleported to earth, he obsessed over what they were doing over there. What did the Phantom Queen know about Doctor Pavarti's work that he didn't?

In America, two politicians made a drastic change in policy and opinion. But it was only on healthcare reform. Nothing sinister. He kept scanning.

"Donovan, Lab 64 is reporting they're ready for testing. Let's go down and watch." Inara called out.

Donovan didn't respond right away, so she persisted. "Come on, honey, you can do that later. This is important."

Donovan reluctantly swiped two fingers together, closing the globe and revealing the floor below them. A massive grid of large cubicle labs that stretched a quarter mile.

He moved to his left and opened a nearly invisible door. The noise of the labs below echoed across the cavernous roof. Smells of chemicals burning, mixing and reacting violently with each other wafted to his nose and he smiled. Nothing brought him more joy than his labs.

Together, he and Inara stepped quickly down the stairs that lined the wall, and down the middle hallway, where the largest cubicles were located.

Lab 64 was retrofitted differently than the others. It was among the largest labs in the whole building. The other labs were made of four thin walls under a ventilation shaft. The walls and roof on lab 64 were built with the strongest materials. The door was a airtight hatch that belonged on a submarine.

The door was open, and they walked in. The room was rectangular. Control panels lined the far wall, observation chairs lined the close wall. In the middle was a giant glass tank.

Donovan stepped in and all of the scientists tensed up. He made a calm down motion and sat in a chair just to the right of the door.

Inara took a seat next to him, clutching his hand in hers with an excited squeeze.

"Do you think it will work this time?" Inara asked.

"I've been looking over the specs, and I have high hopes." Donovan smiled.

Inara let out a fake laugh. "Something other than the Phantom Queen on your mind? I don't believe it."

Donovan nodded to the room in front of them. "Believe it. You know me. I can get distracted sometimes, but I try to make time for everything."

"We're ready to begin," reported an engineer.

Along the far wall, several engineers flipped switches and indicated safety parameters were all in place.

Inside the aquarium, on the left side, a large red circle began to glow brighter and brighter. Then, at peak brightness, a deluge of water shot through the hole and filled the aquarium almost instantly. The water crashed against the wall, but then the water calmed down.

"Everything's holding," an engineer reported. "The portal is stable, and the glass is easily handling the water pressure."

There was a series of cheers and Donovan and Inara stood up and clapped with them.

"Well done, everyone!" Donovan said to the group. "What a remarkable achievement. We now have a portal at the bottom of the ocean. But now for the next task, getting somebody through it. I believe I have a volunteer for the job, and I would like you to get this ready again. We are going to make history!"

The group cheered again, and then shut down the portal. Slowly, the water drained out of the tank, and Donovan and Inara walked down another hall in the maze of cubicles.

"Who's volunteering?" Inara asked as she put his arm through his.

"I am." Donovan said. Then, seeing the concern in her eyes added, "Sort of."

They made their way to another cubicle. Again, different from the others. Locked doors, one way windows, security guards, and cameras.

They looked through the window at the current resident on lock down. A young man with black, curly hair, and skinny arms. Former Councilor Colin. Of course, the person in there did not believe he was Colin. The person in there was planted with the consciousness and memory of a young girl named Skylar Dixon.

"Skylar?" Inara asked.

"She's the one who'll have memories of the location." Donovan said.

"Memories don't persist through portals."

Donovan smiled and opened the door. "I may have found a loophole for that."

Colin, or rather, Skylar, looked up with wide eyes and cowered slightly. "Wh-wh-where's Peter? And the other two we were with?"

Donovan sat calmly in the chair and smiled. Inara sat down to his right. The consciousness implant was recent. To Skylar, her last memories from childhood took place this morning. Memories of running through a portal with little hope of rescue. But those events took place two decades ago.

"Skylar," Donovan began. "I'm going to cut to the chase, because this will likely be our last meeting together."

"Last?"

"Yes." Donovan said. "I've been resetting your brain and interrogating you for the past few months."

Skylar looked down at her pale skin. "Always in this boy's body?"

Donovan shrugged. "It was available when I needed it. My last informant betrayed me, and I had your memories stored away for just such an occasion."

"Stored away?" Skylar asked.

"You first came through the portal nearly 20 years ago," Inara clarified. "Peter and his friends have grown up and moved on."

"Did, I die?"

Donovan cut her off. "I don't have time for your questions. Who is the teleporting girl?"

Donovan took in a breath and closed his eyes. In a flash, a small, red vapor of energy shot out of his chest and latched itself to a similar grey mass of energy sitting inside Skylar's new body. He was still shaky with the practice of soul jumping, but weaker opponents like this could be bent to his whim. Skylar let out a slight bark of a cough and stared back at them serenely.

Not one to waste any time, Donovan forced her to close her eyes and search her memories for images of flying clouds that could teleport anyone anywhere.

No such images lurked in the depths of Skylar's memory. Donovan opened his eyes and the red apparition floated gently back into his chest. Skylar put her hands on the table and steadied herself while breathing heavily.

"No thoughts about the girl. She must not know," He whispered quietly to Inara while Skylar shook her head to clear it.

"Ouch," Skylar complained. "You could have waited for my reply."

"Not interested. Next subject." Donovan leaned forward. "How does one get into Naprea?"

Again he soul jumped her, pressing for thoughts, images, any kind of memory that might lead to any information. And again, he came up short.

"Nothing again," Donovan muttered as he released the soul jump. He took a few breaths to calm himself down and try a new tactic. "One last question. I need to know the exact location of the other side of the portal you fell out of with your brother."

Skylar clenched in anticipation of the soul jump, which did not come. Finally, she addressed them. "Not until I know my brother is okay."

Donovan slid a datapad across the table. On it was a video feed of Peter Dixon shooting and killing a group of soul jumpers on a remote island.

Skylar's eyes started welling up, and her eyebrows furrowed with anger.

"Your brother has not coped well in your absence," Donovan said. "He does not realize who he is, and has become the biggest danger to my people and yours. Tell me what was on the other side of that portal so I can stop him."

Skylar took a look around the room, apparently contemplating what to say. She looked up briefly, as if trying to remember, and Donovan took his chance.

Skylar let out a moaning cough as he soul jumped her again. He shut his own eyes to better focus on her. This time, the images in her mind were clear. He could see where she was the last day they went through the portal. Running through the sandy forest with Doctor Pavarti.

"We have a match," he forced Skylar to say. "I can get there through our new portal!"

"How are you going to get through the portal?" Inara asked.

He made Skylar stand up. "Soul jumpers developed a way to retain their jumps through portals."

"Do you think you can do it?"

"If not, we flood her tanks and try again with another host body." Skylar walked out of the room and back towards lab 64. Donovan kept his eyes closed and held out a hand to Inara. "I need you to guide me to our car. We need to head to the aeronautical plant where Skylar and crew first fell out of that portal."

Inara grabbed his arm and lead him along. He had a hard time keeping two sets of eyes open. It was disorienting for him. He kept his eyes closed and focused on Skylar.

Skylar made it to the lab and a few engineers began dressing her in a special suit. This one was more clunky than the new suits that Donovan and Inara wore, but it still had most of the functionality. The fabric was a synthetic programmable matter. On command it transformed from bulletproof-hard to feather-mattress soft, to fly-trap sticky. Along the exterior and interior of the shin were several undetectable portals, enabling him to carry the whole lab with ease.

The helmet was placed over her head and an electronic Heads Up Display connected her to the interface of the suit's computer. Her vitals, and the suit's menu were displayed over her eyes.

"How's the HUD?" a service technician asked her.

She gave the thumbs up and climbed into the empty tank.

On the wall opposite the portal, a circular class enclosure was opened. She climbed up and strapped herself into the wall. A minute later, an engineer closed the lid, forming a tight dome around her.

The sequence was started, and the wall opposite her lit up in a glowing bright red. All at once, a huge wave of water rushed through the portal at her.

Donovan was guiding Skylar through a soul jump, and he knew if she died, he would still live, but the sight made him jump all the same.

"It's ok, I've got you," Inara said as she guided him blindly up the stairs to the observation room.

He took a few deep breaths and Skylar did as well.

Back in the tank, after the water pressure stabilized, the dome around Skylar was unlatched and she was freed from the straps.

She swam up to the portal and paused. "Here we go."

Tentatively, Donovan guided Skylar to swim through the portal. No memory wipe, no mind reset. It felt less invasive than going through an open door. Both he and Skylar punched their fists in victory.

"Did you make it through?" Inara asked in his ear.

"Skylar is in the ship's command deck." Donovan announced. "Still under my control."

Skylar was now floating in the command center of the submerged coalition ship. A majestic vessel, brought to the bottom of the ocean by a few bombs, and endless waves of tetrapath monsters.

Some of those monsters were still floating, submerged with the ship. Their bodies were mixed in with the bodies of sailors. Some of them halfway through the mutation. Most in advanced stages of decomposition.

Skylar swam through the command deck and to the exit doors. They were sealed shut. She pressed on the glass and a small portal system in her fingers injected acid into the glass. The acid quickly ate away the glass, opening a path to the sea.

Out here, it was dark. Sunlight was only a distant glimmer from the depths where she floated. She pressed a button on her suit and it lit up from head to toe.

Fish swam away and her HUD displayed facts about pressurization, depth meters, fish species, and more. She waved her hands in the water, and most of the extraneous information was swiped away.

"Time to use a trick I learned from Peter Dixon," Skylar said.

She pulled on the fabric on her shoulders, and it stretched out, giving her the impression that she was wearing a tiny parachute. Two portals opened on the inside, unleashing a small amount of super helium and filling the parachute like a balloon.

She shot to the top of the ocean like a cork. The suit automatically calibrated for the pressure, preventing Skylar from getting cramps associated from depressurization.

In seconds, she was at the surface, and then floating in the air. Small portals opened on her back and rockets were ignited.

It was only a short trip to the shore where the seemingly infinite tetrapath army emerged to destroy his ship that fateful night. Where Azurand had betrayed him, and where the activists had conquered.

The beach was empty now. Here and there, the remains of a tetrapath carcass lay rotting into the sand.

He guided Skylar beyond the shore and over the small jungle on the Control Center Island, noting only briefly the state of the western bay where a large portal had teleported some 40 activists to Earth.

Nearly in the center of the island, under the cover of trees, stood a large building. The fabled head laboratory of Doctor Pavarti.

Skylar hovered above of the building and shot more acid onto the roof. A small hole opened and she descended gradually into the very center of the lab.

It was caked with mold, dust, and small bits of unhealthy looking vegetation. Three of the walls were covered with old tools, and the floor was a mix of operating tables, chairs, and chemical lab stations.

Skylar's memories shot again to that day when she was running with her little brother for their lives, when Doctor Pavarti promised them that they would be found on the other side of the portal.

Donovan smiled and allowed her to feel a little bit of anger. To go through the events of that day in her mind.

The memories pointed right to the wall she went through. He could see Doctor Pavarti flipping a switch and turning the portal on.

She walked across the room and made her way to the switch. Just to the left of the switch was a tall sheet covering what looked like a display case.

She pulled the sheet off and revealed a large set of glass cases, almost like aquariums. Inside the cases were models of Cova, Earth, and two solar systems. On the bottom of the display was a topographic terrain mapping out Cova. The large continent on the west, and the small cluster of islands on the east. Everything was intricate in detail.

Every model in the display case was littered with light bulbs. Some were red, others were blue. It didn't take Donovan long to realize that this was a map of every portal Doctor Pavarti ever built.

On top of the largest mountain on Cova, a mountain that could be seen from Cantera Bay, a ring of red lights was glowing. She peered as close to the glass as possible to see. A small crater, with a tiny city inside of it. The ring of red lights was around the rim of the crater.

"So that's what Azurand meant." Skylar tapped on the glass, appreciating the genius of the situation, and the skill involved in the execution. Everything clicked. The city of Naprea was protected by a portal. Try to fly through the top of the crater housing Naprea and you were teleported to who knows where.

"Donovan, we've arrived at the plant," Inara whispered into his ear.

He nodded to her in the car without opening his eyes, and continued to guide Skylar's left hand where she remembered Pavarti had flipped the switch.

The wall to her left hummed and the portal activated. Two red lights flicked on in the bottom display map of Cova. One where he was, and one where Skylar was.

He jumped through the portal and to his aeronautical plant. He looked into the Faraday cage where Skylar,

Peter, Scott and Miranda had fallen out all those years ago.

"Inara!" he shouted to her as he released his soul jump. Skylar fell to the ground as the suit locked her into place.

"I've found Pavarti's map of portal locations," Donovan said through his own voice. He opened his eyes and blinked a few times. "And it even has the layout of Naprea in there."

Inara smiled. "Does it reveal their defenses?"

"It does." Donovan said as his suit pulled up a video feed.

"I wonder what the blue lights represent?" Inara asked as she watched.

"I don't know." Donovan wondered with her. "A different kind of portal, perhaps?"

He pointed at the rim of the crater Naprea was nestled in. "All those red lights indicate that there is a portal on the top of the crater. Always on."

"Where does it lead?" Inara asked.

"I'll need to do a proper scan," Donovan said as he prepared to soul jump Skylar again. "But this should tell us the best way to infiltrate."

"I can't wait to visit Naprea," Inara smiled.

CHAPTER 2: THE PORTAL SMITH

The windows of the library gave off a bright glare onto the street as the mid-morning sun crested around a moon and over the ledge of the valley. Talia put her hand to her eyes to shield them.

She stole a glance quickly at her teacher, who was droning on about history, at the top of a staircase just outside the library. The class was nearly twice the size it normally was. Close to a hundred kids clung to her every word.

Talia could not care less. Behind her blocked hand, a small tuft of purple smoke materialized. At the edge of the city, a larger counterpart cloud appeared out of thin air. Instead of her usual teleporting trick, this produced the effect of having a flying camera at her command. She swooped the mist in the clouds above, looking at Naprea, the city in the crater.

In the center was a large spaceship the town was named after. The back end of it stuck out like a poorly lodged splinter in a thumb. It was green that was almost black, with giant gold letters on the site. "Naprea." Half of the N was cut off, and Talia wondered if it was really called the Vaprea. Neither name made sense to her.

Inside the ship, her older sister Miranda spent most of her days toiling away building weapons to fight the Coalition with.

It didn't take long to figure out that the ship crashed here a long time ago, leaving a massive crater almost tailor made for this city to fill.

The city was divided into circular zones called prefects. The innermost prefect was a park filled with trees, picturesque rocks, and a small man-made river.

Talia and her class stood on the next inner rim, which consisted of the Library, a town hall, and the hospital. Cobblestone streets connected each building. Those three buildings were surrounded by markets and a few municipal buildings.

Just outside of that prefect was the residential loop. Talia spent a lot of her free time gazing at what the people were up to in their home neighborhoods, curious to see what a normal, Naprean life was like.

The outer rim was a mixture of ranch and farm lands, with a few processing mills.

Their class was standing on a cobblestone courtyard just outside the library. They were there as part of a multi-school field trip. A history buff was getting ready to take the stage and explain their heritage, again.

"Talia, now is not the time to go wondering off," the teacher warned.

"I'm not, Mrs. Stanton." Talia turned her attention now to the teacher.

Mrs. Stanton's eyes were following Talia's clouds. Talia pulled both portals back into her quickly, and they disappeared from view.

"Now, onto our next subject." Mrs. Stanton's fake smile returned as she stepped down from her slight perch atop the stairs. "We have a guest lecturer from the historical archive department, Silas Stanton."

A tall man with wavy, graying hair stepped up to the podium. He wore a handsome smile, and looked dressed for a trip through a tropical forest. Several small sections of students let out enthusiastic cheers.

Talia stood up slightly to get a better view of this man. She didn't know why, but she found him very pleasant to look at. His chiseled chin, the way his hair bounced around his head as he nodded.

Silas waited for the crowd to calm before addressing them. "What do you know about the ministering angels?"

An enthusiastic boy to Talia's left thrust his hand high into the air. As he answered, she could not help but notice this boy was perhaps a year too old for this class, and shared many of the striking features she admired in Silas. "They are the angels that would grant certain children of the Keystone extra gifts, based on their actions and good works."

"Very good, Hudson," Said Silas. "It was not long ago, that nearly one of every two children were selected for these gifts. Who knows? Maybe you'll be next."

Talia rolled her eyes slightly. Two months ago, she would have believed all of this. But Scott and Miranda had been whispering about it. Things weren't adding up.

"Something wrong Talia?" Mrs. Stanton asked, a hint of warning behind her voice. Everyone in the crowd looked at her. But the only ones she really noticed were Silas and this boy to her left.

Talia hesitated a moment, and then blurted it out. "Yeah. If there were really angels doing all of that, why did they suddenly stop when Dr. Pavarti died?"

Silas did not miss a beat. "Dr. Pavarti has been taken from us because of the wicked actions of Azurand. And since we are lacking a doctor of his skill for healing, the Angels thought it would be best to wait for a new doctor."

"So these are powerful beings leave children wounded so badly, they need a doctor to patch them up? And according to some, not every kid taken in by these angels actually got new powers. Some of them got sick. Some of them died. Why would that happen?"

"Talia, that is quite enough." Mrs. Stanton looked around at the startled classmates. "If your father were-"

"But he's not!" Talia stood up, and a mist appeared over the crowd to her right. Some girls let out a scream, and Talia rushed to pull it back into her. "He died saving me and my sister. And if you think bringing him up is going to answer my question, then my next question is, who qualified you to be a teacher?"

The words rolled off her lips before she knew what she was saying. Her knuckles were white from clenching. Another portal mist was threatening to pop out of her at any moment. The memories of her father were just too much for her to control.

"What did you say?" Mrs. Stanton asked as the family narrowed their eyes.

"You heard me," Talia answered, coolly. "My father has nothing to do with my question."

Mrs. Stanton's face contorted in rage for a brief moment. "You'll be staying after class to have a word. I don't want to hear another peep out of you until then. Are we clear?"

Talia nodded, tempted to lower her mist and teleport Mrs. Stanton off a cliff. Silas continued his lesson in the delusion that angelic beings cut people open to give them powers. After that, Mrs. Stanton resumed control of the class and they went into the library to practice scribe recording drills.

Talia collected two stones at the door, and walked in. It was her first time inside, and she was not impressed. The library on her home island had huge open widows, and everything in it invited learning and discussion.

This library was dark, with ugly pillars in all the wrong places. There were about seven shelves holding books on the far side of the room, arranged in a half circle. In front of those shelves, a large number of chairs were set out for the students to sit.

Talia walked past the chairs and sat cross-legged on the floor, her back propped up against one of the bookshelves. From here, she had a better view of the boy, and Mrs. Stanton.

"Alright." Mrs. Stanton got the attention of the room. "In here the temperature is controlled, so the only thing you need to focus on is the sensation of sound and light as I go through today's pattern. Let's begin."

Mrs. Stanton pulled out a trumpet and began to play. The noise was high pitched and way off key.

Talia focused slightly on the trumpet sounds from Mrs. Stanton, pulling them into her mind. Then, Mrs. Stanton held up various signs that reflected what little light was coming into the room.

More than once, Talia's eyes wandered to her right, where Hudson was sitting. He was probably their son; he had the same jaw line, ear lobes. He even wore the same hair cut as Silas. She watched as he breathed in and out, focusing on his task of recording.

She snapped back into focus, trying to catch everything Mrs. Stanton was doing.

Once Mrs. Stanton was finished, Talia focused on the memory and picked up a stone. All the hairs in her arm raised in goose bumps and swayed as a glowing green orb floated down her arm and settled in the rock. The past few minutes of her life were recorded and placed into that stone, ready to be replayed to anyone who touched it.

After it was placed into the rock, she walked to the front of the class to give the memory to Mrs. Stanton. Talia was surprised to discover she wasn't the only one with her memory transfer completed already. Hudson was walking down with her. Normally, the other students weren't as advanced as her. But Hudson did seem a lot older. Maybe she could transfer to his class.

Mrs. Stanton took her recording with a sharp tug. Silas took Hudson's with a knowing wink, probably a father and son wink.

Mrs. Stanton's eyes went shaky as the green orb raced up from the rock to her mind, and began playing the memory Talia recorded.

Talia swayed awkwardly while both Mr. and Mrs. Stanton were in recording trances, testing the transfer of memories prepared.

She stole a few glances at Hudson, but he did not seem eager to reciprocate. He was resolutely staring off in the other direction, avoiding her gaze, as if they just had a rough argument.

Finally, Mrs. Stanton resurfaced from the trance.

"You were distracted this time around, Talia." Mrs. Hudson gave her a pointed look, punctuated by a pair of very cross eyebrows. "You only barely recorded the pattern, but next time I suggest you keep your eyes from wandering."

She inclined her head sharply to Hudson, and now Talia felt confident that he was her son.

"Understood."

After class, the rest of the children were excused for lunch. Talia remained behind as instructed.

"Talia." Mrs. Stanton began. "I don't know what was behind that little outburst today, but I don't want it happening in my class again."

"Professor. I am honestly curious. I've seen stuff in this last month that doesn't add up with what is being taught."

"Oh, yes." Silas said sarcastically, stepping in. "The big hero on the island who thinks she's so much better than the other children."

"I can't help it if I was trained to use my powers at a younger age. If you think that makes me better than my classmates, move me up a grade to learn with the older kids."

"Ha." Mrs. Stanton gave another look to her son, who was helping a few of the other students with their lunches just outside. "There you go again. You act out during class, and then expect me to reward you with privilege. Go eat your lunch. You are staying after school for detention."

Talia's feet remained planted for a moment, a protest on her lips. But she let it go. She was hungry and nothing was getting though to her teacher.

All the other kids were off playing in the field and Talia's lunch bag sat alone on the table. She picked it up and saw too late the glowing green orb of a planted memory. The orb traveled from the lunch bag, up her arm and to her mind. A wave of emotions, characteristic of new scribes, washed over her. She was in a memory trance.

In the dreamlike state, she saw three girls from her class standing in a line with their arms folded over their chest. The girl in the middle stepped forward.

"You're a freak, Talia," the girl said. "And a criminal. You broke the archway portal, a sacred relic. I'd tell you to watch your back, but seeing as you're in a trance right now, that won't be possible."

A smirk spread over the girl's face. "Too bad because outside of this recording, I'm going to kick you in the tailbone."

Talia focused hard on her portal mist. While she couldn't move her body yet, she could conjure up the cloud outside of her mind. Within seconds, the recording trance ended and she was completely enveloped in her purple mist. It thinned, giving her a view of four girls backing up slightly, trying to stay outside the radius of her fury.

Without thinking, the mist swept over the girls, and they were gone. Halfway around the world in the blink of an eye. Talia smiled when she realized it would be in the middle of the night on her home island.

"Talia!" Mrs. Stanton shouted as she ran out of the library. "What have you done to your classmates?"

"They attacked me!" Talia shouted back. "Thought they were clever, too."

"Where are they?"

"In my burned down village, on the Helix Cascade Island."

"Bring them back this instant!" Mrs. Stanton yelled.

"Or you'll what? Put me in more detention?"

There was a crowd of people gathering to hear the shouting match. Hudson was there, looking at her with a mixture of fear and confusion. Talia didn't care.

Mrs. Stanton didn't back down either. "Bring them back."

"Are you going to punish them?"

"Punish them?" Mrs. Stanton threw up her arms in exasperation. "For being teleported across the planet?"

"For attacking me." Talia pointed at her lunch bag on the ground. "Their threat was recorded nice and neatly for you there."

Mrs. Stanton made a show of effort to pick up the bag. "I sense no recording in the bag. And none of your pupils are capable of hiding a recording yet."

Talia looked at Mrs. Stanton's hand. The glowing green orb was gone. Talia sighed. The girl who made the recording was still learning how to make them. The memory had already faded out of existence after the first use.

"It was there, and they did attack me." Talia clenched her teeth and waved her purple mist back into existence. The girls on the other side were still screaming as they fell back onto the street in front of the crowd. Talia turned to face everyone. She looked away from Hudson when she said, "Stay away from me!"

Before anyone could reply, her mist swept over her and she teleported to the research station in the Vessel Naprea. The room itself had three rows of tables, organized the way a chemistry class might be. Bunsen burners were lit all over, and several assistants were performing repetitive tasks as instructed by Miranda. Fabric and circuitry lay in organized chaos. Half the tools were on tables and the coffee pots were constantly running.

"Talia! There you are." Miranda looked up from her microscope and picked up a clip board. "I need you to pick up a few more rocks from the mines. I think the suit needs a metal that can channel the energy more effectively."

Without another word to Talia, Miranda turned away and began talking to another assistant. "Good. Excellent progress. Now we need to focus on making the delivery agent work better."

Talia mumbled under her breath. Tears still clung to her eyes, and her heart still thumped with rage. Instead of taking it out on her sister, she calmed herself and formed two mists in her mind. The first one hovered on the delivery platform two rooms down the hall. The second one shot up the mountainside and to a cave Scott had discovered. Like a nimble bird, the mist rushed down the cave and into a makeshift mine shaft.

In the other room, a lab assistant lit a stick of dynamite and tossed it into Talia's closer mist. As the fuse sizzled, Talia focused, and teleported the stick of dynamite into the mine shaft.

The stick exploded, and Talia raced her mist in the mines around to catch the flying debris. Bit by bit, large chunks of rock fell through her portal in the receiving platform.

"Done sis. Now-" Talia was interrupted by a finger.

Miranda was looking over her datapad, reading complicated equations and specs of the suit she was creating.

"Sis?" Talia asked after a minute of silence. There was no response. "Sis! Did you schedule a meeting with the psychiatrist?"

"Mm?" Miranda mumbled as she tapped her fingers across the screen. "Look, honey, now's not a good time. Maybe later for dinner or something. But while you're here, could you bring me another space suit? They're a few floors up, and it would really save me time."

Talia stood with her mouth open a moment. She had another comeback to yell at her older sister, but Miranda was already speed walking off to another assistant.

Talia turned to the closest assistant. "Do you know where Scott is?"

"The only thing I keep hearing is that he's out of town."

With a quick flick, her mist deposited three space suits hard against the floor in front of her. As they landed, her vision went spotty for about two seconds. Then, she focused on her soft bed and brought up the mists to teleport her there.

Instead, when the mists disappeared, she was in the market. Another cobblestone road, this one surrounded by artistic looking houses, supply stores, and restaurants.

Along the side of the road, there were tons of booths constructed for the selling of all kinds of things.

She shook her head again, and spots blurred her vision. She stumbled slightly, hitting the back of a woman who didn't seem to notice.

"Oh. Not now." Talia grunted under the pressure of her growing headache.

From her perspective, it was a wall to wall throng of people. Standing on her toes, she could only barely see over people's shoulders. Back down on the balls of her feet, even the pleasant aroma of fried breads and meats could not overpower the smell of bodies moving in such close proximity.

Talia focused again, and a small wisp of mist levitated above the crowd. She tried to move it around, but it wouldn't obey. She brought up a smaller mist in front of her face, and with it, she saw the river of people from a bird's eye view.

She made her way through the throng of people, hidden by the taller bodies around her. A few booths down, the way was blocked as people were gathered together around an outdoor stage.

"Beware!" Silas was shouting on top of the stage. A giant sign with angels printed on it hung behind him. "Everything you think! Everything you do! Everything that happens to you is captured in the great recorder. And in the end of days, it will be played for your condemnation or your justification!"

Silas continued as she tried to pass. Talia wondered how he got there so fast. "Right among us, there are heathens, not raised in the ways of our God. They have trampled our sacred sites, and yet we treat them like royalty. Our leaders give them access to everything. Meanwhile, they make no efforts to purify our people, making us unworthy for a new doctor to lead us!"

There was a cheer of acknowledgement from the crowd as Silas stomped his foot for emphasis. "If we want our recordings in the great recorder to be favorable for us, we must make the choice. Choose to do whatever it takes to purify this people."

Silas scanned the crowd with a somber look on his face. Then he spread his arms and looked heavenward in the attitude of addressing God. But instead he found Talia's portal mist. He looked back upon the crowd with a smile.

"I know you walk among us, little one." He paced the platform, looking around the crowd for her. "You who claim great, new powers without the touch of the angels. Consider this. If your power didn't come from the angels, where did it come from?"

Talia took a step back and ducked slightly. Her heart was racing again. She found herself breathing heavily, and her vision was going spotty. She tried to pull her mists back into herself, but they weren't obeying.

"Not now." She held her head and stumbled through the crowd. There were so many people.

The mist above the crowd flashed with a bolt of lightning and began moving in random directions. The mist in front of her grew and levitated above the crowd. One mist engulfed a fruit stand nearby, and the other mist threw it out onto the crowd. Just as it left the mist, the fruit stand was struck by a lightning bolt and caught fire. The crowd screamed and tried to move out of the way.

Talia's head split with pain. She collapsed to the ground, and her stomach felt like she was going to be sick.

"There! On the ground!" A man shouted from behind her. Several footsteps ran towards her.

With the last ounce of energy she had left, she raised a mist over herself, trying to teleport to the hospital.

When the purple faded, she was in a dark room. She again fell to her knees, but caught herself slightly on what felt like a couch.

"Oh, it's you," said a voice as the light switched on.

Talia turned to the source. In the shadows of another room, a tall, dark skinned man flicked on another light switch. Peter Dixon walked out of the room, casually carrying a sword.

"What's wrong?" Dixon asked.

"I...I..." Talia took a few calming breaths. "I'm having a black out."

"I don't understand."

"Losing...losing control of the mists." Talia looked around at the furniture. "Things might start disappearing."

Dixon set the sword low to the ground and took a few steps towards her. "Don't you worry about any of the stuff here. What do you need?"

Talia raised an eyebrow at the man before her. The only thing she really knew about Dixon was that he was a ruthless fighter. This gentle, caring attitude was unfamiliar to her.

"Where are we?" Talia managed to ask.

"Hospital." Dixon scratched his face nervously. "Three floors underground in the Mental Health Ward. They uh... they don't think I'm right in the head."

"Any way you could get me to the emergency room?"

A thick mist materialized with a flash of lightning and zoomed around the room like a hungry shark.

"Not for a while." Dixon eyed the mist nervously. "They have me locked up. And there isn't anyone nearby to change that."

"Then your couch is going to have to do."

Dixon picked her up, but the mist swooped down and engulfed the couch. In an instant, the couch was gone, along with an end table and part of a lamp.

"Didn't care for it that much anyway," Dixon said, moving to the back bedroom and placing her on the bed. "Don't worry, new sheets just this morning."

A few flashes of lightning erupted from her mist again as it swooped everything out of the living room one by one.

Talia tried to focus, tried to bring the mist back under her control, she was rewarded only with a larger headache.

Dixon started yelling something in the other room, but she couldn't hear him. The mist came swooping into the bedroom, and she blacked out.

*****

Talia woke to darkness, still laying on top of Dixon's bed. The comforter was inviting, trying to pull her back into sleep.

"Dixon?" She called out.

"I'm here," came a soft voice from the corner.

Talia tried to sit up, but her limbs wouldn't respond. They were too heavy. "Water."

Dixon stood up from his chair and left the room. In a moment, he was by her side helping her to drink the water.

"I managed to contact somebody about you being here. They said they would send somebody, but I'm not sure they believe me so, it could be a while."

The water helped her calm down. But her head was still spinning, and her vision remained spotty.

"Sorry about your furniture."

Dixon waved off the concern. "It wasn't mine, and I didn't like most of it anyway."

"So, does that happen often? Do you lose control of those things a lot?"

Talia shrugged. "Only when I don't drink from the Catalyst Fountain back home. You might have seen it while you were over there. Big font full of purple water?"

"Yeah," Dixon nodded. "I've seen it."

"Well, my dad was always forcing me to drink that stuff. Helped me to control them. The mists, I mean."

"So go get a drink. What's holding you back?"

"Nobody will let me teleport outside of Naprea. They say it's too dangerous."

"They won't let you?" Dixon raised an eyebrow. "Talia, no one here can stop you from teleporting."

"But Miranda has a point about it being dangerous." She let out a huff of resigned frustration. "The coalition could be there."

"I suppose that's true. But what if they are? You took out an army of tetrapaths by yourself! That's more than I could handle."

Talia smiled a little. "Maybe, but Miranda would still kill me."

"Again, I ask how?" Dixon looked back at the entrance door through the living room. "Anyway, lucky for you, nobody would know if you went right now."

"You wouldn't tell?"

"If you let me come along." He gave a shrug. "I need to get out of this place, if only for a little while. I'd stay out of your way while you took out any coalition soldiers unfortunate enough to be there. But, you're up for the trip, right? You're not going to drop me in the middle of the ocean?"

"I should be strong enough for one trip," Talia said. "I'm really familiar with the destination."

"Ok, let's do it."

Talia thought of home and slowly conjured her mists. They came with flashes of lightning and rumbles of thunder. She took a deep breath and they teleported to the Catalyst fountain at her home island, the Helix Cascade.

Talia fell to the ground and her mists started swooping around the ceiling of the temple in random paths.

After a few seconds, a cup was pressed to her lips and she drank. Her headache relaxed and faded. She took the cup from Dixon's hand and he stood back.

After finishing the cup, she stood and refilled it. She drained the cup four times before she felt normal.

"Thanks," Talia said. "It's been too long since I've done that."

Dixon took in a deep breath and sat down next to her. "It feels good to get some fresh air."

"This is still a cave." Talia smiled and teleported them to a field near her old home village. Her heart raced with excitement that the portals were now under her control again. "This is fresh air!"

Her smile faded slightly as she gazed at the village that was mostly rubble. She looked over at Dixon, knowing he had caused most of the destruction.

Dixon was looking down at the ground, a frown on his face.

"Listen," he began, but he couldn't finish his thought.

They stood there in silence for a few awkward moments. Talia wanted to yell at him for what he did to this town, but she also wanted to understand him. The caring person he was now contradicted the madman that burned the village.

"Hey, you want to help me with something else?" Talia asked quickly.

"What's that?" Dixon answered with hesitation.

"I lost something of my father's that day." Talia looked over to where the old capitol building stood. "I've been meaning to get it back, but I haven't had a chance to come back here."

"Sure." Dixon stood up straight and forced himself to look at the village.

Talia teleported them to the scene of her father's death. The once tall building was now mostly rubble. The front section still stood, a testament to how hard her father fought during his final moments. The room was large and the walls were now charred black, with several sections missing. The floor was littered with wooden debris, with most of it piled under large holes in the walls.

"What are we looking for?" Dixon kicked at a bit of the debris near his feet.

"My father's death memory."

"His what?" Dixon asked.

"Oh, right. You never learned about that." Talia knelt down and examined the bits of wood. "When a scribe is dying, they produce one more memory, a last message to loved ones, or if you believe such things, they will occasionally produce prophecies."

"And your dad left you one?"

"Yes." Talia picked up a chunk of wood and threw it aside. "But, before I could save it, or even try and commit it to memory, I was soul jumped. The Phantom Queen made me throw it into this mess you see here."

"And it was one of these chunks of wood?" Dixon asked. "Can't you sense the memory?"

"Death memories are different." She picked up another chunk of wood and started a pile. "Scribes can consciously make memories do different things. Some of them call out to nearby scribes, some are hidden except to the recorder, and some are locked so only a select few can open them."

"And which of these are the death memories?"

"Death memories are hidden and locked," Talia said. "You know how people have their lives flash before their eyes when they have near death experiences? Well, that moment is planted into a memory. Whatever they're holding or touching becomes that memory. But only the one person they are thinking about can access it, and they have to find it."

"So, it could be anything in this pile of rubble, and you don't remember where it is?"

Talia touched her head, trying to pull the memory back to her. "I don't even remember what was in the memory. During the memory transfer, I was soul jumped. And the soul jump lasted for days. Enough trauma to cause me to forget a lot of what happened that day."

She remembered the conversation with Miranda about seeing a psychiatrist about this problem.

"Well, this is going to take a while."

"What, you have plans back in your cell?" Talia asked playfully.

"As a matter of fact, I did have a hot date tonight."

"Oh, my mistake, Romeo." Talia picked up another chunk of wood and tossed it. "If it helps narrow it down, I think the chunk of wood he gave me was at least partially covered in blood."

"That does help," Dixon said. "I'm good at finding blood."

Talia started making a pile of discarded debris. She picked up a few that had blood on them, but they were empty. Just inanimate chunks of wood.

"So, why do they have you locked up in the loony bin?" Talia asked.

Dixon clenched his lips in a tight grimace, and there was a slight smacking noise as his mouth opened again. "Because they think I'm dangerous. There are a lot of accounts of me doing some violent things."

"And they think you're going to do that in Naprea?"

"They're sure I will. So much so, that they cleared the rooms above and below me, as well as the neighbors to the right and left. Keeping me from soul jumping."

"That's paranoid." Talia laughed a little.

"Not when you're trying to contain someone like me. Someone who could use practically any person as a weapon to escape."

"Oh." Talia's smile faded, and she continued to sort through the debris in silence.

After a few hours, she lost track of which pile she had already sorted through. She clenched her fists slightly, but that just pressed in the growing number of slivers on her palms.

Dixon stood up and looked out a hole in the wall. "The sun is setting. We should come back and try another time."

"Yeah, we should be getting you back, I guess." Talia faked a yawn to conceal her frustration.

"Yeah, I'd hate to miss my date."

Talia smiled and teleported them back to Dixon's room, which was now full of doctors rummaging through his stuff.

"What the?" The closest nurse to them squealed.

"I told you Talia was here!" Dixon said.

"But, there's no need for urgent care!" Talia said. "I've fixed my problem. So, I'll just drop off Dixon here and be on my way."

In another instant, she teleported to her bedroom and fell down on her bed. She focused her mind, trying to see the bit of wood with blood on it her father gave her, trying to remember what it looked like, and more importantly, what was in it.

CHAPTER 3:
SCOTT'S ONE HORSE TOWN

Perth looked different from the last time Scott Orr visited the town. Cleaner. Larger. More buildings were established, and the roads were full of more people.

Scott wondered just how long it had been since he left the little town on the side of the mountain. Certainly less than a year. Either way, he was long overdue for a friendly face. And Perth was the best place for that right now.

He stood in the overgrowth of the surrounding forest, something he wanted to chop down so tetrapath couldn't sneak in. He took a calming breath and pulled out a small pill bottle. It was empty.

The scars on his leg itched in protest. The tetrapath infection inside of him was getting worse. If he didn't resupply soon, the infection might finally overtake him.

As he walked the streets, however, most of the crowd moved to avoid him. He reached his favorite diner, and continued to silently count the cold stares from strangers and friends alike.

Last he checked, he was a hero in this town. Responsible for keeping the tetrapath infection from taking it over. Right know he felt like an outcast.

It was still early, so there weren't many customers in the diner. The ovens were baking bread and the stoves were warming up the meats.

Inside, the diner was large and open, with windows cascading in natural light on the tables and booths scattered around.

Scott walked through the small maze of seats to reach the counter where a young woman was polishing some seating areas.

"Excuse me?" Scott said.

The young woman looked up at him and froze. Scott tried to talk to her again, but she backed up slowly, never taking her eyes off of him.

"Clara?" she called out.

A larger woman stepped out from the kitchen door behind the counter. Scott knew her. For years, Clara refused to accept payments for any meals she prepared for Scott because he saved her sister from the infection.

Today though, her eyes narrowed when she saw him. "About time you showed up."

"What did I do?" Scott asked, looking around the diner. "I'm getting death stares from half of these people, and now even you. My friend last time I checked. What's going on?"

Clara nodded to the young woman and she ran off. "The town's changed since you've been here last. It's been moving on."

"Meaning they're fighting tetrapaths without me?" Scott asked. "It's about time they took-"

Clara waved a hand in front of her face and shook her head. "There have been no tetrapaths in Perth since you left, Scott."

"None?" Scott thought of the cleaner looking Perth he just walked through. "Even better. You should still prepare-"

She cut him off again. "And there are many people around here led to believe that you're responsible for any of the attacks we were getting in the first place."

"What, like I caused them?" Scott couldn't believe what he was hearing. "That's ridiculous."

"I know it is." Clara sent down a rag on the counter and looked over his shoulder. "But if you endangered my sister as part of your schemes..."

"I didn't." Scott waved both of his hands down to calm her down. "Look, if people feel that way, I don't have to stay long. I just need to see Tom. Is he in town?"

She nodded to a staircase behind him. "We've added a hotel to the top floor of the building. He's here for a few days. Look, for old time's sake you can have one more meal on the house, and wait for him to wake up. Once your business with him is done though, I want you gone."

"Deal," Scott said. "Just something easy, then. Eggs and pancakes."

Clara pointed to a table nestled under the stairwell. It was a private booth with low visibility. Obviously Clara didn't want people to know Scott was even there.

He sat down and scratched the scars on his leg, which was twitching nervously, something it had been doing since the graves closed. He tried placing a hand on it, but nothing slowed it down.

Memories of that night flashed into his mind over and over again. That was the night he gained the ability to steal talents and powers from anyone just by touching them. But it wasn't as easy as that. It only felt that way at the time.

Stealing talents took a toll on his mind. Stealing powers, like soul jumping or scribe recording, brought out the worst in him. It brought out the tetrapath infection.

Soon his food was brought out, and he wolfed it down. Half a day's journey down one of the steepest mountains on the planet had worked up his appetite.

Just as he finished, a young man in a gray suit sat down in the chair opposite him.

"Hey Tom." Scott said as he finished the last bite.

"Scott." Tom smiled, but there was something sinister behind it. "Glad you see you back in town."

"You're about the only one."

Tom chuckled under his breath. "Maybe. But this town doesn't even know who it is anymore. It's defiantly not the one you left all those months ago."

"How so?" Scott asked.

"Well, for one thing there's a new mayor. Carolyn Bhattarai."

"And?"

"And she thinks you're scamming us. Scaring the town into thinking it needs your protection."

"What do you think?"

Tom moved his jaw like he was chewing on something tough. "I don't know. I just have to do what's good for business. Speaking of business, what's yours?"

Scott pushed his plate out of the way and leaned forward. "I need tetrapath medicine."

"How much?" Tom asked without batting an eye.

"All you have."

Tom leaned back in his seat and scratched the underside of his chin for a moment, and then he leaned back in with a serious look in his eyes. "I'd like to help you, but I can't just give that stuff out anymore. If people see you making off with that medicine, they're likely to think you're up to something again."

"All I want is the medicine, and then I'm gone."

Tom sat in contemplation for a moment. "I can sell you half of my inventory, which is about five standard bottles, for a thousand."

"A thousand?" Scott had to refrain from yelling. "For that stuff? It's not even the real cure!"

Tom's eyes narrowed. "The real cure? If you don't like the product, why are you so interested in it?"

Scott clenched his teeth. "Fine. Put it on hold for me. I'll get you the money."

Tom reached over and patted Scott on the shoulder. "There. Glad we could do business. You know where to find me when you have the money."

Tom stood up and left the diner. Scott leaned back and scratched the warm scars on his leg.

After several minutes of contemplation, Scott stood and made his way back to the front counter, where someone was setting out cups and plates.

"Can you bring Clara out again for me?" Scott asked.

The attendant fled behind the kitchen doors, and Clara stepped back out to greet him.

"I need a job."

Clara raised her left eyebrow. "I don't know Scott. People might go crazy if they knew you were tampering with their food."

"I won't tamper with it," Scott insisted. "And no one has to know. I'll stay in the back and only leave when no one is looking."

"I can give you dish duty. Can you handle that?"

"You're not going to let me cook?"

"Can you cook?"

"As well as you can."

"Is that so?" Clara looked back over her shoulder, and then turned back to him. "I'm sorry, but I can't risk people finding out you're involved with food. Do you want the cleaning job or not?"

"Fine."

She nodded and walked back to the kitchen. As they walked through the swinging doors, he saw two robust women preparing breakfast at a furious pace. They were in sync with each other, chopping, whisking, flipping each item with practiced ease. Sweat rolled off their foreheads. The kitchen was warm from the bread baking in the oven and dozens of eggs frying on skillets.

"Sink's over there." Clara patted him on the shoulder. "The rest should be self explanatory."

Scott found a set of large rubber gloves and got to work. The load was light at first, but the crowd outside grew and grew. Soon, the dishes were piling up faster than he could manage.

"Need more plates!" One of the cooks called. "I've got hot food ready to go!"

Scott scrubbed faster and faster. Soon, others came to help out and the dishes were caught up with the cooks.

Scott looked over at the order tickets and noticed that the cooks were having a hard time keeping up with the orders.

Scott walked passed Clara and tapped her on the shoulder softly. A few grey orbs floated into Scott's mind, and he felt the knowledge and talent of cooking become part of him.

He stepped over to a pan of sizzling sausage and looked at the ingredients, ready to go. His mind flashed and the orb told him this was supposed to be sausage gravy. He stirred the sausage a little and then got the milk ready to pour. Clara shrugged her shoulders and walked off in another direction.

As the time ticked by, he finished the sausage gravy, made eggs of every variety, pancakes, waffles, and cinnamon rolls.

The afternoon rolled on and the meals switched to sandwiches, pastas, and salads.

"Where have you been all of my life?" Clara asked once the crowd died down slightly. "You're like a second me running around. Make yourself something and go take a break. You've earned it."

Scott nodded and put together a sandwich to take out back. There, a young man was pushing a cart full of fish up to the loading dock.

"You're back!" The man ran to him, dragging a huge trail of mud behind him.

"Whoa." Scott held out his hands. "What's going on here?"

"Scott, right?" The man held out his hand. It looked slimy. "The name's Casey. I watched you fight a bunch of tetrapath the other year. I didn't think you would come back."

This was the reaction he was used to here. "Yeah, well, with the less than warm welcome, this may be the last time I visit Perth."

"How long are you in town for?"

"As long as it takes to make enough money." Scott looked at the huge cart full of fish. He pointed to the pile. "Any money in fishing?"

"Enough. But if you want big money fast, you need to enter the big race this weekend!"

"What big race?"

Casey pointed up to the sky. "In three days time, our closest moon will be over the mountain, and a geyser will erupt. The eruption is so powerful, and the moon is so close, it will cause a storm. Not nearly strong enough to be called a hurricane, but there will be a lot of wind."

"Yeah, I've seen that in the city before." Scott looked around. "What's that have to do with a race?"

"Well, depending on which way the wind is blowing, is where the starting line is on the lake, nearby. The race starts with a sail boat leg where you ride the winds to a cove over on the west side of the lake. There, you will dive out of your boat and swim to an underwater cave. The cave is a large maze full of air pockets in the ceiling. You must retrieve an item from the cave, and then race back to your boat. Then you have to paddle the boat to the finish line on the north shore over there."

"Sounds intense," Scott said as someone from the diner came out and began counting the fish.

"Few finish the race at all."

"Anybody die down in the caves?"

"No. We have people stationed at the air pockets. If they see a straggler, they go down and save them." Casey looked down at fish counter with concern for a moment.

"What's the prize?" Scott asked.

"Two thousand even."

"How do I sign up?"

*****

The next few days, Scott made preparations for the race. Most of that time was spent going over the tactics and learning who the competition was with Casey.

"There is a champion for each leg of the race." Casey leaned in like he was revealing a big secret. "There's

Carolyn Bhattarai, the finest sailor in the town, likely the world. She'll navigate the storm like no other. And then Phillip, a master swimmer. And a fair diver too. And then there's me, the master rower."

"Master rower?" Scott raised his eyebrows. "What's so hard about rowing?"

Casey flexed his muscles. "Let's just say you'll need your strength to keep up. If you can even make it that far."

Scott smiled and finished his breakfast. When he was done, he stood up and put his hand on Casey's shoulder and he absorbed a rowing talent. He shuddered a second. "Well, good luck out there today."

"Where are you going?"

"I'm going to learn how to sail." Scott left the diner and headed north to the lake.

The sky was littered with thick clouds, hovering in patches like ships come into harbor. The moon was close, and looked huge. He could almost see the geyser spout between the clouds. The race would be starting soon.

He reached the lake, and found what he was looking for: the other champions practicing. Phillip was doing leisurely laps near the shore, and Carolyn was making preparations to her small sail boat.

As Scott stepped onto the dock, a motor boat pulled up. An elderly couple was sitting in the back while a younger man drove.

The man stepped off the boat and tied it to the dock and gave him a cold stare. "I hear you've entered the race. Are you here to try to get Mr. Parker here to reveal the hiding place of the flag?"

"What?" Scott looked at the old couple. "He hid the flag?"

"Yup." The young man said. "He's the best diver in the town. Knows the caves better than anyone. But he's too old for the rest of the stuff. So he's taken to hiding the flags."

"And I've got them in my best spot yet." Mr. Parker stepped off the boat with a prideful smile. "So good, I dare say you'll never find it."

Scott placed a hand on Mr. Parker's shoulder and took in a diving talent. Deep breathing techniques filled his mind. The only thing missing was the location of the flags.

"That's okay Mr. Parker. That would spoil the fun of the race."

Mr. Parker looked up at the sky behind him. "Looks like we'll be starting soon. Best to get ready."

Scott nodded and walked over to Carolyn. She was busy tying some knots and testing her sail.

"That looks complicated." Scott said.

"It is complicated." Carolyn grunted without turning around. "Too complicated to teach you, so move along Mr. Orr."

"I'm not here to ask for your help." Scott leaned over the doc and extended his hand. "Just here to wish you luck."

She reluctantly took his hand and shook it. He shuddered again as his mind was filled with information on sailing techniques, knots, and more.

"Are you okay?" Carolyn asked.

"Your the first person to ask me that." Scott nodded. "Just a little cold is all."

"Well, you better bundle up, because that storm is not going to be pleasant."

"I'll do that." Scott walked away, with only one more person to target.

There were now a few more people doing warm up laps near the pool. Phillip was pulling himself out of the water, apparently already warmed up.

"Ah, Scott," Phillip said as he approached. "You won't get any tips from me, so you better just be off to the starting line."

"Good luck." Scott smiled and held out his hand.

Another talent, another shudder. This time, his head shook a little more, and he felt a hard pressure building up in his mind. He focused on the four talents he had stolen this morning, and they were shaking all over.

"Are you alright?" someone said from behind him.

Scott tried to nod, but everything blurred around him. He extended his hand and released the rowing talent through his mind and out of his arm. In his vision, he saw a gray orb shot out and popped mid air. No one else seemed to notice.

"I'm fine." Scott shook his head. It was a little clearer now. "Ready to race. But I need to go get my boat ready."

"See you at the starting line." Phillip called from behind him.

Scott spent the next twenty minutes tying knots in complicated patterns that until recently made no sense to him, but he was finished with a few minutes to spare. He felt confident that he could keep up with Carolyn on the sailing leg of the race.

"Almost time," Casey said, stepping into the sailboat next to him. "Take a look at that moon!"

Scott turned around and saw the moon hanging massively in the sky. Low on the horizon, a thick patch of clouds was floating towards them.

"Any minute now." Casey said.

At that moment, the geyser erupted. A shockwave spread out from the center, and a burst of steaming water shot across space and into the atmosphere of Cova.

The clouds down below grew agitated. Some of them grew darker, but they all grew larger and swept up the mountain.

An official shouted something, but the wind picked up ferociously and he couldn't hear the instructions. The sky went dark as clouds and fog covered them like a blanket. Then, when Scott thought they were in the height of the storm, the wind picked up even more.

In unison, the boats detached from the dock and were off. Scott missed the cue to go, so he was a little behind everybody. Just as he detached, Casey slammed into him, turning him sideways and placing him even further behind the pack.

Scott turned his sail and rudder instinctively to right the ship. Once he was facing the right direction again, he let the sail catch the full force of the wind and it felt like a rocket pushing him along the lake.

In moments, he caught up to those near the back of the pack. He passed three contestants without even maneuvering.

Then he ran into a congested crowd. A less experienced sailor would either slow down, or crash into the pack, but with the grey talent orb floating around in his head, he had all the experience Carolyn did.

With a quick maneuver, he stood on the right side of the boat and leaned back, pulling on ropes and holding the rudder steady with his foot. The left side of the boat lifted above the water and he zipped right between two sailors.

The lake was growing choppy, and he readjusted to sail around another pack of racers. This time, he stood on the left and swung his boat in a tight arc around the pack.

Finally, there were only the elite sailors out front. He could barely make out Carolyn in the distance.

Directly in front of him, Casey was neck and neck with Phillip. Scott zipped up to them, and he made sure to veer enough to splash a wave of water into Casey's boat.

Casey turned around, at first furious, and then surprised as Scott sailed past them with ease.

Scott gave him a salute, and then turned to focus on the waters ahead. They were still choppy and Carolyn had a huge lead. But he didn't just have her talents. He had the best of her talents, her talents at her absolute peak.

He watched the waves of the water and his mind automatically charted a path of least resistance between them. The ship bounced slightly as he divided waves and closed the gap.

His hands slipped a few times on the rope, a few fresh burns stinging, but he held on, pulling every last ounce of speed out of his boat.

When he was twenty yards away, Carolyn dived from her ship and began swimming to the caves. Someone at a buoy hopped into her boat and sailed it to the left and out of the way.

As Scott approached the buoy line, he let his ship drift a little to the right. At the last second, he cut a sharp left and flung himself over the line with a great leap. Before hitting the water, he heard the satisfying clang as the ship hit the buoy.

He hit the water with the grace of a legendary sea creature. The next gray orb took over, and he felt his mind and body fill with the practice and knowledge of a world class swimmer. His arms stretched to mimic the most efficient swimming stride. His breathing synched with every stroke, maximizing his energy.

After a quarter mile, his muscles began to burn. Knowledge aside, his muscles were not trained for this kind of strain. He passed Carolyn at the half mile marker, but he still had a mile to go.

A huge wave pushed him to the side and he tumbled underwater. He took it in stride, and pushed his way back to the surface. Another wave came crashing down on him. He extended his arms into a diving position and shot under the wave like a missile.

With a quarter mile to go, his left leg was starting to cramp. He instinctively switched to a different stroke to compensate. But this one didn't favor the choppy water conditions.

Every time a wave crashed on him, he had to maneuver into a better position to avoid getting tossed. On the down swells he would switch back.

Phillip passed him with 20 yards to go. Scott let him go, knowing that he wasn't in a condition to keep up.

Someone else was not far behind him when he reached the cave entrance. He flipped up and treaded water for a moment. When a swell of water rose up, he took in one last final breath. On the down swell he dived under the water.

He used the pressure of the wave to dive faster. He flipped under water, and the wave all but pushed him into cave opening 10 yards under. He twisted his body in subtle ways, steering himself deep into the cave and to the first air pocket.

He reached it and took in a deep breath. With a few quick breaths, he was back under the water and searching the tunnel. His lungs weren't as practiced, but the calmness of the techniques allowed him to swim between two air pockets before needing to breathe again.

After a few minutes of navigating, he reached the first hiding hole. It was a larger cave opening with a floor. He pulled himself out of the water and rested on the rock.

His body ached and he wanted to just quit right there. He rubbed his head, desperate for the race to be over.

After some time, he pushed himself up and started looking around. Most of the area was just slimy rock around the floor and walls. He rubbed his hands along them, and the map from Mr. Parker flashed in his mind. Loose gravel in the back right corner.

He started to stumble in that direction when someone splashed their way up.

"Scott!" Casey shouted. "Phillip's already passed this cave! It's obvious the flags aren't in here. "

Scott slumped to the floor and put his hand to his head, exaggerating his fatigue. "Maybe. I need the rest though."

"Suit yourself," Casey shouted and dived back into the water.

Scott pushed himself back up and made his way to the corner. There, he pulled on some loose gavel until he found the pile of flags. He pulled one and pushed the rocks back onto the remaining pile.

With another deep breath he dived back into the water and swam for the exit. His legs protested and his lungs ached. But he continued his pace of two air pockets per breath. After about six air pockets, he ran into Carolyn, taking deep breaths before moving on herself.

"Where did you learn to sail like that?" she panted.

"No time." Scott panted back. "Flags are in the first cave, towards the back to the right. Under a pile of rocks and dirt."

She nodded her thanks and Scott was back under water and making his way to the exit. It was only ten more air pockets away. Once he got to the curved part of the cave entrance, he pushed himself off of the rocky floor and shot upwards.

His leg seized up just feet below the surface. He pushed frantically with his good leg and his arms. Finally, he broke the surface and took in air. His lungs were on fire.

Someone shouted from behind him and a hand grabbed his arm. He turned and accepted help pulling him to the boat.

"You got the flag?" the man who helped him shouted.

"Yeah." Scott held it up feebly.

"Alright then. Last leg."

"What?"

The man nodded at the oars sitting on the side of the boat. "You need to get to shore. You don't worry about direction. Just try to keep us straight. Fortunately for you, it looks like the waves have already died down some."

Scott took an oar in each hand and rhythmically pulled. Before he got very far, Carolyn was up and getting into her boat. A few others were just starting their dive into the cave. By the time he was a quarter mile into the leg, Phillip and Casey were getting into their boats.

"Half a mile to go."

"This leg isn't so long." Scott grunted.

"Yeah." The man shrugged. "The waves are usually a lot choppier. Last year, the people who came out of the cave first wore themselves out on the heavy waves, and the people in the middle of the pack made up a lot of ground."

"We may have a repeat of that." Scott looked out at the three behind him. They were gaining. "I'm running out of umph."

"Stop talking then." The man looked behind them. "And breathe out when you pull the oars in. Use your legs more."

Scott obeyed, focusing solely on the task of making it to shore.

"Quarter mile."

Scott struggled to maneuver the oars through the water.

"Almost there."

The other three were now even with each other, and gaining. Casey had made up the most ground, obviously making good on his boast of being a great rower.

Finally, the boat hit the shore. Scott almost fell out backwards as the boat caught sand.

"Made it. Now you just have run to that finish line over there."

Scott turned where the guide was pointing. It wasn't far, but he didn't know if his leg would make it. He flopped out of the boat and collapsed on to the sand. With a heavy grunt, he pushed himself up and began limping to the finish line.

People were cheering, but he only heard it in the distance. He limped along for maybe fifty meters when he heard the sound of several boats crashing onto the beach behind him. He didn't dare turn around to look. He just kept running.

Footsteps grew near. He was just feet away. He leapt off of his good leg and then extended the flag past the line just as the others caught up to him.

He had done it. He had won. People came in to help him up. They carried him. Water was pressed to his lips. Someone began rubbing a soothing warmth on his leg. He gained his strength, a little, and then a stronger drink was handed to him.

People were shouting his name and cheering. He raised his glass, finally feeling like he was back in the Perth he left.

*****

Back at the diner, Scott walked up the staircase to Tom's room. He knocked on the door and waited. A soft sound came from behind the door, but it did not open.

"Tom! I know you're in there!" Scott shouted. "I have the money."

Still no answer. Scott scratched the scars on his leg. He contemplated kicking down the door.

"I can't sell it to you," Tom said from inside the door.

"Why?"

"The town needs it."

Scott rolled clenched his fist. "Can't you just get more?"

Downstairs, a loud crash came from the front door of the diner. Someone in the diner screamed.

"We need a doctor!" came a shout.

"That's down the road," one of the waitresses said as Scott was running down the stairs. "Does she have the infection?"

"No, she's been shot a few times by Coalition soldiers."

"What did you bring her here for?" Clara shouted at them as she hurriedly reached under the counter for a gun. "Ya daft idiots!"

"She was at the boarder of Perth when we saw her. We took out the soldiers, but she fainted from the loss of blood."

Scott ran past the onlookers to get a good look at the woman. He could not believe it. Laying almost lifeless on the floor was Olivia. The Phantom Queen's former second in command.

His mind raced to the last time he saw her, in a Coalition float pod, captured and taken to the Underlabs.

"I never thought I'd see you again." Scott knelt down to check for life. "We need to stop the bleeding."

"And fast," One of the men said. "We figure there are still a few of the soldiers out there chasing her."

"How many did you see?"

"Just the two we took out."

Scott looked out the windows and to the sky. No float pods. He stood up and checked the streets. Three soldiers were running across the dirt road to the diner.

"They're here," Scott shouted. "Anyone with something to hide, start hiding. Anyone with a gun or something, I'd be grateful if I could borrow it."

"Here." Clara tossed him a gun from behind the counter. "Keep them out of my establishment."

"You got it." Scott caught the rifle and opened the door.

With three shots, he took out three knee caps and the soldiers were on the ground, screaming in pain. Scott ran out with the gun aimed. He could not see any other soldiers.

The closest soldier pulled out a pistol and pointed it at Scott. Scott shot him in the bicep and kicked the gun out of reach.

"I'd stay down if I were you." Scott knelt down and took weapons from the soldier's suit.

Blood stained the soldier's torso and legs. It spilled onto the road. As Scott helped himself to a few grenades, the blood darkened. The red turned into a rotten green color.

Scott looked over and saw the other two soldiers clutching at their sides. All three of them screamed with a familiar dread.

"Tetrapath!" Scott yelled. "Sound the alarm! Get everyone inside!"

Scott shot all three soldiers in the head. For a moment, they slumped to the ground, lifeless. But then the green ooze pumped out of their wounds, and covered the bodies. The fallen soldiers convulsed, and slowly stood up.

"Well," Scott sighed. "That's new."

Clutching some coalition gear in his arms he ran back into the diner. A few brave men lingered, but the diner was now mostly empty.

"Have some weapons," Scott said, tossing the stolen Coalition gear.

"We should kill the girl too," one man said, pointing his gun at Olivia.

"No." Scott shouted. "That woman has as much reason to fear the Coalition as you do. Now shut up and help me carry her out the back."

"What about the tetrapaths? Aren't you going to kill them?"

"I already did," Scott said. "They just got back up. I'm still trying to figure out how to kill them if they're already dead."

Scott's leg tingled the way it did when tetrapaths were near. He peaked out the window, and only one tetrapath remained in the street. It was still forming, turning the host body into a horrible monster. The spine was now stretched, knees were bent backwards, and there was massive bone growth on the hands, forming large clubs.

"Two of them have run off," Scott said. "There's only one to deal with."

Large, thunderous footsteps raced across the roof. A loud crash came from the back, followed by a scream.

"Or, they're covering all of the exits." Scott checked his gun again. "More surprises from these guys."

One tetrapath crashed through the kitchen, fresh blood splattered on its jaw. Another crashed though Tom's door, bearing an impaled Tom in his spike-like hand.

Scott threw a grenade at the tetrapath upstairs. The tetrapath leapt into the air, and hit it back at him.

Scott leapt just out of the blast radius, but felt heat from the energy. With a roll, he sprang back up and fired a few more shots. They merely annoyed the tetrapaths.

Two of the men were down. He rolled over to grab a heavier weapon. The closest one was a grappling hook, used by the Coalition to trap various tetrapaths instead of killing them.

The tetrapath from the kitchen swung its club hand into the chest of another Perthian. The man was flung all the way out of the dining hall.

The remaining two men charged the tetrapath from upstairs, now on the ground floor. One fired flammable shotgun rounds, while the other fired an assault rifle. The tetrapath impaled one of them with a long, bony spear growing at the end of its hand, and then smashed the other man with his friend. At that moment, the tetrapath from the street crashed through the door. It stood taller than the others, perhaps 12 feet tall.

Only Scott remained. He was surrounded by three tetrapaths with more intelligence than the ones he was used to dealing with.

His mind raced for something to do. The three tetrapaths crept closer, moving in for the kill. He could really use a gifted Soul jumper right about now.

Then it clicked. He had a scribe. She was dying on the floor, but she still had powers. He hefted the grappling hook and shot the tetrapath closest to Olivia. It connected with the shoulder, nailing it to the wall.

With a quick dive, he clasped Olivia's face in his hands. A green orb shot up his arms from her face and stopped in his brain. His whole body tensed up and he nearly fell over.

He had to play this just right. When he absorbed powers, the tetrapath infection was unleashed. It amped up his strength right away, making him almost even with his current opponents, but eventually the true monster would break out of him. It was a fine line.

One of the tetrapath behind him lunged at him. Scott rolled out of the way and the tetrapath crashed through the wall, freeing the tetrapath he had nailed with the grappling hook.

With one motion, Scott picked up a circular table and threw it like a Frisbee at the remaining tetrapath, knocking it back into the bar. His shoulder popped out of socket, and something snapped in his elbow.

He shot his arm, and the tetrapath infection snapped it back together.

He had a few precious seconds before they all got up and charged him. With those seconds, he used the scribe power he had just borrowed to create a new memory.

The two tetrapath that crashed through the wall got up and lunged at him. Scott leaped to his right and ran to the counter of weapons.

He grabbed a long knife, made for stabbing through the thick skin of the tetrapath, and planted a green orb containing his recent memory into the knife.

The spike armed tetrapath reached him and thrust the long spike at Scott. Scott deflected it and pushed it into the tallest tetrapath's leg.

He then stabbed the tallest tetrapath with the knife and leapt over it. The tallest tetrapath slumped to the ground in a memory trance while the spike armed tetrapath tried to free itself.

Scott then grabbed three grenades from the table of coalition weapons and ran back to the entangled tetrapath.

The club hand tetrapath gave chase behind him. With a few quick steps, Scott shoved a grenade down the throat of the tallest tetrapath, and leapt over him again.

The explosion shattered the head of the tallest tetrapath and sent the remaining two flying back out of the diner. Scott pulled the knife out of the leg of the fallen tetrapath and ran to chase down the others.

They both got up and lunged at him. Scott kicked his legs out and slid under the tetrapath. He stabbed the one on his right, and spun to kick the other one away.

The stabbed tetrapath fell to the ground in a trance and Scott shoved another grenade into its head.

The other tetrapath charged again. Scott pulled the knife out of the fallen body and leapt out of the blast radius.

The explosion pushed the remaining tetrapath aside. Scott ran and stabbed it in the back as it landed. With a quick push, the monster rolled over, and he shoved the last grenade down its throat.

Scott stood up and walked back to the diner as its head was blown clean off. He looked down at Olivia, and then at his trembling hands.

He had to cure himself first. He ran up the stairs to Tom's broken room. There on the table was ten bottles of medicine against the tetrapath infection. He pocketed the bottles and put three pills in his hands.

His empty hand extended, and he expelled the green orb of Olivia's scribe powers. It would fade with time anyway, and it was aggravating the tetrapath infection. Once it was clear, he swallowed the three pills and his body relaxed.

When his hands stopped shaking, he walked down the stairs for Olivia.

"You did it again Scott." Clara called from behind the counter.

"Just lucky this time." Scott said, walking back to Olivia. "Can you help me lift her to the doctor's?"

"Sure. We're not going to have any customers for a while." She walked over. "You know this woman?"

"Yes." Scott knelt down to cradle her arms. "She used to run with a dangerous crowd."

"Looks like that caught up to her." Clara snorted as she grabbed Olivia's legs. "You do know that Perth is going to call for your exile now."

"What? Why?"

"Because you show up and the tetrapath return," a voice said behind him.

Scott turned his head to see the mayor. "In Coalition soldiers. The coalition brought it."

Carolyn was not convinced. "It's a good story Scott. But I want you and your bleeding friend out of here."

Scott adjusted his grip among the slippery blood. This brought up again the last memory he had of her. Bleeding and slipping out of his arms.

"She still needs a doctor." Scott protested. "She'll die if she doesn't get medical attention right now."

Clara ran for the kitchen, and then returned carrying a medical kit. "I will help you patch her up. But after that, the both of you have to leave town."

"Fine." Scott reached into his pocket and pulled out the prize money from the race. He tossed all of it at the mayor's feet. "This was never about personal gain."

CHAPTER 4: THE ARCHIVE STONE

Miranda's alarm beeped and she sat up in her cot. She touched the data pad on the table to silence the alarm, took in a deep breath and got back to work.

A screen popped up on the desk in front of her, asking how she felt.

"I feel great." She recorded. "Week three of the sleep cycle experiment appears to be working. My body has adjusted, and according to the data, I went through a full sleep cycle in 20 minutes. Now, where were we?"

The screen switched and Miranda continued pouring over wiring diagrams and physics papers. Then she consulted the real notes. Her notes.

On her left wrist she wore a bracelet of rope holding together polished stones. At the top of the bracelet, there was one stone that was larger than the others. It was in here, that Miranda had figured out how to store an almost infinite number of memories into one object.

With her finger, she rubbed on the rock, scrolling through the dozens of recordings stored in there already. She came to the one she wanted, a memory of the last field test of the suits. She pulled the memory up, but instead of floating up her arm, it rested in mid air, playing for her like a holographic projection just above her wrist.

The movie showed a test subject pulling a Bunsen burner through a portal in her pocket. That worked. The power readings confirmed that the suit was receiving power transferred through the portals. Meaning, as long as the ship had power, and the suit was connected to the ship via the portals, the suit had power.

So far, so good. She fast forwarded the recording until they got outside. There, the test subject was strapped to a harness and instructed to try to scale the outside of the ship.

The test subject made it up the smooth surface for 20 feet, but then began slipping. She fell, was caught by the rope, and then lowered gently to the ground. The test subject reported extreme lag in the nano fiber response time.

The next test was with the suit on a dummy. They pointed a small hand gun at it and fired. A hole tore through what would have been a torso. The gun was fired three more times, and the suit did not harden to block the bullet until the final shot. Serious lag time.

"Miranda!" whispered one of her assistants impatiently. "You have a visitor!"

"Is Scott back?" Miranda pressed her hand to her bracelet and turned to her assistant.

"No." The assistant continued to whisper. "This is Silas Stanton. Head of the Historical Preservation Project."

Silas was tall, with a wide chin and wavy brown hair that was graying in sections. His eyes were wide, but that looked more like his natural facial features, rather than any surprise at the moment.

"Hello, Silas." Miranda forced a smile. "How can I help you?"

Silas returned the smile, and walked calmly towards them. "I hear you have a little girl who can get things."

"That depends on what you want." Miranda said, with a slight warning in her tone.

He held up his hands in front of him. "I mean no harm. It's just that, well, we can't get back to the Helix Cascade with the traditional portal, and there are some things over there worth preserving that I'd like to bring back to Naprea."

"I agree." Miranda nodded. "I would have attempted a similar project myself had I not been so busy. What specifically are you hoping to get?"

"Adjacent to the temple there is an archive hall," Silas started.

"I know the one," Miranda interrupted. "A big hall full of shelves and stones, right? Miles of them?"

Silas' face scrunched up in confusion. "And just what were you doing in the hall?"

"Scott and I needed a short cut to the bottom of the mountain. Seemed like that one would work."

"A short cut!" Silas grabbed his hair and turned away for a second. "That is sacred ground!"

"Sacred?" Miranda raised an eyebrow. "It's a glorified hall of records."

Silas made a show of biting his tongue and brought his rapid breathing under control. "Did you touch any of the stones?"

"Yes," Miranda admitted. "Well, technically no. We had to use a few of them to put some activists into a trance."

"You used the archives as weapons?"

"It was either that, or let someone die. I hope you don't hold those stones more valuable than a person's life. Now, do you want to lecture me about an antiquated belief system, or do you want to talk about getting the archive stones back?"

Silas grabbed the edge of the table and squeezed. After a few seconds, his smile returned. "You're right. Forgive my manners. How were you to know? It seems, ultimately, that we want the same thing. To bring the history over here to preserve it."

"That we can agree on," Miranda said. "But I'm really busy."

"Then let me lead the team," Silas pleaded. "It's my job anyway. We'll keep your sister safe, and bring back everything."

"No." Miranda shook her head. "I can't let her leave. There are too many dangers."

"I don't think you understand the seriousness of the situation." Silas pointed a finger. "We have a duty to those records and-"

"And I will personally make sure they are eventually returned. You can come along when the time comes." Miranda turned her back to him, agitated. She started typing on a screen.

"When the time comes?" Silas asked.

Miranda let the silence grow for a minute, and then turned back to face him. "Yes. Eventually. They're not in any danger where they are right now, are they?"

"The Coalition has been to the islands." Silas picked up a random Bunsen burner and fiddled with the knob. "Who's to say they won't return for more?"

"It would take weeks for them to do that," Miranda said.

Silas set down the Bunsen burner. "Look, I'll level with you. I have some smart people at my disposal. I'll send them up here to help you with your work for the next few days if you agree to take us to the temple, say, a week from today."

Miranda tapped on her keyboard, thinking about what she would be doing in the next week. "Can any of them manufacture circuit boards?"

"Probably not. But they're quick learners."

"Send them over tomorrow. If they're any good, we have a deal."

"Thank you." Silas nodded and left the room. The assistants around her got back to work.

Miranda took a calming breath and sat in her chair. She resumed her routine of analyzing mass amounts of data, consulting with assistants, and endlessly changing and refining her formulas. After a few hours, her datapad beeped again, displaying the message:

[4 hours has passed. Time for another sleep cycle.]

With a yawn she moved back to her desk, pulled out the cot from underneath it, and instantly fell asleep.

Twenty minutes later, Miranda deactivated her alarm and rolled off the cot. As she sat up, she noticed half of the assistants were gone. And the ones who were still there were huddled together talking.

"Is it everything already?" Miranda asked the room.

The closest assistant looked at Miranda with concern for a moment, and then decided to speak. "Scott's back, and he brought a girl with him."

"A girl?" Miranda stood up and changed her lab coat for a light leather jacket. "Who?"

"I don't know. Some blond girl. About your age. Maybe a little younger. They're at the hospital right now, she was hurt very badly."

Miranda felt a twinge of anger, but she didn't know why. "I'll be back. Don't run any tests without me."

"You mean, you're actually leaving the ship?"

"Yeah. Why is that weird?"

"Well, it's been like two or three weeks since you've been out of this room."

"Oh," Miranda looked around at her work. Had it really been that long? "Well, when someone new comes into town, we have to make sure she's safe."

"You know..." The assistant hesitated. "Brea used to take care of herself. She was much more productive when she was fully rested."

Miranda looked over at the wall where a memory of Brea, the former lead scientist, was kept. "I don't have that luxury."

Miranda left the room and walked for the ship's exit. As she traveled down the ramp, she had to shield her eyes from the glaring sun, something she had not seen in a long time.

The hospital was close, but there were a lot of people in this section of the town. Small food vendors lined the busy streets, vying for the attention of travelers. Amidst the confusion, she had to take an extra lap around the inner ring of Naprea, trying to find the hospital.

The hospital was perhaps the most impressive building in the city. The only thing taller than it was the crashed spaceship that Miranda called her home.

The doors opened automatically and she walked across a linoleum floor to a receptionist's desk.

"Hi, I'm looking for my friend Scott, and I think he brought somebody here recently."

"Yes." The receptionist nodded and stood up from her chair. "Talk's been all over the town. Poor thing was really hurt. She's down the hallway behind me. Room 107 on your left."

"Thanks."

Miranda walked around the desk and pushed through a set of double doors. Doctors and visitors were walking in and out of rooms and she did her best to stay out of anybody's way as she navigated herself to room 107.

Inside, a group of nurses were tending to a blond woman laying on the bed. The woman looked familiar, but she couldn't quite place why.

"Miranda!" Scott turned around. "Aren't you supposed to be hibernating or something?"

"Very funny." Miranda scrunched her lips in a fake smile. "I hear you brought a girl home with you."

"Yeah," Scott said. "She was shot up pretty bad by the Coalition. She's been unconscious since I found her."

"So you got to be the big hero and save her from the mean soldiers?"

"Tetrapaths, by the time I got to them," Scott said nonchalantly.

Miranda smirked. "I thought you were going to get medicine."

"I did. And Perth didn't want her to stay."

"Why?"

At that moment, a nurse turned around. "We've got the bioportals out, and the trackers. We're adding more blood back to her system. Hard to find her blood type among the Scribes though."

"Why does it need to be scribe blood?" Miranda asked.

"Well, because she's a scribe, dear." The nurse shook her head like that should have been obvious. "We can't go mixing tribal blood."

Miranda pulled up her sleeve. "I'm a universal donor blood type."

"Perfect." The nurse directed someone else to bring a needle. "Sit down on that chair."

She did as directed, and a needle was plunged into the inside of her elbow.

"So, Scott." Miranda licked her lips. "Anything else about this woman that you want to tell me? Before she wakes up?"

"You're not getting jealous, are you?" Scott asked. "Because last time I checked, our arranged marriage wasn't a high priority."

"This has nothing to do with that." Miranda scratched her hand nervously. "I'm..simply concerned with the safety of our city. Stop dodging the question."

"We'll have to keep monitoring her," the nurse said. "Being that she escaped from the Underlabs, there may be something new they put into her body."

"She escaped from the Underlabs?" Miranda tried to stand up, but a nurse pushed her back down. "Why didn't you tell me?"

"I was about to," Scott almost shouted.

"Well, were you two cell mates or something?"

"No." Scott shook his head in annoyance. "She was one of the Activist handlers. She was caught while I was running around with them."

The room went silent and everyone looked at each other with a touch of nervousness.

"She's an Activist?" Miranda broke the silence.

"Yeah," Scott said. "But she's one of the more sensible ones. I think we can turn her around."

"I don't believe this," Miranda said as the needle was pulled out of her arm. She tried to stand up. The nurse pushed her back into the chair and placed a cookie in her hand.

"What?" Scott said.

"Don't you think it is a little suspicious that an Activist broke out of the Underlabs?"

"I did it. You're not suspicious of me, are you?"

"Yeah, but..."

"But what?" Scott interrupted loudly. "Was I supposed to just let her bleed out, or turn into a Tetrapath?"

"Will you two cut it out?" the nurse yelled. "We are trying to save a woman's life. If you insist on continuing that conversation, do it outside. Preferably on the other side of town. We will monitor her, with guards on hand. Come back and visit when you've calmed down."

"Come on, let's go," Scott said. "We're supposed to meet with Clarinthia and Kiri for lunch pretty soon anyway."

"What? No, I need to get back to-"

"They're insisting." Scott stood up and walked to the door. "They have important business."

"Ok, but I do have to get back to work."

They stepped out of the hospital and once more into the blazing afternoon light. Miranda's eyes took a few minutes to adjust.

Scott led them through town. The noise of people yelling and moving and setting up shop was at first deafening and then inviting. It reminded her somewhat of the Oldtown market she used to frequent when working for the Coalition.

"How long has this been going on?" Miranda asked.

"The market?" Scott gave her a look of disbelief. "They've always had this. Since before we got here. You really need to get out more often."

Miranda sighed and continued to follow Scott. After navigating the market, they arrived at a quaint outdoor cafe. Clarinthia and Kiri were already there, and food was brought out as they arrived.

"Greetings, friends!" Clarinthia gestured to three open seats. Her hair was a bright silvery white, and had thinned significantly since last Miranda saw her. "I trust your morning is going well."

"Actually," Miranda said as she sat down. "There is the matter of this girl Scott has brought into the walls of this city."

"Yes." Clarinthia smiled. "I always knew she would return in her own time. I am so glad you found her, Scott."

"But she's a known activist!" Miranda demanded. "She was involved in plots to take down Naprea."

"We knew her heart was not in it," Kiri said with a croaky voice.

A thick cloud of purple smoke appeared in an empty seat at the table and Talia teleported into it.

"What are you doing out of the ship?" Talia's eyes were wide, and she tussled her hair nervously.

"What are you doing out of school?" Miranda folded her arms and narrowed her eyes.

Talia looked down at the table cloth. "Oh, uh, I'm on a morning break."

"It's the middle of the afternoon," Scott said.

"Oh, right. afternoon break. You know, for lunch." Talia twitched nervously in her seat. "Anyway, I have to get back. Those lunch breaks sure are short."

Another flash of purple, and she was gone. Miranda looked to the sky and saw a purple cloud form over them. She stared at it until the cloud vanished.

"Anybody else think Talia got a lot older all of a sudden?" Scott asked the group.

"Children her age are prone to growth spurts," Clarinthia said.

Scott shook his head slightly as he finished another mouthful of food. "Not like that, they aren't. She looks years older than the last time I saw her."

"That was a long time ago," Miranda said. "Kids grow up when you're not around."

They sat in silence for a while and ate.

"Okay, what do you want?" Miranda asked Clarinthia after she finished her plate.

Clarinthia set down her fork. "We would like to ask a favor of you."

"I probably don't have the time," Miranda said curtly.

"But you are uniquely qualified." Kiri squeezed her hands as she talked. "Unless, that bracelet of yours does not hold multiple recordings?"

"What, this?" Miranda held up the bracelet. "Yes, it does. But what does that have to do with anything?"

"A war is brewing in Naprea." Clarinthia said. "And we have been trying to stop it for a long time. Your gifts, aided with others we can give you, will put you in a position to stop it."

"How?" Miranda asked.

"I, too, have a unique gift." Kiri said. "I can see hidden recordings even as they are being made, for miles."

"With this gift," Clarinthia continued. "We have been able to find all of the original plans of the activists. But we think there may be more hidden from us."

"Our bodies grow too old for the constant traveling." Kiri tapped her back. "But if we gave you my powers, you could find them all and put them into one recording. Play it for all of Naprea to see. Help them see that these Activists were not on a religious errand, but acting out of selfish ambition."

"Even if I had the time, how would you give me your powers?" Miranda asked.

"Through Scott." Clarinthia nodded her head towards him.

Scott dropped his fork and scrunched his lips. "I uh, don't know how to do that."

"A routine procedure. I'm sure you'll pick it up." Clarinthia waved off the concern. "The important thing is, that we get these powers to you as soon as possible. In a week's time, there will be a public gathering. We hope to expose the real intent of the Activists at that gathering."

"So, you think there are still people wanting to join the Activists?" Miranda asked.

"Yes," Clarinthia said. "There are more now than ever before. the Report that they went through the Archway

Portal and may have found their salvation on the other side is quite appealing to most members of this town."

Miranda stared back at the two elderly ladies. She pulled up a napkin and wiped the edge of her lips, cleaning off excess food. "Look, you two have been good friends to me. But I have more pressing issues. I have to find a way to contend with the coalition and beat them to Earth."

"It will not matter who gets there first if this town kills itself." Kiri said.

"This town is not savable!" Miranda pounded the table and her cheeks turned red. He ear was pulsing with every heart beat, but her next words were more restrained. "Sorry, but it's not. They hold onto weird grudges, they follow a nearly suicidal religion that was obviously made up by Doctor Pavarti. There is no amount of truth that can undo the brainwashing that has taken place here."

"All of this does not mean it is not worth it to this town to try." Kiri stood up and walked away.

Clarinthia looked after her, a pained expression growing on her face. "Please reconsider. There is only so much we can do for this town on our own."

Clarinthia stood up and followed Kiri back into the crowd.

"I should probably get back," Miranda said. "I haven't had a chance to work on the suits yet today."

"Why do you need those so badly anyway?" Scott asked before she could stand.

"Did you see what your friend did with one of those suits?" Miranda asked. "He was unstoppable."

"He's your friend too," Scott said. "And yes, I did. But Dixon can do most of that without a suit. He's got a knack for that sort of thing."

"We need every advantage we can get."

"We have a little girl who can teleport anything anywhere!" Scott said emphatically. "And by the looks of that conversation you just had with her, you are alienating her! And everybody. Azurand found a way to beat the suit, and you can too. But you shouldn't do it at the expense of everybody who cares about you."

"You want to talk about alienating?" Miranda refolded her arms. "Where have you been all of this time? And why did you leave?"

Scott looked away. "You know why I left."

"I'm not in the habit of asking questions I know the answers to." Miranda now unfolded her arms and leaned in close to him. "I know that I asked you for help, and then you left."

"You were asking for help I couldn't give."

"What do you mean?" Miranda raised her eyebrow. "You are a talent snatcher! Any talent of mine can be yours for a handshake! Or a hug, or a kiss."

"And I want to. Help you, I mean. Not necessarily the..." Scott's face grew red as he scratched the back of his head and looked away. "But I can't. I have a problem... taking talents from scribes and soul jumpers."

"A problem?"

"It aggravates the tetrapath infection in me." Scott said. "That's why I left. I went to find medicine to help with that."

"Scott, I... I didn't realize..."

Scott stood up from his seat. "Well, you should try listening more. If you can find Talia, practice on her."

"Are you leaving?"

"I'll be in town for at least a week." Scott said. "Clarinthia made me promise to stay here for the big meeting. But right now I have to go clear my head."

Scott walked away, leaving Miranda alone at a table for five in the middle of a busy outdoor diner. She looked back to the ship in the center of the city, and with resignation, made her way back to the laboratory.

CHAPTER 5: OLIVIA'S QUEST

Pain. She felt a lot of pain. Or was it he? She checked. She. There was a small swarm of people poking and shoving and shouting around her. Someone shined a light in her eye. Her stomach lurched and she couldn't even warn the people. But they were fast. A bucket materialized and caught everything she expelled.

She took in a deep breath, and someone shoved a straw in her face. She drank, and the external noises and bright lights softened a bit. The people around her were talking, but not to her, so she paid no attention.

The room was a hospital of some kind. But where was she? The nurses wore unusual garb. There was absolutely no skin showing. The gloves were almost green, and the hats looked like chef hats.

Her throat burned with pain on the first attempt to speak. But she couldn't even react to the pain. She drank more water and forced herself to calm down.

"Olivia?" One of the nurses placed a hand on her arm. "Do you need anything?"

Was her name Olivia? It was hard to tell if the nurse was talking to her behind that mask. She tried to respond, but no words came. She tried to scratch her arm, but she couldn't move.

"Olivia?" The voice came again. "You need to rest. I'm going to give you a sedative. When you wake up, you should feel better."

Nothing seemed to matter. Nothing except rest.

*****

When she woke up again, the room was empty and silent. Small conversations could be heard just outside the door.

She tried her arms, and this time, she found the strength to lift them. She tried her throat, and she managed a soft whisper, but only to prevent herself from being heard. She could tell her voice worked just fine now.

Her nose itched, and she let out a loud sneeze. She brought her hands up to her face and felt the thunk of something large dislodged from her nose. Her first reaction was to flick it away, but it was glowing green.

Goosebumps ran up and down her arms, and then to her shoulders and neck. Thousands of images rushed through her mind. Garbled sounds. In moments, relevant information filled her thoughts. Inara: her real name. Olivia: her cover name. Donovan: her husband and co-architect behind the heist she was in the middle of.

A nurse came through the door. "Olivia, are you alright?"

Inara shot her a wide eyed look. "Who are you? What's going on? What are you doing to me?"

"Olivia..." The nurse calmly raised her arms to show she meant no harm. "We brought you back from the Coalition. We think they did something to your mind."

"My mind..." Inara reached for her head, and took in a sharp breath. "I don't... I don't understand."

"I can get the doctor if..."

"No!" Inara shook her head. "No, I feel fine. I just don't remember anything."

"Maybe I'll arrange for some of your friends to visit." The nurse left the room.

Inara placed a finger on a nostril and blew her nose. A small ring shot out and landed in her other hand.

"There you are." She placed it under her pillow as the doctor approached.

"Sorry, I hear you say you don't need me." The doctor picked up a stethoscope and walked up to the bed. "But I have to screen you."

Inara widened her eyes again. "Screen?"

"I just need to look at the monitors and find out how much longer you need to stay here."

The doctor tapped on a few machines and looked at some charts. Then she ran a series of tests for reflexes and responsiveness.

"I can't believe it." The doctor set a few papers down. "You are fully recovered. Ready to go. Everything about your blood tests look fine."

"Really?" Inara scratched at her arm nervously. "I don't need to be in here anymore?"

"No. You're fine. There's just the matter of your memories." The doctor reached out to touch her on the head.

"Please don't." Inara recoiled back. "Please, I feel cramped in here. Can I leave?"

"Leaving you on your own right now is probably a bad idea."

A tall man with wide eyes strode through the door. "I can take her."

"Silas?" The doctor turned. "What are you doing here?"

"She's a family friend." Silas smiled. "I heard she was brought back into town, ill, and without her memory."

"This wouldn't have anything to do with your son leaving town on account of her?"

Silas' eyes flashed angrily for the slightest moment. "Be that as it may, the girl still has a soft spot in my heart. I am here to help. Maybe I can help her remember what happened to my son."

"Olivia, do you feel comfortable with this man?"

While the doctor was turned to her and talking, Silas winked at her. What was he doing? Without really knowing who that man was, it was hard to determine if he was dangerous or not.

"Yes, I think so. If I'm a family friend."

The doctor shook her head in futility. "Ok. I'll take care of the paper work. You get dressed and be on your way."

The doctor showed Silas out, giving Inara some privacy. After she was dressed, she pulled the small ring out from behind her pillow and rubbed it between her fingers. This made the molecular compound change and the ring turned elastic. She stretched it out as wide as a dinner plate and it turned into a portal. A small box fell from the other side. She popped it open and examined the contents.

Several spray bottles, a taser, and a pair of contacts. She put the contacts on and an augmented reality appeared in her vision. She calibrated the movements and they began responding to her. Then she stuck the taser in a pocket in her provided shirt.

The screen on her contacts flashed. Donovan sent a message.

[Welcome back Inara. How are you doing?]

"Just fine dear. Not much time to explain. Just follow along." Inara placed the rest of the gear back into the box and shoved the box back through the portal. With a little twisting, the portal turned off, and the ring shrunk back down. She placed it on her ring finger and left the room.

In the lobby, Silas nodded for her to follow him, and didn't say anything until they were a block away from the hospital.

"So, how much do you remember?" Silas asked.

"Nothing."

Silas clenched his jaw for a moment, but kept walking. He led her into a library a few blocks down. It was modest, with maybe ten bookshelves in it. They were arranged in an open circular pattern around a set of tables.

"Well, I can help you with the first chunk of your life."

They walked to the back wall of the library, where a large row of reference materials were stacked in random intervals on shelves.

"Not a lot of books here," Inara casually mentioned.

Silas chuckled. "You really don't remember, do you?"

"No."

"You used to be my most frequent guest." Silas reached in his pocket and pulled out a set of keys as they reached a locked door at the back wall. "You understood then, as you will again, our society doesn't much need to keep history in written form."

They walked through the door and into what looked like a warehouse. The room was easily twice the size of the library, but there wasn't a single book. Dozens of industrial shelves stood in organized rows, and they were full of stones.

They walked to the right and down a few rows. Silas looked thoughtfully at signs tagged on each of the shelves and navigated his way to a particular one. There, he pulled out a small box labeled 'family.' He opened the lid and it was divided into fifteen sections, each with a name on it. The first one Inara saw was 'Olivia.'

"Like I said," Silas picked up the box and handed it to her. "You were a family friend."

[This is looking very promising.] Donovan typed into her message screen.

Inara reached in and picked up the stone with her name. Again, thousands of images and sounds poured into her mind. In moments, all of Olivia's memories were downloaded into Inara's brain.

She looked back at Silas, this time with hundreds of memories of family dinners, stolen kisses with his son, and the formation of the Activists in her mind.

"This was taken about a year before you left," Silas admitted. "But it's better than nothing."

"I'll say!" Inara smiled and jumped to hug Silas. She had many memories of Olivia doing that.

"Welcome back." Silas returned the embrace. After the hug, he said, "Do you remember what happened to my son?"

"No," Inara shook her head. "All I remember is that he did not approve of the Activists. He wouldn't even come to the meetings or hang out with Brooke."

Silas' face sank and he nodded his head in understanding.

"So, all those reports I heard about people traveling to earth, that was us? It worked?" Inara said, desperately wanting to change the subject.

"Yes. Yes it did. The Phantom Queen is over there now. Do you know what she was planning to do?"

"Actually, I planned it." Inara chose carefully what she was about to say. Plucking what she knew about Silas from Olivia's memories. "She was going to bring back power. Power to restore Naprea's faith in the gods."

Silas' eyes flickered with excitement. "Really?"

"Yes." As big a lie as there was. Olivia was actually trying to bring back proof of the falsehood of their unfounded religion. It was the very lie that fueled the Activists in the first place.

"What kind of power?"

"I can't say just yet," Inara whispered and looked around the room. "But we need to be ready."

"How can I help?"

"Well, you can start by inviting me over to another wonderful family dinner, and bringing me up to speed on everything that's happened in the last year." Inara smiled. "And then we can plan out how best to prepare this town for the days ahead."

*****

"Dinner is ready," Hudson Stanton said, peeking his head around the window.

Inara stole a quick glance, but saw him clench his jaw. She tentatively made her way to the table where Silas and Mrs. Stanton were taking seats.

"It is so good to see you again," Mrs. Stanton said as she poured a ruby red drink into a wine glass. "I had feared we had seen the last of our family dinners."

"She never actually became family," Hudson said bitterly.

"Don't take that tone, boy," Silas warned. "We may have had our differences a year ago, but she is our way of finding your brother again."

"So..." Inara trailed off, trying to change the subject.

[Ask about their political system.] Donovan typed into her eyes.

"So how is the political landscape?" Inara blurted out. "Ready to accept that changes need to be made yet?"

"Yes, and no." Silas set down his own glass and buttered some bread. "I think you would have three times the volunteers signing up to be Activists today than you did a year ago. They've been so impressed that the Phantom Queen made it through the Archway portal."

"That sounds great!" Inara said as Mrs. Stanton and Hudson exchanged sour looks.

"Yes, but there are still strong numbers opposing such moves." Silas shook his head. "If there was only a way I could make a greater influence on the city."

"What's standing in your way?" Inara asked.

"A few big things," Silas admitted. "I am one of the next in line for a position of Elder in the government. But all of the seats are filled, and they only way they vacate is through death."

"So, if someone died..."

"Honestly, dear." Mrs. Stanton interrupted. "You're talking like you're planning to murder someone!"

"Oh no." Inara placed a hand on her chest. "I would never do that. I'm just trying to understand how the government works is all."

"Yes." Silas smiled a bit too broadly, trying to calm the tension. "If a member of the Elder circle passed, then the next in line would be up. But there are four of us with equal rank. So, there would be a month trial period where we would have the powers and responsibilities of an Elder of the Circle. In addition, we would campaign to the city, and at the end of the month, the city would vote on who gets in."

"And what would you do, if you became an Elder of the circle?"

"I would purify the town with fire." Silas set down his fork. "And I would start with our young heroes from the islands. They have been a scourge upon us long enough."

[Let's get this guy elected!] Donovan typed into her screen.

After dinner, Hudson and Mrs. Stanton retired to another part of the house to study. Silas poured a glass of wine for the two of them and they walked out to the back patio. His yard was small, but it rested at just the right point to have a good view of the valley.

"I think we should plan your election campaign," Inara began.

"Somebody has to die for that." Silas sat down on a lounge chair and gazed up at the starry sky. "And if you're thinking of killing somebody, I want no part of it."

Inara sat in another lounge chair and joined him. "No. That's not what I am saying. I am saying, I think you are right that this place is in need of a great purge. And it can't wait for the Phantom Queen to return home. We need to take action now."

"But what can I do?" Silas raised his glass aimlessly. "I don't have the authority to do what is needed."

"When the voice of the people agree with you, our leaders will have no choice but to carry out the deed." Inara leaned forward in her chair. "We need to show these people how much they need Scott, Miranda and Dixon out of this town."

"Don't forget Talia."

"Who?"

"The teleporting girl."

"Oh, right." Inara took a long sip of wine.

"How would we change the dynamic of the city?" Silas asked. "Get them all to realize that they are holding our people back spiritually?"

"I seem to remember you had an ability to plant false memories into people." Inara took a stab in the dark. Olivia's memories were sporadic on the subject, but there was enough evidence to support the theory.

"How did you know about that?" Silas turned to face her, his eyes growing wider.

"I didn't," Inara admitted. "Just something I've always guessed."

"Well, I don't. I can send real memories through the air. But someone who can work in the world of false memories lives under this roof."

"Mrs. Stanton?"

"No. Not my wife. My aunt. Known to the public as Professor Kiandoli."

"Where is she?"

"Where she's been the last few years." Silas turned and looked at a lit window on the upper floor. "Hiding in her room."

"Why?"

"That is a long story. Why are you interested? She can't implant the whole town with false memories."

"Not the town, our heroes." Inara let out a smile. "Get them to act completely irrationally, tarnishing their reputation, and then the people will do the rest for you."

Silas hesitated, his eyes darting back and forth. Equal parts excited and nervous. "Even if we could do that, should we?"

"Silas," Inara said it softly as she set her drink down. "Right now those four are working around the clock to stop Brooke. To either find a way to Earth or a way to stop the Phantom Queen she they returns. They will frustrate our plans."

Silas took a long drink and let it swish around in his mouth. After a few moments he swallowed and set down his drink. "I will bring you to Kiandoli. We will see if she is up for the task."

They stood up and walked back through the glass door. He guided her through the kitchen, the living room, and then to the staircase up front. They walked up the stars and to the left, where a lone door was sitting at the end of a narrow hallway. Silas knocked on the door softly. Inara heard nothing, but Silas must have, because he entered.

Inside a woman was rocking on the edge of the bed. She was older, with wisps of grey hair flowing everywhere in a tumbled mess. Wrinkles were dominant around her eyes and forehead. Her eyes were very faded gray-blue. She was currently muttering to herself and staring at her hands like they were caked in some kind of mess.

"Aunt Kiandoli?" Silas asked as he tentatively held out his hand.

She took it and Inara could see green rivers of energy pass between the two of them. Her eyes fogged over into a complete gray. Her cheeks lost what little color they had.

After a moment, the green streams of energy stopped and Kiandoli's eyes snapped into focus, staring hard at Inara.

"What do you have planned?" She reached out her hands for Inara to take.

Inara recoiled, knowing one touch would ruin everything. "Sorry, I'm still undergoing memory trauma. Why don't we get comfortable and I can explain it?"

"Uh. Boring." Kiandoli scoffed. "If you must child. But fair warning, I will interrupt when you do not give me information in the right order."

Inara shut the door and sat down against the wall. For the next four hours, the three of them began to lay out the plan to take back the city.

*****

Three days later, Inara walked through the entrance hall of the hospital. The receptionist waved her on, knowing that she was here for the regular check up. When she got to the elevator however, Inara hit the down button instead of going up.

The elevator let her out, and the hallway looked like it was cut out of a cave. She walked along the rocky floor and reached room 618.

She knocked quietly and then turned around to face the wall opposite the door. She pulled the portal ring off of her finger and stretched it out again. A small box fell out of the portal. Inside the box were two spray cans.

The can rattled as she shook it, and then she sprayed a circle on the wall. It was colorless, and odorless.

When she finished, a wave of energy slammed into her from behind. She let out a weak cough and then allowed the soul jump to take over.

"Who are you?" Dixon shouted into her mind.

"You can read minds while soul jumping. You tell me," Inara responded playfully.

Inara's memories flooded to the surface as Dixon invaded her mind.

"I'm going to hold you here until a worker comes by." He said through the door.

"And tell them what? That I'm a spy from the Coalition?" Inara rolled her eyes. "No one will believe you."

"I'll make you show them that box and reveal your true memories!"

"Read my mind again. You know what I just did to the wall behind me."

"You made a portal?"

"Yes." Inara smiled. "I did. Keep probing."

She focused on a particular memory so that it was brought to the top of her mind. A false memory created by Kiandoli. It was a memory Kiandoli had to give Silas, who in turn planted the memory into her through the air.

"You have Talia?" Dixon shouted through the door. "How?"

"Doctor Pavarti had ways of containing all of his experiments, and we figured out the way to contain her." Inara said. "Now, you know if you don't let me go, my absence will trigger an explosion that will kill her."

Dixon let go of his soul jump and pounded the door. "What are you using that portal for? You can't send an army through without wiping the memories and destroying their minds."

"Contingency." Inara yawned and walked back to the door. "You'll probably never see it open."

CHAPTER 6: PARANOIA

Peter Dixon lined up several boards of wood in the center of the room. They were nothing more than shattered remnants of his old furniture which he insisted on keeping.

Most of them were little more than fragments, subject to the abuse of his constant practicing. He looked at the pathetic assembly and cracked his neck. His eyes drooped momentarily and then he shattered the boards with a roundhouse to each one.

He took in a couple of breaths, and then shot a red ghost out of his chest and into the hallway just outside his door. The ghost took a quick look around and then shot back into his body.

Still no one. Inara created that portal three days ago, but it remained unused. Not even when the hospital workers came by to deliver him meals or medication did it activate. Why put the portal there if she wasn't going to use it? Why let him know she was here? She could have hid the portal anywhere in the city and he would have never known. That was risky to the operation.

After calming down, Dixon picked up the now completely useless shards of wood and carried them to the trash can.

Just as he dumped the wood into the trash can, a knock came at the door.

"Enter!" Dixon shouted.

Nothing happened. This was usually when the set of keys would turn the lock. Dixon shot out his ghost again, and entered into the body of the hospital worker. He let out a shudder and gained focus of the hallway.

The portal was opened. Dixon forced the worker to look left and right, but no one was there. Then, a flash of red streaked in front of him as a figure jumped through the portal.

Dixon had to do a double take through his soul jumped worker, as he saw who it was. The old Coalition councilor, Colin. Someone Miranda insisted was dead.

"What are you doing here?" Dixon asked through the worker.

Without a word, Colin pulled out a gun, shot the worker in the stomach and ran down the hallway.

Dixon forced the worker to crawl backwards to the door and unlock it. As soon as the door was opened, he let go of the soul jump and ran after Colin.

He ran down the hallway, and to a set of stairs. He crashed through the stairwell door and looked up. He could hear the faint echoes of footsteps above. He shot a ghost up the stairs and reached Colin. But someone else was already soul jumping him and they blocked his attempt to possess the body.

Dixon's ghost retreated back in his body and he ran up the stairs at full speed. After a few flights of stairs, Dixon saw a gun laying on the ground. Without thinking, he picked it up and continued the chase.

He passed a few people who gave him worried looks. Dixon ignored them and reached the sunny surface.

The air was warm and dry. The exit area of the hospital was noticeably empty, making it easier to follow Colin, who he was gaining on. He leapt over a few benches and dodged around trees as they made their way around the tight loop of the inner circle road of Naprea.

At last, they came to a crowd, gathered around the front of the town hall. It was a big building, and everyone was watching as several of the elders in the government spoke.

Colin was nowhere to be seen. He focused on his ghost vision. Part of his soul jumping powers allowed him to see the ghost of every person within his field of vision. And luckily for him, the ghosts were color coordinated. Scribes were green, snatchers were white, and soul jumpers were red. And since Colin was being soul jumped at the moment, his ghost would be red.

The crowd clapped at something the presenter was saying. Dixon shot ten ghosts out of his body, each jumping into a separate person in all directions of the crowd.

He scanned the group through ten sets of eyes, each looking for the red ghost, but only seeing each other in soul jumped form.

And then he saw him. Clinging to the wall of the building opposite the government officials. His legs were bent and his back was to the wall. After a second, a portal opened on his thigh, and he pulled out a long rifle.

Dixon tried to shout, tried push his way back through the crowd, but no one responded. There was too much ground to cover. The intruder pulled the trigger. Nothing happened. No gun shot, no noise.

Dixon pulled out his gun he found and fired.

The crowd yelled in panic, and many people got out of the way. With a clear shot, Dixon now opened fire on Colin. Colin smiled, then dropped to the ground and ran into the alley behind the building. Dixon gave chase and Colin looked like he pulled along someone with him into an ally.

The extra perspectives of his ghosts were starting to make him dizzy. He pulled them all back in and continued his pursuit. His ears perked up and his senses kicked back into gear. The smell of baking bread was trapped and amplified in the alley. He knew without his ghosts that this was a dead end.

"It appears you have me," Colin shouted, as he threw his hostage to the ground. "You haven't lost your touch."

"Who is the soul jumper behind you?" Dixon stopped 15 yards from him.

Colin smiled. "I didn't hire you just because you're good at running people down."

"Donovan?" Dixon clenched his fists and teeth.

Colin gave a slight bow. "Using your sister's powers to come say hi, maybe you'd like to talk to her."

Colin tossed three guns to the hostage and then a portal opened on the wall behind them. Obviously Inara had planted that one as well.

Without warning, the red ghost in Colin shot out and rammed into the hostage.

"Peter!" Colin fell to the ground and held out his hand desperately. "Peter! It's Skylar! They've trapped me in this body!"

"What?" Dixon stood rooted on the spot, failing to comprehend what Colin was saying.

The hostage picked up the gun and aimed it at Dixon. Without thinking, he shot her in the shoulder, forcing her to drop the gun. The hostage let out a hiss and leaped at him. Dixon shot her again, this time in the stomach, and the red ghost shot out of the body and back into Colin.

"What a touching reunion," Donovan said through him. "But now it's time to go."

Dixon sprinted after him, but something in the portal sucked Colin through like he was attached to a large magnet. The portal turned off, and the ring burned up like a line of gunpowder lit with a flint.

The hostage convulsed on the ground, gagging and coughing up blood.

"What have I done?" Dixon dropped to his knees to help her.

But it was too late. Her blood was pouring onto the street. Within moments, her eyes glossed over, and her heart ran out of blood to pump.

A group of people came rushing in behind him. Dixon saw the hostile intent in their eyes, and he knew there was no explaining his way out of this one. The murder weapons were still in his hands. He had to escape the city.

"We have another confirmed dead," someone shouted.

"Who else is dead?" Dixon shouted and tried to rack his brain.

"Like you don't know, scumbag." Someone said as they formed a perimeter around him. "The hospital worker you shot during your escape. And Elder of the Circle Kiri suffered a heart attack, right as you were shooting."

"No one else in the square is dead?" Dixon asked. "I saw him pull the trigger."

"You were the only one shooting a gun today."

Someone threw a ball at him. Dixon shot it out of the air, but it turned into powder and enveloped him. It wasn't until he was encased in it that he realized that it was a memory cloud from a scribe. He fell to the ground, caught in a trance.

CHAPTER 7: PRESERVATION OF POWER

Talia had the whole island to herself. It was a quiet afternoon. The sun was beating down with humid warmth and there was a slight breeze. She tossed another shard of wood over into the discard pile.

The setting sun was casting long shadows, it was almost time to go home.

"First, time to set a new personal record."

Talia stood up and the floor of the room was blanketed in her purple mist. She fell through it and into the sky, now falling from hundreds of feet above the ocean. The wind ripped through her hair and she shouted at the top of her lungs, "Wahoo!"

She moved her body into a perfect diving position and opened a portal on the surface of the water. She fell through it and shot out of another portal aimed at the island like a bullet, parallel to the ground.

A cliff face approached rapidly. Another portal opened along the wall and she went through it.

The other portal was now on the beach and she was launched thought it, straight back up to the sky. She shot out another portal as high up as she dared to go. She went though it and let herself fall again.

"This is amazing!" she shouted as gravity pulled her back down to the surface.

Again she opened a portal on the surface of the water. She went through it and was launched straight back up through another portal on the beach.

This sent her flying up so high she could see some of the other islands in the distance. "Wahoo!"

Just as her launch was running out of momentum, and just before she started falling again, she teleported herself inside her temple, right next to the Catalyst Fountain.

She was a little dizzy on the landing, but there was only a slight wobble in her legs as she picked up the goblet and began to refuel her growing thirst. After several refills, she teleported back home with a gentle landing on her bed.

It was predawn here, meaning she at least had three to four hours to sleep.

*****

Talia felt something scratching her face in the dark. She readjusted how she was laying, trying to go back to sleep. But whatever she was laying on scratched her even more as she moved and startled her awake.

She pushed herself up and looked around. She was laying on a large branch of a very tall tree. Her left hand slipped and she fell from the branch. In an instant, her mists were conjured, and instead of landing on the hard ground, the landed on her soft bed back in Naprea.

She lay there for a moment, calming her breathing and wiping the sweat and tree splinters from her face. It was morning here, and night whereever she had been sleeping. Had she teleported while sleeping? She had never done that before.

Talia considered grabbing another drink from the Catalyst Fountain when a knock came at the door.

"Talia, it's Scott, are you there?"

Talia sat up in the bed and checked to see if she was dressed. Yes. "Come in."

Scott opened the door, and he was dressed in a black suit. "Hey, not sure if you knew, but there's a funeral today for Kiri."

"Kiri?" She stood up from the bed. "What happened?"

"She had a heart attack during a conference the other day." Scott was giving her a funny look. "If you want to go, you should get dressed. They'll be starting soon."

"Ok, I'll meet you down there." Talia said. "But, why are you looking at me like that?"

"It's just that you seem a lot older that when I saw you last week." Scott said. "Are you growing out your hair?"

"No, I-" Talia reached up and touched her hair. It was curlier than normal, and about two inches longer than the last time she had paid attention to it, which was a while ago. "I just haven't gotten around to cutting it."

"Ok, well, see you down there." Scott shut the door.

Talia breathed in deep and began to look for her funeral attire. It was hanging in her closet, with a few other robes. This one was a long black dress, made of wool. Her skin grew itchy just thinking about wearing it.

She didn't spend a lot of time making herself presentable. Just a quick splash of water on her face, hair tied in a ponytail, and some chap stick for her dry lips.

The dress was itchy, and her skin complained as she pulled it over her head. But it was much tighter than it was at her father's funeral. She sucked in her stomach and looked down. It only went halfway down her calves. The last time she wore it, she had to hold the dress up to keep it from dragging along the ground.

There was no time to change, so she teleported to her seat at the funeral, which was held at the large stadium like structure nestled up against the rim of the crater. Miranda was sitting next to her, barely containing her jump in alarm from Talia's startling teleport.

"You've got to find out a way to warn me you're going to do that." Miranda half giggled.

"I'll try to make it more subtle," Talia said. "How are you holding up?"

Miranda's eyes were red, but not from crying. They looked heavy and weary.

"I'll manage." Miranda looked forward resolutely.

Somewhere along the way, the funeral started. Talia snapped awake as someone let out a strangled sob a few rows behind her. Scott was now sitting to her left, leaning forward, with his chin resting on his hands.

"So, I hear you're not attending your classes," Miranda said.

"The teacher gave me a pass, said I already knew everything," Talia lied.

"That doesn't sound like something your teacher would do. And besides, what have you been doing with your time?"

"I've, uh..." Talia's mind raced for a lie. Anything that would make Miranda think she had stayed within the confines of the walls of the city. "I've been hanging out with Dixon."

"Dixon?" Miranda looked at her skeptically. "My friend who scares you because he's violent?"

"Yes." Talia hesitated. "I found him with my portals and he was nice to me so, we've been hanging out."

Miranda kept one eyebrow raised and looked back at the funeral proceedings. "Okay. Well, why don't you come spend some time with me at the lab?"

"Oh, I uh..." Talia grabbed the back of her head and felt her ponytail, again trying to create a lie to end the conversation.

"And now, the bestowal of the death memory," a woman said at the center of the pavilion. "A sacred experience of seeing the last message conveyed by a passed loved one. Usually reserved for the person whom they had the strongest bond with. Often a message of comfort for those who live on. Some of them have been known to contain prophecies. Let us pray as we pass this onto the rightful recipient."

Talia turned to the center and watched as Clarinthia stood up and walked over to the casket holding Kiri's body. A tall woman standing next to the casket extended her arms, holding a pillow with a small, black box on top of it.

Clarinthia's eyes were red and puffy, and it looked like her nose was raw. She took the box and opened it. Inside was a simple handkerchief. Clarinthia pulled it out and closed her eyes, extending her arms as if addressing a higher being.

A short time passed, and then Clarinthia opened her eyes. She turned to the tall woman and said something. The tall woman nodded her head. Clarinthia's face sunk in despair. She put the handkerchief back in the box and barely made it back to her seat.

The woman called up another funeral helper who touched the fabric of the handkerchief, and then he had a conversation with the tall woman.

"Talia?" Miranda whispered intensely. "So, do you want to..."

"This death memory belongs to Miranda Whitlock," said the tall woman. "Will she please step forward?"

Talia and Miranda both looked at each other in surprise. Scott was saying something behind her, and eventually, Miranda stood up and made her way to the center stage. Meanwhile, someone had to escort Clarinthia back to her seat. She was half fighting, half slumping in dejection.

Talia brought up a small portal along the underside of the casket, just to hear what was going on.

"This can't be," Clarinthia moaned.

"Miranda, there you are." The tall lady said with a hint of relief. This wasn't broadcast to the crowd, but kept between them. "You don't have to take in the memory here if you don't want to, but it's yours. It won't play for anyone else."

Miranda held out her hand, and the tall lady handed Miranda the box.

"We have found the rightful heir for Kiri's last memory."

Miranda took the box and returned to her seat.

"What was the memory?" Scott asked as she sat down.

Miranda fiddled with the velvet covered black box. "I haven't opened it yet."

"Now." The tall lady resumed the proceedings. "It is time to send Kiri to her final resting place. Due to her unique talents, she is qualified to be sent to the Master Graveyard, the graveyard reserved for those whose abilities went beyond the ordinary."

A portal turned on under the casket, and Kiri was slowly lowered to her final resting place.

"Perhaps Kiri's greatest gift was what she called the Fog of War. Kiri could open another sense of vision to see where hidden recordings were kept. She could even see where they were from 20 miles away."

"Hidden recordings?" Talia leaned forward in her chair. A way to find her father's death memory. "Any recordings?"

"Yes," Scott said next to her. "Kiri wanted me to transfer that power to Miranda the other day to find recordings hidden by the Activists."

She turned to face Scott. "Can you transfer powers from dead people?"

"I can take them from dead people. So, theoretically I could. Why?"

"I need those powers."

"Too late now." Scott nodded at the casket, which was just disappearing completely into the portal.

Talia stood up, her hand stretched out longingly, but the portal turned off, and the casket was gone, leaving behind only the faint afterglow in the circle.

The crowds around them stood up and made their way to the exits. Talia teleported to where the casket was and touched the surface with the palm of her hand.

"Excuse me, miss?" She said to the tall lady. "Can you bring her back for just a second?"

"Bring her back?" The tall lady turned back around and looked at Talia with disdain. "She's dead, little girl."

Talia shook her head. "No, not back from the dead. Back through the portal."

"Those portals are one time use. A new one is set up for every grave. A security measure for the likes of Azurand and your soon-to-be brother in law." The lady put her hands on the table and leaned forward, her eyes narrowing. "Doctor Pavarti wanted to prevent grave snatching. Which is what I assume you are doing."

"Actually, I just wanted to pay my respects," Talia lied. "But I don't think that's any of your business."

"Whatever, honey. Just know, there is no way to get to that corpse now. I guess it wasn't such a good idea to break the machine that opened them for you, now was it?"

Talia clenched her jaw, and almost without thinking, teleported a small glob of mud right over the tall lady's head.

Before there could be any kind of retaliation, Talia teleported back to her seat. Scott and Miranda were already gone, so she scanned the crowd for them. They weren't together. Talia decided to catch up with Scott.

"So, do you think you could help me get those powers?" Talia asked as she teleported into stride right next to him.

"I don't know how to open those graves anymore. They're locked." Scott scratched his head. "Besides, I have enough to worry about trying to get Dixon out of prison."

"Prison?" Talia stopped walking for a moment. "Why is he in prison?"

"He killed somebody."

"Killed?" Talia started walking again, her hands clenching up. "That can't be."

"You don't know him very well. They caught him over a dying woman in the streets." Scott looked around the crowd. "Holding the guns that shot her and a hospital worker. And a scribe stole a recent memory of his and confirmed that he pulled the triggers. Multiple times."

"What prison is he in?"

"Why, you thinking of breaking him out?" Scott scanned the crowd again and lowered his voice as he spoke.

"Tonight." Talia said. "When there's fewer people watching. But I need you to help me with this talent. I need it to find a recording."

"Ok. But we'll have to figure out how to open the grave before we go over there. I don't want you to spend too much time away from the city."

"Don't worry, I won't." Talia smiled and began to conjure her mists for another trip to the island.

"Hold on. Could you give me a lift to the hospital? I need to see how a friend is doing."

"Sure."

They teleported back to the center of the city and just outside the hospital. There was a large crowd gathered, facing the library on the other side of the street. At the base of the stairs of the library, a large podium was built. Silas was bowing and the crowd was applauding.

"Thank you all for coming out today." Silas waved to the crowd. "As I begin my journey towards becoming an Elder of the Circle, I want to make one thing clear. Our city is in desperate need of help. I have the vision to fix it, and together, we can find our salvation!"

Silas raised his hand and the crowd cheered. He paced across the podium a few times, pointing at people and smiling.

Silas was about to continue his address when it started raining. Talia touched the top of her head as drops of water tricked down it. She looked up and a drop fell right in her eye.

She blinked the water out, and let out a gasp as she was staring up into a smoking volcano.

"Where did that come from?" Talia asked. But when she turned, Scott wasn't there.

Smoke filled her lungs, and the heat burned .The volcano erupted and tons of lava started falling out and splashing into the city. The hospital was smothered, the library caught fire, and a huge tidal wave of lava came rushing down the street towards them.

Talia threw up a huge portal mist, trying to catch as much of it as she could. Huge chunks of debris was sent hurtling through the air, she caught it and sent it to the ocean. A baby fell from a mother's arms towards a river of lava. Talia sent in a mist, catching the baby and setting it down in the woods just outside the city.

Talia blinked again, and just as suddenly, everything was normal. No lava, not even rain. All of the buildings were fine. She looked at the crowd, most of which were laying on the ground, shaking in nightmare trances. The rain was full of recorded memories.

Scott stood up next to her, shaking a little bit.

"Where is my baby?" a woman screamed from behind her.

In panic, Talia sent a portal back out to the woods and confirmed. She had been actually teleporting things during her trance. Quickly, she teleported the baby back to her mother's arms.

The mother looked around the crowd, furious. Talia adjusted her hair to hide behind it.

"What was that about?" Scott asked as he looked up.

The rim of the crater was glowing red, dust swirling around in agitation around what was now an apparent portal.

"It looks like there's a huge portal around the rim of the city." Talia said. "Something must have come through it."

"Memory trance rain?" Scott asked.

"That didn't feel like a memory trance," Talia said. "Usually I can tell when I've entered one."

The rest of the crowd slowly stood up.

"You see?" Silas shouted as pointed at the sky. "Long has that portal been a protection to us, sending anything attacking from the heavens out to the darkness of space. But now, it is a curse upon us, because we allow filth in this city. Filth like Scott, Miranda, Peter, and Talia. They destroyed the most sacred portal of all, and we are now seeing the ripple effect of their actions. We must take action to purge them immediately, or we will see more of this evil raining down upon us."

"Time to go." Talia said as more and more eyes in the crowd turned their way.

She teleported them to Clarinthia's house. It was a two story house, modeled after a suburban home on earth. It was blue with a wraparound porch and a two seat rocking bench out front. "She'll know what to do."

Scott walked up and knocked on the door. There was no answer, but the door opened slightly, exposing the inside. The entryway was a mess. Clutter was all over. A pile of shattered glass from a light bulb was sprinkled along the lower steps of her stairs.

"Careful now," Scott whispered as he edged inside the door.

Talia followed him in, but sent a small mist ahead of them to have a look for intruders. Beyond the entryway, things were a little cleaner, until she got to the kitchen. It looked like someone had dumped three houses worth of junk into it.

Open shoe boxes were stacked as high as her head, leaning precariously against walls and other stacks of boxes. Most of the contents were spilled onto the floor or the table. Old shoelaces, combs, sea shells, small rocks, chunks of wood, animal teeth and claws, crumpled up pieces of paper, children's toys, leaves, and broken picture frames highlighted the list. There was no organization to it. Items were not grouped together by similarity.

Just behind it all sat Clarinthia. Her eyes were glazed over and she was holding a crumpled candy wrapper tightly in her right arm. When they entered the room, she could see the faint glow of green orbs.

"Clarinthia?" Scott waved his hands in front of her non responsive eyes. "Do you think she's drugged?"

"No, just in a memory trance. We should probably go."

"What is all of this stuff?" Scott pointed at the piles of garbage.

"Old memories." Talia rubbed her shoulder. "Probably of Kiri."

Just then Clarinthia snapped out of the memory trance with angry, puffy eyes. "What are you doing here?"

"We've come for help." Talia stepped up and interrupted Scott. "Silas is campaigning to be an Elder of the Circle and killing us is his pretty much his campaign slogan."

Clarinthia let out a snort. "I'm too tired to do anything about that. Just let me live out my life in peace."

"Clarinthia, I know you're in pain." Scott said.

"You know?" Clarinthia snapped. "Miranda knew this town was beyond saving."

She set down the wrapper and picked up a small glass jar. A small green orb began to glow at its base. "Maybe she was right. Maybe there's nothing left to do but revisit the happy times. I've got a life time of it here. Of me and Kiri. I'll probably die before I get through it all."

"But-" Scott started.

Before he could complete the protest, her eyes were glazed over again.

"Come on." Talia conjured up another portal. "We should probably go."

"I want to stay here." Scott walked out to the living room and sat on a couch with a floral pattern on it. "Make sure she doesn't do anything drastic."

"It looks like she is happy to relive the memories while she can."

"Just the same, she looks like she could use somebody to take care of her." Scott stretched out comfortably on the couch. "But where are you going to go?"

"To find out how to open that grave," Talia said as she teleported back to her island.

CHAPTER 8: THE ARCHIVE DIRECTIVE

[It has been 4 hours. Time for another sleep cycle.]

Miranda was tired, but she stood at the counter of her lab and fiddled with the velvet box. It remained unopened. She looked around her laboratory, full of circuited fabric, but empty of individuals.

Where were her helpers? Did they expect to have the whole day off to grieve? She needed to give them instructions before she slept.

With resignation, she walked to the end of the counter and poured another cup of coffee.

The stimulants did little for her alertness, and when she pulled up the equations for the suits, her mind was unable to focus. She finished the coffee, set it down, and then rested her head on the counter.

Miranda was startled awake by a gentle coughing. She blinked her eyes open and saw Silas standing there, smiling.

"You may have noticed a less than stellar turnout to work this afternoon." Silas gestured to the empty room.

"Weren't you supposed to send some help?" Miranda sat up and looked at her watch. She had slept for three hours.

"I was, but I've given them the day off." Silas sat on one of the bench stools. "Three deaths in the span of five minutes."

"And now you're looking for four more." Miranda picked up her data pad and pretended to swipe between formula sheets.

"So you have been paying attention to the news." Silas smirked. "Well, I'll just cut to the chase then. Here is a recent recording I made."

Silas held out his left hand, cupping some sort of stone. Streaks of green energy floated out of his right hand and hit Miranda with a gentle coaxing. The waves collected themselves into a sphere and then shot up into her mind.

Darkness flashed and she saw Scott sitting on a couch surrounded by candles. The girl he rescued came into the room and sat on his lap. They began kissing.

Miranda watched through a window of a house. It was raining outside, but that didn't bother Scott, it only fueled him further.

Her alarm chimed and she sat up from her chair. She checked her watch, and found that it was only one sleep cycle. Her blood raced in anger as she thought about Scott and what he was doing with that girl, Olivia. She hated Silas for showing her that, but at the same time, she was glad she knew Scott wasn't faithful. Now she could focus on more important things without the guilt of neglecting Scott.

The absolute quiet in her lab was a bit unnerving. She tried to rack her brain about where her assistants were, but she couldn't remember.

"This town is falling apart," Miranda muttered to herself. "Time to switch gears."

She walked over to a closet and opened it. Inside was a perfected, but broken suit, one she had stolen from the Coalition and used for nearly a month.

She pulled it out, and placed it on a dummy. The suit activated and hardened to its bulletproof state.

"If I can't make one of you, how do I disable one of you?" Miranda said silently to herself.

*****

[It has been four hours, time for another sleep cycle.]

Miranda stifled a yawn as she looked at her work. It had taken nearly two hours just to get started. She spent that time painstakingly deactivating any cameras, microphones, portals, or any other sensor that Donovan might still be able to tap into. This meant a limited battery life, because all of the energy was delivered to the suit via teleportation from a central hub in the Underlabs.

After she was satisfied there was no way Donovan could discover her intentions, she pulled out and analyzed the schematics to find a weak spot, something she could use to deactivate the suit, not just the programmable matter, and the HUD interface, but everything. She wanted Donovan to be helpless when she attacked.

Miranda hit the acknowledge button on her data pad and continued to work. After another 20 minutes, her alarm rang.

[You have not slept. Please take twenty minutes to rest.]

Miranda hit the acknowledge button again and started walking to her cot. On her way, she emptied her pockets and pulled out the small velvet box.

The thought occurred to her that the memory trances were like enhanced dreams. Maybe she could cut her sleep time in half with them.

She opened the box and found the handkerchief. It was silver, or maybe a white gold.

Miranda reached for it and allowed the green orb of energy to go to her mind.

The trance was quick, but not very vivid. She was standing on a small island, no bigger than train car. The waves crashed gently, but they looked more like mist than water. The sky was pitch black, and her visibility only extended as far as the island.

Suddenly, a large vision of Kiri's face appeared in the sky. Under Kiri's face, a small grass field materialized.

"The Archive shall be the one to save humanity." Kiri said.

"The Archive?" Miranda asked.

"You Miranda." Kiri responded. "You who have the power to store infinite memories into a single object. You will save us all."

"Save who?" Miranda asked. "Nice try Kiri, but this isn't going to work out. I hope you're done soon because I have work to get back to."

"You have already stopped the menace Azurand from taking absolute power. Tomorrow, you will reunite your sister with her parents."

"Her parents are dead," Miranda said curtly. "So are mine, just for your information."

"You must accept your fate, Miranda. There are more things in store. But I cannot reveal them to you now. They will be buried in your subconscious. You must not fight it, but embrace it."

Miranda snapped out of the trance and she was awake again. Seconds later, the alarm beeped.

[You have completed one sleep cycle, but your sleep appeared erratic. How do you feel?]

"Like I just sat through the most pointless movie ever." Miranda walked back to her lab station.

[Was the sleep cycle sufficient?]

"Good enough." Miranda cracked her neck. "Satellite images show an increase of coalition activity on the islands. We need to figure out how to stop them before they get to earth. There has to be a way to shut these suits down."

CHAPTER 9: PRISON BREAK

The Control Center Island was swarming with Coalition soldiers. Talia sat hesitantly in the shadows, wondering what her next moves would be. Too many soldiers to just teleport out of there, but she needed to get to the beach to reach the graves that contained Kiri's corpse.

"Well, I'm not going to reach the grave by day."

She left the sunny beaches of the Control Center Island and teleported back to the library in Naprea. It was dark there, and most of the patrons and angry mob had left for home.

Now she had time to study, time to learn all she could to find another way to open those graves.

She quietly stalked the shelves of books, flipping through records and trying to find any bit of information that she could.

In the darkness, she opened a portal on the other side of the world and sent rays of sunlight through it to read properly, and find the books she needed. But book after book was useless. None of them contained anything about the graves.

"You don't see many people reading the books anymore," A voice called out behind her.

It was Hudson Stanton. He was casually leaning on the shelves behind her, arms folded and biceps were in a half flexed position. Talia turned back around.

"It's a library," Talia droned sarcastically.

"Are you looking for something specific? My name is Hudson, and my dad runs the place." Hudson walked around to the other side of the table and sat down. He glanced casually at the things she was reading.

"I know who you are, and who your dad is, and you should know who I am. By default we should be mortal enemies or something."

Hudson chuckled a little. "That's a bit dramatic."

"Not for people like your dad. He's made it pretty clear I'm not wanted here."

Hudson nodded his head. "True. But he and I don't see eye to eye on a lot of things. And I was actually hoping I could ask you to help me."

Talia looked at him over the top of her book. Last he saw her, he wouldn't give her the time of day. And now he was being friendly and asking for help.

"I have problems of my own, thanks."

"Yes, you do," Hudson agreed. "And at least one of them is finding a bit of information, which I can help you with. I know all of the ins and outs of the library. Just ask me what you want to know and I can get you that information."

Talia shut the book in front of her and leaned forward. "How do I know you're not going to trick me?"

"Because my dad is going mad with power, and this city might be brought down from the inside by him, or the outside by the Phantom Queen and her gang."

"You think that?"

"My brother ran off with Olivia a few years ago, and I suspect he died." Hudson paused and took in a heavy breath. "Now, my dad is blindly following her to his destruction. I need to stop him for his own good."

"And you think I can help?"

"Yes." Hudson leaned in. "It will take a lot of work, but your gifts will make it quick. In advance of this, as a show of good faith, I will help you with whatever you are trying to do first, and then we will tackle my problem later."

Talia licked the insides of her teeth, and looked at the increasingly useless pile of books spread out on the table.

"I'm trying to find a way to open the graves, now that the control panel is smashed apart."

Hudson gathered all of the books into one pile. "You won't find out how to do that with these books. Who's grave are you going after?"

"Kiri's."

"Why?"

"I have my reasons. Are you going to help or not?"

"We could do it right now." Hudson stood up and shelved the books. "I know how to open the graves."

"Not right now. It's crawling with soldiers from the Coalition. And I have other things I have to do." Talia opened a small portal to have a peak at Clarinthia's house. Scott was asleep on the couch. "Take a walk around the block right after breakfast. I'll send a portal for you and we will go then."

"Sounds good. After we have finished there, I'll have my request ready."

Talia nodded slightly and teleported back to Clarinthia's house. Clarinthia was still sitting at the table, lost in memories of happier times.

"Scott!" Talia shook his shoulder. "Scott! Wake up! It's time to get Dixon!"

Scott slowly opened his eyes, straining and stretching in a tired frenzy. He sat up, groggily looked over at Clarinthia and scratched his face.

"I guess she'll be alright for a few minutes." Scott yawned. He bent down and tied his shoes. "Let's go."

Talia teleported them just outside prison, conveniently nestled between the library and the capitol building. It was smaller than the library by a considerable measure. Fake pillars were inlaid into the front wall, and bars lined the windows.

"You go make a scene in there, demanding to see Dixon," Talia said. "The louder the better. I'll teleport him out of there while they aren't looking."

Scott nodded and walked into the front door. He kicked it open and started shouting demands.

Talia looked at the back side of the prison with her portals and began sifting through the various cells, looking for her friend.

Most of the cells were empty. One man lay curled up on his provided mattress, another paced next to the bars.

She saw him. Close to the front of the prison, his cage looked like a large glass box. She rammed her portal into it to claim Dixon. But her mists just tumbled gently over the box.

Dixon looked up at her mists from his cell, and quietly pointed down at the drain at the bottom of the concrete floor.

Talia understood. This cell was soul jumper proof. Her mists would not penetrate it. She sent her mists through the floor and looked for the drain pipe underneath. But her mists would not penetrate that either. She followed the pipe along to sewage, and reached the outside vent next to where she was standing. Her mists jumped out of the ground and into the vent like a fish leaping out of water.

Back through the pipe, she made it to the cell. But when her mists collected around Dixon, nothing happened. He stayed right where he was.

Talia grew dizzy. She fell to her knees, and then she fell forward so that her hands had to catch her. A few people walking around her stopped and looked at her.

With no time to see if they were hostile she pulled the mists back into her body. Then she shot a mist out to catch Scott, and she teleported them back to her island for a refreshing drink.

Instead, they fell out of the portal and into Miranda's lab. Miranda barely stirred as she slept on the cot.

"What are we doing here?" Scott asked.

"It was a mistake." Talia said. "I'll get us out of here."

Before the mists could be conjured, Miranda's alarm woke her up.

"Talia?" She asked as she sat up. "Perfect timing. I need you to get me to an island."

"Sure." Talia shrugged her shoulders and teleported them all to the catalyst fountain.

Before anyone could protest, Talia crawled to the fountain and filled her cup.

"She was on her hands and knees, obviously in pain, and you didn't even ask what was wrong?" Scott shouted. "Just straight to your needs."

"You're one to talk!" Miranda walked over and slapped him on the face.

"Ow!" Scott shouted. "What was that for?"

"Silas saw you and Olivia."

"Saw me and Olivia... what?" Scott asked, holding his jaw.

Miranda ignored him and turned to Talia. "I didn't mean this island."

"You'll have to be more specific next time," Talia gurgled through her drink. "Are you two done? I'm on a bit of a schedule, and I'd like him in one piece."

Miranda's expression turned from stone cold heat to curiosity. "What are we doing here?"

"Don't worry about it." Talia refilled another cup. "Which island do you want to go to?"

"The Control Center Island."

"Me too." Talia finished another drink and set the cup down, feeling refreshed again. "So here's the deal. You help me go grave digging in about six hours, and then I'll leave you to do whatever it is you need to do there."

"Grave digging?" Miranda asked.

"Yeah. I need a particular talent of the dead."

"Where's Dixon?" Scott interrupted.

"Still in his cell." Talia turned to him. "Its soul jumper proof. So Dixon won't be able to soul jump anybody outside of his cell."

"So? What's that to you?"

"So, my mother was a soul jumper. And I get my mists from her. Meaning if you trap me in that box, I can't teleport out. And if you hide something in it, I can't teleport in and get it. We'll have to find another way to get him out."

"Talia, have you been leaving the town to come here?" Miranda asked, looking around the temple. "I told you I don't want you leaving the city."

"That city is way more dangerous than it is out here!" Talia teleported them back to the lab. "They're one bad look away from conducting a manhunt on all of us." Talia pointed between the three of them furiously. "They lucked out with a reason to snag Dixon up earlier, and it is only a matter of time before they come after us. So get over me making an executive decision about my safety. Get some rest. I'll be back in six hours."

Miranda's mouth fell slightly open, confusion on her face. Talia didn't give her sister time to sort her thoughts, however. She teleported to her bed and got some rest herself.

*****

Hudson, on the sidewalk, walking behind a row of trees. Miranda, asleep on her cot. Scott, doing pull-ups in his room.

All three were teleported back to her island, next to the Catalyst Fountain. Talia finished her last drink of the morning and set down the cup as the three of them materialized in front of her.

Scott landed in a crouch and then looked around. "Any chance you can bring my gear?"

Another mist appeared at Scott's feet. Out of it came several knives, a hand gun, a rifle, and a shirt.

Miranda slid her fingers across a datapad and didn't look up. "What's he doing here?"

"Scott, or Hudson?"

"Hudson." Miranda stood up and cracked her neck. "Is he your boyfriend or something? Introducing him to your parents?"

"Actually-" Hudson started. Talia raised a hand to him.

"First of all, neither of you are my parents." Talia corrected. "You're my sister, and Scott is only pretending to be engaged to you. And Hudson knows how to open the graves."

"How?" Scott asked. "Did you study with Azurand?"

"Learned it on my own." Hudson smiled. "I live in a library."

"Wait." Miranda interrupted. "Are you Silas' kid?"

"I-" Talia held up to stop Hudson from speaking.

"He knows what we need to do," Talia said. "That is enough for now."

"Before we go, I want my suit and my gear too," Miranda said. "Teleport me back so I can get dressed."

"You have five minutes." Talia teleported her back and clicked her tongue in irritation.

"She's nice," Hudson said sarcastically.

"Can it, you." Talia rolled her eyes and walked back to the Catalyst Fountain for another drink.

"Does that stuff taste good or something?" Hudson asked.

"It doesn't taste like anything, but it makes me feel good." Talia sat on the stairs next to the fountain and drained the cup.

"Uh, you should probably-" Scott started.

He was interrupted by the mists teleporting Miranda back, looking almost the same has she had done before. But Talia could see the faint outlines of the suit she was working on.

"I thought that didn't work yet." Talia said.

"It has some serious lag issues." Miranda conceded. "But it's better than nothing. What's the plan?"

Talia teleported them all to the beach, a far ways off from any patrolling soldiers. The night was dark, but the sand was visible with the blue light of several full moons.

"Miranda, use your suit to check out any Coalition chatter, if you can." Talia looked around. "Scott, use your gifts to find Kiri's body."

The four of them began walking along the beach, following Scott as he scanned the area for Kiri's particular talents.

"So, are you their leader or something?" Hudson asked, stepping into stride with Talia.

"What?" Talia looked at Scott and Miranda, who were doing their best to avoid each other. "No. They're usually giving me orders. This is kind of new for me."

"I wish I could talk to my dad the way you just talked to your sister. You know, really put him in his place."

"I know what you mean." Talia giggled and combed a strand of hair between her ears. "It is kind of liberating."

"Here." Scott stopped and pointed to a flat patch of sand. "That's definitely the talent you're looking for."

"Okay Librarian." Talia gave Hudson a soft nudge with her elbow. "You're up."

Hudson pulled out a small shovel and knelt down where Scott was pointing. "Okay, we'll have to take turns to get to the casket."

Talia rolled her eyes and then teleported Hudson behind her. "If we have to dig, I can handle that part."

Her mists sank into the sand, and then slowly, the sand disappeared around the casket. Another portal floated above the ocean, draining the sand away.

"Oh." Hudson stood back up and pulled out a small, silver disk. "I guess we could do that."

He set the disk on the casket and pushed a button. Gold lines illuminated the disk, and the casket began to activate.

"Tetrapath aren't going to pop out of that, are they?" Scott asked.

"No." Hudson said. "This disk is one of Pavarti's toys. The tetrapath are more of a deterrent for people opening the graves without his permission. This grave thinks we have permission and will only open the casket."

The casket lid popped open, revealing Kiri's body. The signs of her body rotting weren't visible yet, but she was starting to smell.

"Let's get this over with." Talia looked at Scott, who took a few tentative steps towards the body.

Scott reached his hand to Kiri's head, and the other hand to Talia's head. He gave out a loud grunt, and then Talia's head grew warm. Something inside her clicked, and her head went dizzy.

Bright colorful orbs danced around the grave site, illuminating death memories that weren't passed on. The whole graveyard beach lit up with glowing orbs of memories, all calling out to her. Her mind was overloaded.

She teleported the group back to the Catalyst Fountain to get away from the memories, but this was the former temple of the scribes, and she was again assaulted by memories. They were everywhere, and her new sense was screaming at her, telling her where each of them lay.

"How do you turn it off?" Talia clutched her head as the pain grew more intense. She teleported them back to the grave site, hoping to lessen the pain.

"Turn what off?" Miranda asked.

"Someone's coming," Hudson said behind her. "We have to go now."

"Leave me here." Miranda said. "I have something I need to do."

"We can't just leave you here with all these soldiers," Scott said.

"Aw." Miranda said sarcastically. "I appreciate the sentiment, but I can handle myself. Leave me and I'll make contact when I'm done."

Talia teleported all but Miranda back to Naprea. Here, the onslaught of her senses was at its peak. What felt like millions of memories were pulling at her from every direction. They glowed in dozens of shades of green and were almost blinding, collectively. She collapsed to her knees, and sent the two boys out of her room.

With a shaking hand, she reached for the top of her bed to pull herself up. Her vision went spotty, and her breath fell short. She needed to teleport to a place without memories everywhere.

With one more strain of effort, she teleported to Cantera Bay, just a few blocks down from the Illurium building where Donovan and the Coalition spent their time.

Buildings as tall as mountains surrounded her. People were walking everywhere. Lights and billboards flashed messages in nearly every square foot of her vision.

There were three recordings in a twenty mile radius. Her head was relieved of pain, and she could again think clearly.

"Well, that's going to be a problem," she said as a few pedestrians gave her odd looks.

CHAPTER 10:
THE PURGING OF PETER DIXON

Dixon sat quietly in his all glass cell, watching the guards, looking for patterns. The room was simple enough. A short front entryway that lead right to a front counter. That counter served as a blockade to those wishing to visit. No less than three guards had been at that post since he arrived.

Just on the other side of that was a scattering of filing cabinets, where three to four people were constantly filing. But the filing looked even more repetitive than it should have. They lingered in the same areas for far too long. Dixon counted them as more guards.

Finally, there was the traditional prison bar partition that led back to where the criminals were kept. Here sat two guards on the public side and two guards on the prisoner side.

They were nonchalant for good reason. Dixon was one of three prisoners. The other two were asleep, and he was stuck in something he had never seen before. His cell was a perfect cube of glass. The only door was barely visible. What was worse, he could not soul jump anyone outside of the cell. All of his ghosts refused to go past the walls.

The front door of the jail crashed open. Dixon stood up and watched as Scott belligerently made his way through the first wave of guards. What was he doing? He wasn't attacking, just walking around, making noises and otherwise drawing attention to himself.

Dixon turned around and saw a thick cloud of purple rushing to his cell and understood. He stepped closer to the edge and prepared to teleport.

But the mists rolled over the glass walls. They couldn't break through! Just as his soul jumping powers were blocked inside the walls, so were Talia's mists.

Then Dixon saw it. A drain pipe, mostly used to pump air into the cell, sat in the left corner. Dixon quietly pointed to the grate that covered the pipe. Talia must have understood because the portal mist dropped through the floor. Seconds later the mists shot back out of the grate, inside his cell.

Dixon again prepared himself to teleport, but the mists wouldn't cling to him. He was completely enveloped, but nothing was happening. For the briefest moment, he thought he heard Talia screaming in pain.

And then the mist was gone. Scott was gone too and the temporary chaos was replaced by silence.

"Some friend," one of the closest guards said to Dixon. "Doesn't even come up with a plan good enough to get through the second line of defense."

Dixon said nothing and sat down in the center of his cube again, contemplating whether he should just go to bed.

No sooner had he sat down, however, than the front door came crashing open as two people came to the desk.

"Silas?" Asked one of the front counter guards. "What are you doing here?"

"Is Peter Dixon still here?" Silas barked.

"Yes."

"Oh, good." Silas ran his hand through his hair quickly.

"Scott's attempt to rescue him was very poor," another front desk guard said.

"He was only trying to distract you." Silas pointed to the back cell. "Talia was trying to get him out while you weren't looking."

"What?" Several guards in the room asked at once.

"The big question is, why wasn't she successful?" the blond woman, who had entered with Silas, asked.

"Who are you?"

"Olivia." She answered. "Silas' Campaign Manager."

"I'm not sure how Talia's powers work, but as you can see, we still have the prisoner."

"We have to move up the time table," Silas said. Olivia nodded.

"Move up?" a guard asked.

"Yes. Peter Dixon is dangerous, and we need to purge him before his friends figure out how to break him out of here."

"Purge?" Said a front counter guard. "I don't care what he did, we don't have the authority to execute somebody!"

"I'm not talking execution." Silas put his hands on the counter. "Eventually, yes. But not here, not tonight."

"Then what are you talking?"

"Memory reconditioning." Silas smiled and looked back at Dixon.

"Your aunt is on her way." Olivia said. "She said she would be a few minutes behind."

"Memory reconditioning?" A guard asked.

"All I'm talking about is adjusting his behaviors so that he is not dangerous to society. If this goes right, he could be useful to society, for a small amount of time."

"I don't think I am comfortable with that either," the guard said.

The guards at the filing cabinets all stopped filing and stood to look at Silas in unison. The threat was more than implied. They intended to protect the Dixon until the trial.

"You can't be serious?" Silas chuckled a little. "We know beyond doubt that he killed that woman. He goes on about how the Coalition came in here and somehow killed Kiri by giving her a heart attack. Nonsense. His friends will find a way to get him out of there. And when they do, if he is not reconditioned, he will kill again."

At that moment an elderly woman walked through the door. She was wearing a purple business suit with a skirt. From where Dixon was standing, he would have guessed velvet.

"Are we ready?" The woman asked as she walked through.

"These men here say they're uncomfortable with you using your talents, Kiandoli." Silas gestured his hand across the room.

Kiandoli put on a smile like she was visiting her grandkids and walked up to the counter.

"Why, hello there," Kiandoli said as she extended her hand to the closest guard. "You may not know who I am, I don't really get out much."

She laughed at her own remarks as the guard took her hand. He was immediately paralyzed. Dixon stood back up to get a better view. Kiandoli kept shaking the hand, but that was the only part of the guard moving.

When she let go of the hand, he slumped face first onto the counter. She walked casually to the next guard and offered her hand again.

This guard backed up and pulled his hands away. "What did you do to him?"

Silas extended his hands and started waving his fingers at that guard. Suddenly, she jumped reflexively to the counter like she was being chased, and then she too fell unconscious, face first onto the counter.

Kiandoli walked up to her and put her hands her head.

The remaining guards had seen enough. Four filing cabinets were slammed closed simultaneously and they rushed the intruders. But, just as suddenly as they did, the two fallen guards stood up straight and began to attack their peers.

Silas, Olivia, and Kiandoli waked calmly around the counter and in the middle of all the chaos. One by one, Silas and Kiandoli moved people to their side, until they were standing in front of Dixon's cage.

"Are you sure this will work?" Silas asked.

"Yes," Olivia responded. "To stop Scott, we will need all of his friends against him. We already have Miranda. Dixon is next."

"But how will this turn the people against him?"

"This won't." Olivia turned back around to the guards, who were standing in formation behind her. "The tetrapath infection will."

Silas turned around. "You're going to infect somebody just to get Scott?"

"No." Olivia held up her hands in protest. "Scott is. He has the infection resting inside of him right now. And we need to quarantine him before there is an outbreak."

"Ah." Silas nodded his head in understanding and turned back to Dixon.

"Visiting hours are over," Dixon said flatly, sitting down onto the edge of his mattress.

"That didn't stop your friends from trying to say hi." Silas put his hand to the door.

Dixon said nothing. He eyed the handle as it turned, readying his ghosts to capture everyone in the room. Silas too, was steeling himself. The lock clicked into place, and Silas held the door handle with his left hand. He took a few deep breaths and opened it.

Dixon instantly shot out all of his ghosts. One slammed into Silas, the next into Kiandoli, and then a few of the guards and Olivia.

Just as Dixon stood up, he felt a gut wrenching wave of emotions flood into his mind. A few images flashed in front of him. He blinked, and then he was in the library, filing objects in the back room. It was a repetitive dream, set on a loop.

Dixon tried to escape, tried to do anything in the memory that would help him get out, but he was a powerless observer.

Then, the dream stopped. Dixon's own memories started flying in random directions. Everything went black, and Dixon found himself standing on a poorly lit courtyard. After a few seconds, Kiandoli appeared in front of him.

"I thought I recognized you," Kiandoli said nonchalantly. "I've worked on you before. Doctor Pavarti had big plans for you."

"I've never met you before." Dixon lunged at her, trying to disrupt her mind.

A large tail that looked like it belonged to a whale appeared out of thin air and swatted Dixon to the side like a child.

"I'm in control here!" Kiandoli sneered. Then she gestured to their surroundings. "This may be your mind, but it is my domain."

Dixon rolled on the ground for several yards and hit a small stone planter's box.

"I am surprised at how much of my work made it through that portal. Even if it remained subconscious, it was always there." Kiandoli continued as she walked calmly towards him.

"What are you talking about?" Dixon grunted. He tried to get up, but he felt like a weight was pulling him down.

"As a child, Pavarti brought you to me. He instructed me to make you a fierce warrior. Pathologically so. To force you to build up your skills to be the ultimate fighter, and then have an army of snatcher's copy your talents."

"You're lying."

"No. I drove you to be what you are. Before you came to me, you were a peaceful boy." Kiandoli put a hand on his head. "And then I gave you pain."

A memory flashed into his head. The image of seeing his mother die. Stabbed through the chest by a tetrapath. And then his father was shot in the eye.

"There, you see?" Kiandoli continued. "I planted these memories in you. Your parents never died. And reading your thoughts since that day you fell through the portal, I see most of the pain is related to your sister. But the effect is the same. You became a ruthless killer. And now, it is time for more conditioning."

Dixon's mind felt a searing pain as new memories were written. He could see Scott shooting his sister Skylar in the stomach. Miranda plotting with the Coalition to kill him. Talia almost injuring him with her portals.

He screamed out in pain, trying to fight it, but he couldn't.

He woke up, alone in his prison. Sunlight flooded the prison like it was the middle of the afternoon. The guards were filing paper work like nothing had happened. Dixon checked his heart rate. It was elevated, like he had just been attacked, but the office looked normal.

He shrugged his shoulders, and rolled back over in his bed, plotting the ways he would break out of this prison, and then kill Scott, Miranda, and Talia.

CHAPTER 11: COALITION PRESENCE

The purple fog cleared, leaving Miranda on her own on the beach. A flashlight swept the ground nearby, two guards were talking.

Miranda leapt into the pit containing Kiri's grave and activated the active camouflage function of her suit. Her Head's Up Display turned on, displaying a virtual interface in her vision.

[Active camouflage loading.]

A progress bar popped up in the corner of her eyes. Twelve percent. The footsteps drew closer. Thirteen percent. The flashlight beam reached the top of the casket. The status bar dropped back down to ten percent.

Miranda canceled the active camouflage command, got into a crouch position and weighed her options. Going bullet proof was out. She couldn't hit them with a memory trance because they were covered head to toe with thick tactical gear. She had to buy more time.

She slowly crawled to the far side of the casket. Waiting for her moment. The light was now covering the hole and there were two coalition soldiers standing at the edge.

"Sir, it appears someone has dug up a grave," a soldier said into a radio.

"What?" came the static response from a radio. "Are there any tetrapath?"

"No sir. I don't see anybody around."

"I don't like it," the commander replied. "Search the area. Report back as soon as you learn anything."

"Yes, sir."

The radio was cut.

"You heard the boss," the soldier said. "We get the whole beach to ourselves tonight!"

"I love where your mind is," replied the other soldier. This one was female. "But knowing the commander, he'll probably send out more people to help us with the search. He gets paranoid about these things."

"Yeah. He does," the male soldier said. "But it will be at least 10 minutes before anybody can get here."

There was a pause. The woman responded. "That will give us five minutes for us, and five minutes to check before we have to give our report!"

There was a rustling of gear and Miranda risked a quick look over the top of the stone casket. The two of them were stripping their gear off. They weren't looking at each other while they did this, and more importantly, they were looking away from Miranda. She cautiously made her way to the other side of the casket.

"In the ocean, or the sand?" The man asked.

"Sand. They'd notice if we were wet."

Miranda climbed out of the hole and crept behind the woman on the right. With her right hand she scrolled through her memory archive and selected a good long one. Once it was pulled out, she touched her hand to the soldier's exposed back. She fell down face first into the sand. Miranda cautiously reached down and pulled out a hand gun from her gear.

"Yeah," the man said over his shoulder, as he tossed his shirt onto the ground. "But sand will get everywhere if we do it on the beach."

"Try the casket." Miranda cocked the gun, and the soldier held up his hands. "Not very giving, but nothing says sexy like a graveyard, right?"

The guard tentatively turned his head. Miranda pointed the gun at him and he turned back around.

"Don't bother with anything." Miranda took a slow step towards him. "All your gear is at your feet. Help isn't coming for seven minutes."

"So, are you going to shoot me?" the man said.

"No." Miranda walked up behind him and touched his back too. He fell to the ground, landing on bits of his armor.

She scanned the suits on the ground and her HUD showed the dimensions of the suit. Most of it would fit her convincingly. Instructions popped up on her HUD, and she figured out how to dress herself quickly. She was grateful that the suit left her forearm exposed enough that she could use the portals there readily.

Once suited up, she knelt down and touched the female soldier's face. A green orb shot up through her mind, but she did not go into the trance. She immediately shot it back down into the archive stone, storing the soldier's life memory there.

Once that was done, her suit scanned the face and hair.

[Scan complete. Rendering facial replication.]

As the suit loaded the program, she pushed the woman into the hole and covered her with enough sand that she hoped would hide her until morning.

Then she turned to the man. She opened a portal on her arm and pulled out a small syringe.

"Sorry, big guy," Miranda said as she knelt down and pulled off his boot. "But this is not going to feel good when you wake up."

She held up his foot and stabbed him really hard at the base of the ankle, where the Achilles tendon attached. The foot began to swell almost immediately.

She dropped the foot and looked behind her. Three more flashlights were making their way up the beach.

On the top right of her HUD, the facial replication render showed a 67 percent progress bar.

"How long until the drugs take full effect?" Miranda asked out loud.

[Your subject should be in cardiac arrest in less than a minute.]

"No time to waste then, is there?" Miranda stood up and waved her hands wildly. "Help! Over here! Hurry!"

The flashlights moved faster, and the crew reached her within a few moments.

When they got there, Miranda was pumping the fallen soldier's chest, trying to keep him going with CPR.

"He doesn't have a pulse!" Miranda shouted.

"What happened?" one of the guards asked.

"Does it matter? This man is about to die. Do any of you have a defibrillator?"

"I can get one."

Miranda was about to turn around and say there was no time when a small, flying drone swooped in and dropped a defibrillator.

"I'll use it," one of the guards said. "I'm a medic."

Miranda backed up and checked her HUD. [Facial Replication Render: 94%]

But all of the other guards were looking at the fallen soldier. It took three shocks to restore the pulse.

"His heart is working again, but he's still not responsive," the medic said. "We better get him to a medic station."

"I'm calling in an evac-floatpod." Someone else said.

[Facial Replication Render complete. Changing your face now.]

Miranda blinked, and hoped the computer made her face look more like the female soldier that was laying at the base of the casket.

A few eyes turned to her. They didn't seem disturbed at all.

"What happened to him?" the medic asked.

Miranda touched her archive stone and let a little bit of the fallen soldier's life memory flood into her. It was enough to know all of their names and the protocol for this island.

"He, uh, we went to look at this casket, and a bunch of spiders came rushing out," she said, knowing that more than a few of the soldiers here found spiders creepy. "I tried to burn them all, but one must have got into his boot. He was screaming and holding it as he fell into the sand."

"Why is his upper armor off, Samantha?" Rick, the medic asked. From the memories Miranda knew his name, where he was stationed, and why there was a tone of jealousy in the question. Samantha, the name of the woman Miranda was impersonating, had slept around. And Rick thought it was more serious than it was.

"He, uh," Miranda looked at the other faces. "He thought more spiders had crawled into him, that's all."

Rick was not convinced. He gave her a scowl and then turned to help the others move the half-naked soldier. The evac-flaotpod flew into view, lighting the beach with the bright glow of halogen.

The soldier was laid in a gurney strapped to the pod. Bronson, another person Samantha knew a little too well opened the hatch and then looked down at her.

"Samantha, the sergeant wants a report of this incident from you," Bronson said.

"Oh. Uh, I should really finish my search out here." Miranda forced herself not to look at the real Samantha laying at the bottom of the sand pit.

Bronson gave her a confused look. "We'll have the drones do the search. Everyone is heading back."

As he said the words, a large utility transport vehicle drove up and the rest of the group got onto the truck, while a small army of flying drones swarmed out of the back and scanned the area with lights, thermal sensors and more.

Miranda scratched her head and grabbed a hold of the latch of the float pod. They ascended rapidly and headed back to base camp.

"When's your shift over?" Bronson asked through the speaker.

"Not right now." Miranda took a look back and her HUD selected the drones back on the beach.

"Let's see if Donovan even bothered to change the passwords," Miranda said under her breath.

It wasn't long before she was logged into the system giving the drones orders. She gave the drones a new set of instructions, similar to their original instructions, but the grid search now had a significant gap in it. It would not do a thermal scan of the open grave. Just one quick picture from the other side of the tomb.

Relieved she had a little bit of time, she turned back around to see where she was going. Base camp was in sight, and it was huge. A large, old looking building sat in the middle of a sprawling military village. The place was crawling with vehicles, tents, soldiers and scientists.

"How did all of this get here?" Miranda asked under her breath as she held her hand over the archive stone. A holographic projection of Samantha's memories hovered above her bracelet. The first memories she was assaulted with were about Samantha's extracurricular activities. Miranda fast forwarded through those and scanned others to find out how she got here.

Before she got that far back in the life recording, the floatpod dropped dramatically and landed in the middle of a gated landing zone. The half naked soldier was carted away and Bronson hopped out of the pod.

"Sarge is this way." He pointed to the big building in the center of the base and walked towards it.

Miranda followed, bringing up frequencies and itineraries of the Coalition on her screen. People and soldiers were going all over the place, talking about all kinds of things. There were about three dozen email and radio conversations happening at that moment about portals alone. She decided to run a subroutine in her computer to check for any female scientist that needed an escort to a remote location.

After passing several large tents containing sleeping soldiers, weapons, and vehicles, they reached the main building. It was probably three stories high, and covered with moss, rust, and some filmy substance. Miranda took a look around, wondering how she missed this building when she was here the last time.

They walked through the main door and down a narrow, dimly lit hallway.

"Seriously, when's your shift over?"

"I meant it, not tonight, Bronson."

"I just want to talk this time."

"Yeah, well, I don't want to listen."

Bronson let out a huff and opened the last door in the hallway. On the other side was an expansive lab. In the center, there was a cluster of operation chairs, which were surrounded by experimentation tables. The walls were covered with odd tools and she had no idea what they were for.

"My orders are to take you to that room over there, just in case there was a new tetrapath outbreak."

"What?" Miranda looked where he indicated. A glass room with only one door. "That's ridiculous."

"That's why I only wanted to talk." Bronson kept walking. "You were next to an exposed grave. Anything could have happened."

They passed the tables and entered the cluster of chairs. They were old, some of them cold metal and rusty. The clamps looked very ridged.

[A councilor Marie Blake is scheduled to go to your home island, the Helix Cascade, and examine the memory stones. She is trying to go unescorted, but the Coalition insists she bring one soldier along. No one is assigned.]

With a quick motion, Miranda fell down at the base of one of the chairs. Bronson reached down instinctively to catch her, and then tried to recoil in fear of the potential tetrapath infection. But it was too late.

Her archive stone grazed the underside of his palm, and she sent out a two hour block of Samantha's memories into him. Miranda tried to make it time Bronson and Samantha spent together.

He fell forward, and she helped guide his body to land comfortably on the chair in front of them. She took a quick look around, but no one seemed to notice.

"Assign Samantha Walther to Councilor Blake's mission and show me where I am to report. And erase all restrictions Samantha may have due to suspicious tetrapath contact." Miranda said into her computer.

Seconds later, a marker was displayed on her HUD. She navigated the room, through a series of chairs and tables. Other scientists and researchers were walking around, buried in their own work.

She reached the marker point just twenty feet from the isolation tank Bronson had been trying to take her to. Councilor Blake was already there, tapping her datapad with a repetitive tick.

"Councilor Blake, I am here to escort you," Miranda said.

"About time," Blake huffed. "You tell me I can't go without somebody, and then you make me wait while you send somebody. Such a waste of time."

"Let's go. I am sure a floatpod is ready to take us there."

"Floatpod?" Blake looked at her with a sour expression. "Why would we fly there? Honestly, just don't talk for the remainder of this trip."

Councilor Blake turned around and pressed a few buttons on a control panel against the wall in front of her. As she did so, a section of the wall began to glow. There were other parts of the control board that began to glow as well. But Miranda was only paying attention to what was in front of her. They were going to go through a portal. She readied her memory bracelet.

As the portal stabilized, Miranda noticed it was a little different than the ones she was used to. Instead of the purplish red hue, this one was gray and hazy.

"We're going to be over there for a long time, soldier," Councilor Blake said. "This portal closes behind us and can only be opened from this side. I have asked that it be opened for us in four hours."

Then she walked through the portal. Miranda summoned her courage, and took a tentative step behind her.

She walked out the other side like she had just gone through a an ordinary door. She was now standing in her home temple with no adverse effects.

"Come along now, Soldier." Councilor Blake said behind her. "The stones are up this way."

Miranda turned around and saw where the other side of the portal was. On the center stage of her temple, there was a stone archway. Each stone was made of a mysterious material that Miranda could only describe as petrified water. She could see through each stone. While the portal was on, there were glowing red dots in the middle of the stones. Then the portal shut off, and the red dots stopped glowing and revealed the depictions of islands that Miranda remembered seeing the last time she was there.

They walked through the stage at the bottom of an amphitheater in the center of the temple, and they made their way to the Hall of Records.

"What do you want with the stones, anyway?" Miranda asked as they entered the tunnel and approached the first set of shelves containing the stones.

"I want to find out how they do it," Councilor Blake said, putting on a pair of gloves. "But like I said, don't talk for the rest of this trip. I need to concentrate."

Miranda rolled her eyes and tapped the end of her bracelet stone to the back of councilor Blake's neck. She fell down face first onto the pile of stones.

Dozens of green orbs shot into Blake's mind, all vying for her attention. She shook slightly for a few seconds and then fell to the floor.

Miranda pulled all of the memories in Blake's mind into a hologram above her head.

"It looks like she'll be in a trance for at least 12 hours, if she comes out at all." Miranda said.

She then put her hand to Councilor Blake's cheek and downloaded her life memory into her archive bracelet.

"I want a full body scan of councilor Blake, ready to render as soon as possible." Miranda said as she removed the extra soldier gear.

[Scan complete. Estimated full body render time: 2.5 hours.]

"Good enough." Miranda tossed the last of the armor aside and opened a small portal on the underside of her wrist.

On the other side were seven small disks.

"Do you think Donovan has updated his suit?" she asked.

[A good Councilor would.]

"I hope these things will work on the one he is wearing."

[It proved successful on the suit you stole from him.]

"Yeah." Miranda sat on a pew back in the temple and ran her hand through her hair. "Right now, it's our only shot. The Coalition has to be stopped. And that starts with Donovan's assassination."

CHAPTER 12: THE DEATH MEMORY

Talia clenched her teeth sharply as she stood on the beach of the Helix Cascade. Her head pounded under the sheer number of recordings littered everywhere. In the trees, under rocks, in broken down houses, and in the temple. She scrunched her eyes shut, but she could still see them. Ghostly green orbs imbedded in inanimate objects all over.

There were so many here, that Talia felt she could still safely walk across the island without opening her eyes. Each recording was a bright spot in her vision, even if the recording was blocked by a mountain, or buried in the ground.

Each one cast a slightly different shade of green. Before, when she did see a memory recording, they were all the same color, and their glow would not even light up a dark room.

Her head ached, and she could take no more. She teleported herself back to Cantera Bay, the thriving city where her sister had grown up a Coalition scientist.

She was in the rubble of some former building by the ocean. Most of the inner walls were crumpled, and quite a few of the outer walls as well.

In the middle, there were rows of chairs facing a stage. Maybe this used to be a temple of sorts, Talia thought.

Here, she regained her peace. In her vision, there were only five total memories in her current 20 mile radius. Some were high off the ground, probably in a building somewhere, while others were low, like they were underground.

Her stomach rumbled, and she considered teleporting Miranda to help her navigate the urban terrain in front of her. But bringing either Scott or Miranda here would set off alarms too big to handle. They were wanted fugitives here.

Still, she ached for food and another drink from her fountain. She walked to one of the still standing chairs and sat down.

She had no where she could go until she figured out how to deal with her new powers. She had already tried her island ten times, but she couldn't even handle the beach.

In frustration, she rubbed her hands on her face and looked in the direction of the city, eying the five recordings. With nothing better to do, she decided to find all of the memories in the city and hoped she could use them to train herself to see things better.

The closest one was in a bar three blocks down, along the beach. She teleported to the back entrance and looked around. The back door was open, and there was a cook dumping a vat of grease into a can.

He finished and then walked back in the door. Talia crept inside the door and saw where the memory was. It was imbedded in a glass cup at one of the tables. She teleported a napkin into her hand, and then she grabbed the cup through another portal with the napkin so she did not go through the trance right there.

Before the chef turned around, she teleported to the broken building. She placed the cup in one of the cup holders on the chair, and teleported back out.

The next recording was in a multi story building a few blocks inland. It was some sort of office that catered to the public. There were people coming in and out everywhere. Talia more or less waited in a line for something while she scanned the area for the memory.

The line turned a corner and she saw what it was. The memory was embedded into an entire chair where people would wait when they were told to do so.

The chair was currently occupied. Talia waited in the line and watched the man in the chair. He was reading a magazine, yawning, and his eyes were droopy.

She drew closer to the front of the line and started to feel people staring at her. She nervously combed a strand of hair behind her ear and risked a quick glance at other sections of the room.

People were staring at her. Did they know who she was? Were they about to report her? The person in front of her was called to the help desk, meaning she was next.

She contemplated, not for the first time, just teleporting the chair out from under the guy and leaving. But she did not want to let the coalition know she was in the city if she could help it. She had no idea how long she would be here.

She looked back at the chair, and noticed a huge flock of birds swaying between the buildings outside.

She closed her eyes and conjured a very thin layer of mist on the floor wrapping around feet and furniture so as not to let people fall through it, hoping it would be imperceptible.

Then, when the birds flocked up, she conjured another portal above them.

Squawks and shrill shrieks filled the room as dozens of birds flew through her portal. People jumped up from their seats, swatting the bird filled air with magazines and furniture cushions.

In the pandemonium, the man in the memory chair jumped up and ran away in the crowd. Talia teleported herself and the chair back to her base.

She took a couple of deep breaths and looked for the next one. She closed her eyes and focused on the glowing green orb. This one was moving. Quite quickly.

With a flick of her hand, she conjured a mist and followed it. On the mist in front of her, she saw a high speed commuter train zipping along an elevated rail system. She teleported herself to an empty section of the train and cautiously began to move through the cabins towards the orb.

Once she reached a cabin with a bigger crowd, she was once again the subject of attention. People were staring at her, like they somehow knew she did not belong among them.

She navigated the crowd and made her way to the center, where the orb was dangling from the ceiling. It was imbedded in a hand hold for people to keep themselves steady as the train traveled.

The handhold looked like it was firmly stuck in the roof, so Talia would need to examine it here if she wanted to know what was inside it.

She reached up and grabbed the handle.

The green orb shot through her hand and to her mind. The images were dark and blank, and then she was standing on a jetty back at the beach. A tall woman Talia would never forget was standing at the edge of the jetty during a time when the waves weren't so bad.

He hair was multi-colored and sections of it were tangled in knots. He clothes didn't match, and looked barely qualified to cover her body.

"Hello. I am the Phantom Queen," She said. "And if you are seeing this, it is because you have a gift. Maybe you know about it, maybe you don't. Either way, I can guarantee that gift is being blocked, and I want to do something about it. If you want to find out more, head to that bar at sundown."

She pointed down the beach and whoever was actually making the recording turned to look at a bar. It was a different one than Talia had visited that morning.

Talia blinked, and she was back on the train, holding the handle. The train had stopped, and people were getting off or on at the moment. Most were looking down at phones or talking to each other.

Reasonably sure no one was watching, she looked around for the next closest orb and teleported. This one was underground, somewhere dark. She stumbled around for it, reaching her hand out to try to keep from running into anything.

With the cloth from her shirt, she shielded her hand and reached out for the orb. It was buried under a few soft things. By the feel of it, a pillow, a mattress and then a wooden panel. Talia took the pillow case off the pillow and used it to store the orb.

She teleported back to her base. As she stepped out of the mists, a thunderous crack erupted from them, pushing her down to the floor. Dust and debris stirred up, creating a dust cloud.

Talia rolled into the first row of chairs and then looked back at her mists. They were thick and dark, but there was an almost electric energy humming though them.

"Beware!" A man was shouting through her mists. "Everything you think! Everything you do! Everything that happens to you is captured in the Great Recorder, and in the end of days, it will be played for your condemnation or your justification!"

Talia recognized the speech. With hesitation, she reached out her hand to part the mists slightly. The mists opened, revealing Silas preaching on the stage. She could even see herself, panicking and losing control on the street.

The man looked up at her through the mists in the sky.

The mist cracked again and then Talia pulled it back into her. She collapsed to the concrete floor with exhaustion.

It took her several minutes to calm down. When her breathing slowed down to a normal rate, she sat up and looked at her hands. Were the mists storing recordings now? Or had she imagined it?

She rubbed her hands over her face to try to calm down some more and noticed a faint ringing in her ear, almost like the sound Miranda's computers made when they had been on for too long.

She looked at the three memories she gathered hoping they were her salvation. They were at least the source of the ringing in her head. She moved chairs to be closer to them.

The glass, the chair, and a mystery object in a pillow. Each was a different shade of green. The orb in the glass was a dull green like a leaf that had fallen off a tree a few days ago, while the orb in the seat had more of a yellowish hue to it, like a lime gone sour. Talia reasoned that these two objects, found where crowds of people gathered, were likely more propaganda from the Phantom Queen.

She was attracted most to the mystery object. It looked like a ball of glowing moss. This one was found hidden in the dark, away from prying eyes. This memory trance had a secret.

Cautiously, she opened the pillow case and peered inside. The mossy green orb was planted inside a silver necklace. The pendant on the end was a large sphere that looked like it opened. Talia reached down into the pillow and willed the orb to shoot into her mind.

This trance once again took her to a small room. Most of the lights were coming through the door, but Talia could see the reflection of a mirror. A woman was crying.

"Cal. I... I heard you are leaving Naprea. Don't. Stay home." She looked quickly over her shoulder, and then returned to face the mirror. "Things have changed. I'm no longer in control of the activists. Brooke is. She's... She's calling herself the Phantom Queen, and there has been violence. It's too late for me. But if you leave now, there is no telling where you will end up."

The Phantom Queen burst through the door, kissing a man aggressively.

"Olivia, what are you going here?" Brooke shouted with a drunken slur. "I have this hunk of love under a soul jump, and I was gunna, you know..."

Olivia's face grew sick and the memory trance ended.

Talia took in a deep breath and dropped the necklace back into the pillow case. After scratching her head for a moment, she realized the ringing in her head was lessened. She looked back at her three objects, and while they were still glowing, they weren't glowing as brightly. Could she be developing a tolerance?

With a little bit of trepidation, she touched the other recordings in the room. They were propaganda, as Talia guessed, but with each one, the ringing in her head lessened.

After finishing all of the memories, she conjured a portal and jumped to the village on the Helix Cascade. Her mind was assaulted. Thousands of memories were crying out to her.

Her mists were crackling with lightning. She ran through the rundown buildings, to the first memories she could find.

They were death memories. A dark night, explosions, gun shots. Screaming people everywhere. Each one was painful to go through, but with each memory trance she picked up, her senses grew calmer. After five memories, she could think clearly. But her mists were still out of control.

She teleported back to the Catalyst Fountain. Along the way, her mists crackled, and voices could be heard through it.

"Sorry about your couch." she heard herself saying.

"Don't worry about it, Dixon replied.

Her hands shook as she lifted the cup out of the Catalyst Fountain. Slowly, the mists relaxed as she drank the purple water. Five glasses later, her mists were inside of her and her memories weren't playing on a loop.

She sat on the edge of the stairs and looked over the island. Thousands of memories were still shining, but she was adjusted to it. Still, it was hard to see anything besides the glowing green spots.

Now it was a matter of remembering her father's lessons about cultivating unfamiliar powers. When she had first displayed her ability to conjure portals, there were no step-by-step instructions on. Nobody had ever done it before. Nobody could do it, except for her.

It was the same thing with these powers. No one alive could show her how to use them. She focused and closed her eyes. She let out a loud breath and opened them again.

The countless memories were gone. She closed her eyes and took in another breath. When she opened her eyes, the memories were back, but her senses were okay with them there.

The confidence rose with her as she stood up and teleported back to the scene of her father's death. The room was still in chaos, with chunks of wooden debris everywhere. But there was only one bit that had a memory embedded in it.

The orb was still sitting under a pile, and it was glowing a very deep green. Talia thought of a field of small blades of grass that stretched on forever.

With no hesitation, she reached down and picked up the memory, waiting for it to wash over her again.

The memory took her to the exact room, but it was night. Explosions were happening all over. More of the walls were intact, but large holes were already blown out of them.

Her dad was sitting where Talia remembered seeing his body. He was breathing heavy and looking at chest wounds and blood loss.

"Talia, sweety." He coughed up a bit of blood. "I'm not going to make it. Your sister is here for you now. Stick with her. Keep her close."

The wall exploded in front of him and most of it fell down. Her father picked up some sort of weapon and shot it out into the darkness. A softer explosion went off in the distance and silenced the night temporarily.

"Talia, I am so proud of you." He took in a sharp breath and his vision grew spotty. "Your mother would be too. She had a gift for you. Got lost in all the funeral proceedings. She wound up buried on her home island with it. I was... I was going to take you there. Or.. you know what I mean. When you were old enough. In a few years."

He coughed violently and his vision went completely black. "Her cloak. Her cloak has a memory. Go to it. Learn more about your mother."

The memory ended and she was brought back to the present. The glowing orb returned to the bit of wood in her hand.

"Oh, Dad." Talia stifled a sob as a tear ran down her cheek.

CHAPTER 13: SCOTT'S FAMILY

Scott stared at the entrance to the prison. People moved around him in the street while he resisted the urge to scratch his leg.

Dixon was still being held in there without the typical Naprean trial. No scribe took a life memory to see what Dixon was doing through his own eyes just before he killed those two people. Something wasn't adding up.

He stepped inside, expecting to be escorted out, but no one moved. The guard at the counter looked up at him, waiting for a response.

"I'd like to talk to Peter," Scott told him.

The guard nodded his head in understanding. "I'll get the paper work."

The guard left his post, and took another guard from in the filing cabinet area with him.

Scott focused his thoughts on the gray orb that was the collective talent of the guards in the office. The last time he was here, there was plenty of contact for him to steal talents. He knew everything they watched for, every fighting technique, every security measure. And now there was a gaping hole in the defense.

Scott quickly jumped the over counter and crossed into the filing cabinet area. A small tennis ball was lobbed at him.

He picked up the chair behind the counter and swatted the ball into the exposed arm of a guard who was charging at him. The ball rolled back to him and Scott swung the chair like a golf club at the face of the next guard over.

The last guard in the filing cabinet area ran around to flank him on his left. Scott ran alongside the right wall. The guard caught up to him and there was only one cabinet that separated them.

Scott turned, jumped his back into the wall, and then kicked his legs out into the cabinet. That slammed into the guard and started a domino effect, with the last cabinet slamming into the left exit door where the first guard had gone to get paper work.

From his cell, Dixon slowly sat up and stared at Scott with a confused look.

The remaining two guards from the counter ran up behind him, and the three guards at the gate rushed him from the front.

Scott reached into the nearest cabinet and pulled out a long staff with a ribbon attached to the end of it.

All of the guards stopped in a circle around Scott, hesitant to take the next step.

Scott swung the staff in front of him. The guards leaped back to avoid contact with the ribbon. The guards behind him took that moment to charge.

He leapt forward, twisting and swinging the staff back at them. The ribbon connected with two of the guards on the first swing and the last one on the second swing. They all fell to the ground in a memory trance.

He spun back around, lashing out with the staff. In short order, the rest of the guards were on the floor.

"How long will they be out?" Dixon asked casually from his cell.

"Only about two minutes," Scott said, as he reached into another filing cabinet and pulled out the keys to Dixon's cell. "But we should be gone by then."

Scott unlocked the cage and Dixon shot out of it like a cork. Scott's stomach collapsed as Dixon slammed his fist into it. As he toppled over, Scott reached out and grabbed Dixon's arm.

The red orb of Dixon's soul jumping power shot into him. He could now see Dixon's soul. Dixon tried to soul jump him and Scott blocked it with the newly acquired powers.

Scott held off a choke hold while the tetrapath infection amped up his body. "What are you doing?"

"This is for my sister!" Dixon shouted as he soul jumped all of the guards in the room.

Scott threw Dixon back and ran back out towards the exit.

Under Dixon's power, the guards were standing up to block the way.

Using the strength of the tetrapath, he kicked one of the filing cabinets. It flew like he had just kicked a soccer ball and slammed into two of the guards.

"Don't make me do this!" Scott yelled as he picked up another guard and threw him across the room with one arm. "I won't be able to control it!"

"I don't care," Dixon said as he grabbed Scott from behind, trying to get him in a head lock.

With a quick twist, Scott flung Dixon over his shoulders and over the front desk. The remaining guards shook their heads in confusion as Dixon let go of the soul jumps.

"Stand down, and no one has to get hurt!" Scott yelled.

At that moment, loud, rapid gun fire broke through the window and the guards started falling down. Scott dropped to the floor and rolled behind a filing cabinet.

The gunfire stopped and Scott wasted no time picking up a cabinet and throwing it full force through the window. His shoulder popped out of socket and something snapped in his back.

The window glass was not completely shattered, but Scott could tell he missed the assassin.

There was a cut on the inside of his palm from where he had gripped the cabinet. The blood was still too thin to be true tetrapath blood, but his hand was already starting to heal, the way it did when he was amped up. His shoulder and back snapped back into place as his body corrected itself.

And then he caught himself scratching his scars. They were itching the way they did when tetrapath monsters were lurking about.

Scott looked around, stood absolutely still, hoping it was just him amped up on the infection.

Under one of the filing cabinets, a guard was convulsing. He was also bleeding, but the blood was thick and dark, with a shiny coat of green.

"The new ones?" Scott ran towards the front counter, eager to get out of the room.

Dixon sprang up to his feet, a bunch of red ghosts shot out from him, and into the soon to be tetrapath.

"Hold it right there." Dixon said as he assumed a defensive stance.

"Dixon, we have to alert the town," Scott pleaded. "The tetrapath with consume this city."

"Don't worry." Dixon grunted a little bit as the forming tetrapath behind Scott stood up. "I have them completely under my control."

Scott turned back around in time to see a filing cabinet flying at him. Even with his enhanced reflexes, it hit him square in the chest and knocked him back against the counter.

Another tetrapath ran up, grabbed him from under the cabinet and threw him to the prison.

His ribs cracked in pain like they were broken. He turned around in time for a second filing cabinet to smash into him, pinning him down. He lifted it a little bit to allow room for his ribs to set back together. Fast healing or not, it was painful.

The closest tetrapath crawled forward slowly, like a pack of predators assured of victory over a an injured kill.

Scott let out a grunt and used his enhanced strength to throw the cabinet into the first wave of tetrapath.

The cabinet collided square with one and tripped another. But more came in to take their place as Scott pushed himself up along the bars of the jail.

The next one was still mostly on hind legs, and its left hand looked more or less the same. The right hand, however looked like a two sided battle axe.

"That's gotta be a Coalition upgrade," Scott moaned.

It leaped into action, swinging the axe arm with precise fury. Scott ducked and rolled behind the jail cell bars. The monster slashed out again, cutting the bars cleanly. In two cuts, there was a hole for it to jump through.

Scott leapt to the monster's right and through the entrance gate before it could get a good backswing in. Once he was outside of the cell, the remaining tetrapath engaged.

Scott picked up the fallen bars cut by the axe monster and threw them at other tetrapath. Because of the angle of the cut, some of the bars were now pointy on one end.

Two monsters were impaled through the head, and another through the shoulder. The remaining tetrapath had blocked the bar with a shield-like appendix.

"You forget just how good I am Scott," Dixon cried out derisively. "Even the dead ones are subject to my powers."

Scott looked around, and then realized that even the tetrapath with impaled heads weren't laying on the ground dead.

He had to get out of there. His heart rate increased again as the tetrapath inside him brought out animal instincts for survival.

He ran to the closest filing cabinet and kicked it at the tetrapath to his left. It was blocked, but it gave Scott enough time to engage the next tetrapath to the right.

This one had two spiked hands and lunged for him with both. Scott pushed the spikes out of the way and grabbed the bar that impaled the monster's head. With a quick spin, Scott picked the monster up, broke its neck and slammed it into the next tetrapath.

He let go at just the right moment and the two tetrapath were launched at Dixon. The axe monster swung from behind. Scott ducked and leapt towards the front of the building.

Dixon managed to duck to avoid getting hit, but it gave Scott enough clearance to leap out of the building and into the street.

"Tetrapath!" Scott shouted to anyone that could hear. "Take cover!"

The immediate crowd did not seem to know how to respond. The just stood there until the monsters leapt through the front walls of the prison and gave chase to Scott.

The only way he was going to stop these creatures was to take out Dixon. And the easiest way to do that was with to put him in a recording trance.

Scott shot out his own ghosts and soul jumped the closest people. As he ran down a few city blocks, he used his soul jump to make his people throw recorded memories at Dixon.

Dixon reflexively caught the first one, and fell to the ground asleep.

The dead tetrapath fell to the ground behind him and Scott used his ghosts to soul jump the remaining few. He was about to use them to kill themselves when a small platoon of men and women came charging out of the hospital, shooting the tetrapath with some sort of spear guns.

Seeing all was contained, Scott pulled out a few pills from his pocket and swallowed them. But then a member of the platoon shot him with a spear. Scott blocked it and used his soul jump to attack. The closest tetrapath slammed the platoon member with its massive clubs. He went flying end over end and slammed into a nearby wall.

The clubbed tetrapath was impaled through the neck by a spear, but Scott kept it going. Then, Scott felt something hit the back of his neck. Everything went dark as a memory trance washed over him.

*****

Scott woke up from the trance in a large room with cold, steel walls. He rubbed his head and pushed himself off the floor and looked around.

The tetrapath carcasses were scattered on the floor, their thick blood trickling like drying mud everywhere. The rest of the room was empty.

Scott stood up and tested his body. His ribs were swollen, but fine, and his shoulders worked, but they hurt a lot.

There was no noise from outside the walls, but Scott could see faint ghosts, meaning he still had Dixon's powers. But for how much longer, he didn't know.

Based on where the ghosts were, Scott there was a hallway outside of his cell with more cells on either side.

After gaining his senses, he finally realized that the ghosts were white. Pure, bright white. Just like his.

Tentatively, he reached out and soul jumped the closest ghost. The jump was allowed, no forcing. But once Scott was in, thousands of thoughts flooded his mind all at once.

[Sick! Snatchers! Kiandoli! Help! Don't let her touch us!]

Scott pulled out of the soul jump and tried the closest on the right. This one was calmer.

[One of us!] Was the thought of the man. [Help. We need help. We can escape.]

The man kept repeating this mantra in his head over and over again.

[Stay with me.] The man said distinctly to him. [They are coming.]

A slit opened on the wall where Scott had not seen one. The hole was now large enough for Silas' head to be seen.

"You brought the plague with you," Silas sneered.

"I'm not a carrier. Someone else planted this." Scott protested.

"I'm afraid the only other witness was your former friend, Dixon. And he's already testified that your blood infected those men and women."

"You're believing him now, then?" Scott asked.

"Well, he did aid in the killing of all of the tetrapath."

"He was using them to try to kill me!"

"He's earned the town's trust, for now." Silas continued. "As for you, Naprea has decided that quarantine is not enough for you. You must be cleansed."

Scott looked as several large hoses dangling down from the ceiling.

"Those are fire hoses." Silas said. "We're prepping them with oil right now. Soon, they will be burning everyone in there."

Scott looked from the hoses to Silas. Silas was sneering, enjoying the moment. There would be no reasoning with him. Scott's only option was through the dead tetrapath. He soul jumped them, using Dixon's power while he still had it. At once, they leapt up and sliced at the hoses.

Scott walked to the edge of the room as hoses started gushing out oil. Then he focused on the front door, and sent all of the tetrapath over to smash a hole through it.

Silas backed away from the window as the noise levels in the room rose to a crescendo. The walls around the door cracked and crumbled with every blow.

A solitary red ghost appeared at the end of the hallway. Dixon. Scott pressed harder on his tetrapaths and they smashed through the wall. Out of triumph, Scott made them roar as they charged through the new hole.

A dozen people ran around the corner , shooting automatic weapons.

Scott rolled out of the path of the door and took cover.

The tetrapath charged, almost unfazed by the gun fire.

Dixon sent out a soul jump to attack Scott. Scott blocked it with one of his own, but he had to let go of one of the tetrapath to do it.

Dixon quickly took control of the freed tetrapath and made it fight the tetrapath under Scott's control. Scott diverted two of his own puppets to attack Dixon's.

Dixon's puppet tripped one tetrapath, and slammed a second to the wall with a massive force. With a quick twist, it impaled another and started running down the hallway. Dixon tried again to soul jump the other tetrapaths in Scott's control, but this time Scott held his ground and stayed on the defensive.

Meanwhile, Silas and the others were hammering his tetrapaths and wearing them down. They were dead, but there was only so much mass to them. Soon they would just be shattered bones.

Scott felt Dixon's powers of soul jumping start to fade. It was only a matter of time before Dixon and Silas would wear him out.

With a last ditch effort, he let go of one tetrapath and it slumped to the ground. Dixon picked that one up, but then Scott sent his free soul at Silas. Dixon swatted his soul away with ease, preventing Scott from making the soul jump.

He was out of options. His next instinct was to aggravate the infection within himself even more, but that was worse than death. From his crouched position he looked around the room for any weapons. Eventually, his eye caught the white ghosts lining the hallway.

He had snatchers with him. Real, talented snatchers. With one last effort he controlled his remaining tetrapath puppets to smash open the doors of the hallway. Dixon's two tetrapaths stopped in confusion, assessing the threat.

Scott let go of the mangled tetrapaths and they fell to the ground with a large, sloppy thump. The gun fire ceased and Silas let out a panicked shout. Dixon soul jumped all of the tetrapath.

Not knowing how well he could trust the snatchers to fight in their mental condition, he soul jumped them. They seemed to sense that he was one of them, that he could be trusted. They let him in.

"Kill everyone in those rooms!" Silas shouted.

The tetrapath split up, entering separate rooms along the hallway.

Scott controlled his snatchers and they each took defensive positions near the doors. As the tetrapaths marched, or in some cases, hobbled in, the snatchers came in from behind and touched the tetrapaths. They had truly strong talents, and with one touch, the soul jumps on each of the tetrapaths was broken.

"I'm out," Dixon shouted. "Something's happened and I'm out. I have no control over any of the tetrapaths."

Silas swore. "Retreat!"

"What?" Said another man beside him.

"I said *retreat!*" Silas shouted and ran in the other direction.

The other armed men followed suit, but Dixon lingered, not one to back down from a fight.

"Back away now, Dixon." Scott stood up and walked into the open doorway. "Some of my new friends can neutralize talents in others. And you've already seen your soul jumps pushed away like nothing. Without your fighting skills or your soul jumps, I think even I could finally best you in a fight."

"Silas won't stop." Dixon said. "He hates us. Hates you. He'll use this to create greater fear of you. The town will have your head if he has his way. Which, I'm inclined to believe, he will."

"So, what does that make us? Seeing as your his henchman now."

"Come on, Scott," Dixon said with a tone of frustration. "We were never really friends to begin with. Not since you got me expelled from the orphanage, and then killed my sister."

"What? I didn't kill your sister!" Scott shouted.

"I see that I am outmatched at this gathering," Dixon conceded. "But we'll see each other again soon."

Dixon turned and walked in the other direction. Scott weighed his options. He wouldn't be able to hold these snatchers in a soul jump forever, but he couldn't just let them stay in here now. Silas might come back to kill them.

So he ran out of the prison with them. He had to get them to as safe a place as possible for now. Cautious and frightened stares greeted him as he made his way out of the lobby with his new friends.

Before rushing them out of the hospital, Scott let go of one soul jump and used it to scan the outside crowd for snipers.

Sure enough, the team was waiting by the entrance, ready to fire. Scott soul jumped one of them and made him shoot into the air. People in the crowd screeched in panic, and ran in different directions.

Scott let go of that soul jump and jumped into another gunman. He repeated the process three more times, firing the guns into the air.

After there was sufficient confusion, Scott ran out with all of the snatchers in tow. He spread them out, and they navigated the crowd, keeping a low crouch to stay out of sight.

Eventually, they reached a clothing store, where Scott made them trade in their raggedy clothes for new ones.

"We'll still have to do something about your hygiene." Scott said. "But this should buy us some time."

After everything calmed down, they made their way to Clarinthia's place. He had nowhere else to go.

But one of the main problems with Naprea was overpopulation. The main roads were always clogged at this time of day with people scrambling to shop and get home.

As they inched their way to the destination, Scott felt Dixon's powers fade. The snatchers in his soul jump were suddenly lost to him, the ghost in everybody fading out.

He scanned the crowd, looking for the snatchers. They weren't anywhere to be seen. His instinct was to keep them spread out so they were harder to follow, but now he was regretting that decision. He stood on the tips of his toes, trying to spot them, but he couldn't find one of them.

The crowd kept moving on and Scott found himself propelled to the neighborhoods. Here, the crowd thinned as they split in different directions.

He made his way to Clarinthia's house, as he'd intended. The wooden steps creaked as he approached the door. He stopped, with his hand on the handle, and then he turned around, looking back into the city. He had to save his new found family. With a quick stretch, he walked away from her house and began his search.

CHAPTER 14: THE FOUR RELICS

Talia stood on the shores of the Island of the Crimson Reef, her mother's birth place and her final resting place. Behind Talia, ocean waves gently lapped at her ankles.

In front of her, the island was overrun with death and danger. The sand at her toes was pitch back, the vegetation was all rotting and even the weeds looked a sickly black. The reef, just offshore, was blood red.

With a few tentative steps, Talia walked closer to the graveyard at the center of the island. Her feet crunched in the sand, giving off more noise than the entire island.

Something moved in a blur out of the corner of her eye. She conjured a portal above her so that she could get a good view of her surroundings.

She spotted over two dozen tetrapath monsters within striking distance of her. Most of them appeared to be asleep, but there were a few stalking her.

Talia slowly reached out her hand and conjured another portal around it. She reached through the mist and pulled out a burning candle from the Naprean library. She then rerouted the portal to a sage plant on a small island to the west. The candle caught the plant on fire and two tetrapath charged her.

Talia teleported them one hundred yards off shore. She then swooped up all the dead dry wood on the island and teleported it into a circle around her.

Several more tetrapath leapt over her crude barrier. Talia teleported out of the circle and into the sky. As she fell, she opened the portal by the sage plant up again. There was already a roaring fire there.

She teleported the fire onto the wood and it caught slowly.

The tetrapath tried to jump out of the fire, but Talia focused it onto them, burning them to the ground.

Once they were taken out, she teleported herself to shoot up into the sky again, and then teleported back onto the beach once her momentum was slow enough to land.

She was on the other side of the island, where the graves were. She ran through the graveyard, looking frantically for her mother's name.

The tombstone was small and flush with the ground. Talia dropped to her knees and put her hand on it. She could see the death memory resting there, waiting to be reclaimed. But Talia had no means to open the grave and her portals would not penetrate the casket.

The fire had attracted more tetrapath. They were in the distance now, each looking around for the source.

Something snapped behind her. She turned around, and a small pack of tetrapath were charging right at her.

Her mists opened up and huge fireballs rained on the tetrapath.

The creatures screeched in pain as Talia sent fireball after fireball engulfing them. The heat was so intense, they shriveled up like burning bugs on contact.

But more tetrapath were coming. She kept twisting around in circles to see them all. They were so fast, and they were getting closer. The heat pouring out of her portals was beginning to warm her skin.

With little else to do, she spun the fiery mists in a fast circle around her. It swooped around with enough speed that she was holding a temporary barrier against the tetrapath.

A thunderous crack roared from her mist, spinning her in the air and launching the tetrapath back.

When the burst died down, Talia crashed hard against the black sand. Her mist floated motionlessly, unyielding to her command.

"This is perfect!" Came a shout from the other side of the portal. This time, it was the Phantom Queen's. "But how does it work?"

"I don't know. There are no instructions. I guess it is assumed that whoever made it here would already know how to use it."

"Well we don't so you're going to have to figure it out!" the Phantom Queen shouted.

"Me?" the other shouted back.

"Because I'm busy keeping everyone off of our backs. Start a notebook, and tinker with it. Figure it out. We have to get this baby running for our return trip to Naprea!"

The mist disappeared and the tetrapath were again surrounding her. Without a second's thought, she teleported back to her island and started drinking from the Catalyst Fountain.

She cursed at herself for being so stupid, and puzzled over her mist's new abilities. They weren't playing recorded memories. She had no memory of the Phantom Queen saying that. Had it opened a way to Earth?

She picked up a pebble and a small green orb traveled down her arm and rested in it. Once the memory was made, she placed it inside one of her pockets, and made the return trip to Naprea. She would ask Miranda what she thought about her mist's behavior.

She stepped out of the mists into Naprea, where once again her senses were assaulted with thousands of memories. But she calmed herself and managed to turn that part of her vision off.

Her target was walking towards her, his head in a book.

"Hudson!" Talia snapped in a sharp whisper.

Hudson looked up from his book, and stopped in his tracks. A mixture of comprehension, fear, and annoyance fell over his face. 'You finally came back, huh?"

"I need you to open another grave for me."

Hudson shut his book. "Not until you've helped me, or have you forgotten our deal?"

A ping of regret developed in her stomach. "Oh, yeah. Yes. What do you need?"

Hudson looked around the street. Although it wasn't crowded, it wasn't deserted either.

"Not here," he said in a low tone.

Without another thought, Talia teleported them back to the catalyst fountain.

"This is pretty isolated," Talia said as she once again took the goblet in her hands and drank. "What do you need?"

"It's not what I need." Hudson said as he sat cross legged on the floor. "It's what Naprea needs."

Talia rolled her eyes. "Okay, what does Naprea need?"

"Defense." Hudson set his book down in front of him and flipped through the pages, looking for something. "The Phantom Queen is coming with power. And my father is busy distracting everybody from preparing for it."

"What kind of power?"

"I don't know." Hudson shrugged, not looking up from the book. "When Olivia started the Activists, she promised big power to the soul jumpers. Power that could conquer Naprea, take it as theirs. But she never told anybody what it was. Not the Phantom Queen, not even my brother."

"Why would she tell your brother?"

Hudson stopped flipping the pages and looked up. "Because they loved each other."

"Oh." A ping of regret washed over Talia. She thought about the last message Olivia left in the city and conjured a mist and teleported the pillow case containing necklace imbued with a memory trance. "Have a look at the memory in that pillow case. I think that was meant for your brother."

Hudson flipped the book upside down to keep his place, and then cautiously reached into the pillow case. He hesitated just inches from the necklace for several moments, but then he withdrew his hand.

"I'm not sure I want to see it. I can't bear to see her talking to him right now." He flipped through a few more pages in his book and then motioned for her to sit down next to him. "Here we go. The four relics."

"What are those?" Talia asked as she sat down next to him.

"Crowd control." Hudson pointed excitedly at the page. "In here it talks about how these relics were gifts from the gods. Wherever they were from, Doctor Pavarti used them to keep his creations in line."

"So, what are they?"

"The Catalyst Fountain, which is right there." Hudson pointed in the direction of the fountain. "It's used to power the other three, which are the Ancestral Branch, the Dominion Rod, and the Ascendant Shield."

"Okay, obvious question: What do they do, and how are they going to stop the Phantom Queen?"

"They each do a lot, but they were used specifically to neutralize the powers of one of the three types of tribes." Hudson turned the page. "The Ancestral Branch neutralizes any scribe by shooting out orbs that block memories, the Dominion Rod traps a soul jumper's soul in the body, and the Ascendance Shield spreads talent in the area around evenly for a short period of time. Armed with those, we would at least stand a fighting chance."

"You really think Naprea is going to be wiped out?" Talia raised a skeptical eyebrow.

"Yes." Hudson said flatly. "People there are too reliant on the security, and that makes them blind to the growing powers of those who wish to rule it, or to destroy it."

"Which do you think the activists will do?"

Hudson took a deep breath and looked at the fountain. "I think Brooke will try to rule it, but if she can't, she will burn it."

****

Talia spread a map she had teleported out of the library onto the floor, and Hudson kneeled over it. It was an old, hand drawn map, complete with an illustration of a sea monster. All eight islands were arranged as accurately as Talia could have hoped for. The seven islands formed an arch around the eighth. The apex of the arch was to the east, with the two ends to the west.

"So, where to first?" Hudson asked.

"I want to go to the Nebulous Reef." Talia pointed to the island towards the point, just to the south. "We should get that one out of the way."

"Is that where your next grave to open is?" Hudson asked pointedly.

"Yeah, so?" Talia said.

"So, there is a chance we can use the branch to help us with the tetrapath on that island."

"Really?" Talia asked skeptically.

"Yes." Hudson pulled out his book again. "Of the four relics, the branch has perhaps more functions than any of the others."

"Such as?"

"For one, it can shoot out memory trances like a cannon. Handy for neutralizing any oncoming tetrapath." Hudson scanned the text of his book. "Oh, and it can shoot out recording orbs into inanimate objects!"

"Come again?"

"Let's say you shoot an orb from the branch into one of these benches, for example." Hudson pointed to the amphitheater seating around them. "It just rests there, taking everything in like it was a real scribe."

"So you can observe without ever being there!" Talia finished.

"Exactly." Hudson wore a smug smile.

"I still think we should go after the shield first," Talia said. "I need to get in that grave."

"No chance," Hudson said. "You ran off on me the last time we dug open a grave for you. Besides, I need another one of those grave openers."

"Why don't you use the one we used last time?"

"Because you left it at the last grave, and they only work once."

"Well, when can you get one?" Talia reached for another mug of water from the catalyst fountain.

"Tomorrow." Hudson said. "I know where my dad keeps them, and he will be out campaigning all day tomorrow."

"Fine." Talia said as she finished another swig of her drink. "Where do you suggest we go first?"

"To Cherubim's Perch." He pointed to an island on the north tail of the arch, second from the last to the east. "After the branch."

In the picture, the island was mostly flat, with a thin, sheer cliff towards the east side. She got the image of some large angelic bird perching atop that cliff. A picture of an old tree was on the flat side of the island.

"According to legend," Hudson pointed at the tree, "that's where the Ancestral Branch will be kept."

"Yeah, but I think the odds of the legend matching up with reality aren't good." Talia rolled up the map. "We'll have to count on Pavarti hiding the weapon somewhere safer than a tree."

"Agreed." Hudson stood up and looked out Talia's window hesitantly. "So, when do we leave?"

Talia bit her lip and looked at Hudson with apprehension. "Soon. I just want to go over some ground rules."

"Oh?"

"First," Talia held up a finger, "if there is any danger, I'm bringing us back here, and that will happen without warning."

"Danger?" Hudson protested.

"Trust me, we have a good chance of running into the Coalition while we're there." Talia thought of her sister, out there alone against the army. "Anyway, second, we need to get these things as fast as possible. And third..."

Talia trailed off, hesitant to bring up her last rule at all. The trip would only be a few hours anyway. Not enough time for Hudson to get any ideas about their relationship, as boys sometimes did.

"Yes?" Hudson asked.

"Nothing." Talia brushed her hair behind her ear. "The last one wasn't important."

"Two rules?" Hudson asked. "That's it?"

"Everything else is implied." Talia waved her hands and the room began to fill with her purple mist. "If you slow me down, or do anything stupid, you're back in Naprea in an instant. Are you ready?"

Hudson grabbed his backpack and slung it over his shoulder. "Ready."

Talia closed her eyes and teleported them to Cherubim's Perch. They were stationed at the westernmost beach, looking up at the mountain to the northeast.

From here it looked like a large wall, built to scrape the clouds. The sun was still low enough that the mountain was blocking it. The water behind them crashed in the sunlight, but a dark shade still rested on the shore.

Talia had already scoped out the island with her mists, there was no Coalition presence to speak of. There wasn't a lot of tall vegetation. A few patches of trees sprung out here and there, but the landscape was mostly bushes and shrubs.

Hudson pointed to the base of the cliff. "I think I can see the tree from here."

Talia raised her hands to conjure her mists. But nothing happened.

"What's wrong?" Hudson asked.

"I can't teleport." Talia pursed her lips in frustration. "My mists are staying inside me for some reason."

"That's weird," Hudson said. "I mean, this island is locked against soul jumpers, but I don't see how-"

"Locked?" Talia let out a slight chirp of anger in her question.

"Yeah," Hudson hesitated. "Soul jumpers can't use their powers on this island. There's some sort of interference signal that keeps the soul in the body."

"Why didn't you tell me before?"

"Because you aren't a soul jumper?" Hudson backed up slightly and held up his hands. "Didn't think it would come up."

"My mother was a soul jumper." Talia sat down in the damp sand. "It's where I get my teleporting powers from. Those mists you see flying around everywhere when I teleport? That's my soul."

"Oh," Hudson's eyes grew wide with recognition and worry. "So... we're stuck here?"

"Until we can find a way to shut the signal off." Talia sighed. "Do you know where that might be coming from?"

"I don't know for sure." Hudson kneeled down and began drawing idly in the sand. "But my guess would be from the top of the cliff. That's where I'd put it. Are you feeling any other symptoms?"

"I'm a little dizzy, now that you mention it." Talia reluctantly pushed herself up as the sun crested over the cliff. "Come on, let's head to the tree and see if we can find that branch."

The trail was mercifully flat and soft. It was mostly sand for a few hundred yards, and then it turned into an elaborate stone road. The road was surrounded on both sides by wooden hand rails, which Talia gladly used.

"While we're just killing time," Hudson started, "how about some more history on the branch?"

"It couldn't hurt." Talia said.

"Great. Let me sum up the religious back story of it." Hudson held out his hands excitedly. "Hundreds of years ago, shortly after the birth of the scribes, there was a young, talented family who died tragically. They were wrapped in cloth and buried in the dirt, arranged in a circular pattern, with their feet pointing out. A tree seed was planted in the center of the circle. The branches and roots grew out in all directions. Some of the roots even grew into the bodies of the family, drawing on their fallen energy.

"At the height of maturity, the tree was struck with lightning. What was left was a stump and a tangled mess of branches. A gifted scribe took one of the pieces and made an ornament out of it. It was later discovered that the cluster of branches held great power, the power we talked about earlier."

"That's an interesting myth." Talia grunted.

After a half a mile, they came to a set of two log-cabin dwellings. Inbetween them was a stone well. Out of habit, Talia tried to send down a portal to check for water. But again, no mist came.

"I think these were the ceremonial buildings." Hudson pointed at the houses. "People would have to wash themselves with water from the well, and then go through some rituals in one or both of the houses."

"The houses look identical." Talia sat at the edge of the well and gathered her breath and her bearings. "Probably meant for the busier times so they could accommodate a lot of people."

Hudson eyed her with concern. "You feeling alright? We haven't gone very far yet."

"Yeah, it must be that signal," Talia clutched her stomach like she was going to be sick. "It's making me dizzy."

"Let me pull up some water for you." Hudson walked around the well and reached for the rope.

"Thanks," Talia said. "I would have packed my own, but I'm not..."

"Not used to packing anything?" Hudson gave a tug on the rope. "Why would you be when you could have access to anything with just a thought?"

"Exactly." Talia hugged her stomach and listened to the squeak of the pulley.

"So, can you soul jump?" Hudson asked as he continued to pull. "Or see other people's souls?"

Talia shook her head. "No, for some reason I can't. Maybe if I got a hold of the soul jumper's keystone, but for now, teleporting and the scribe's power are all that I have."

"Is that when your mists appeared though?" Hudson brought the bucket to the top and rested it on the lip of the well. "When you touched the keystone of the scribes?"

"Yeah," Talia said. "My dad said it was a gift my from mom, something to remember her by."

"Uh, Talia?" Hudson backed away from the well.

Talia jumped back as the most enormous spidery crab she had ever seen leapt out of the bucket and scuttled her way. Talia pointed her hand at the crab, but failed to teleport it.

The crab took a snap at her fingers and she yelped in alarm. She ran backwards, watching and avoiding its large claws and barely staying out of striking distance.

Hudson ran towards the crab and kicked it off into the bushes. He was laughing uncontrollably until he saw her face. His laughter faded, but he still had a smirk.

"Sorry, but you've got to admit that was funny." Hudson shrugged.

She gave a sneering fake smile and turned to enter the house on the left. The front of the room was mostly blank with a circle of chairs in the middle, surrounding a circular table. On the other side of the wall was a short hallway that lead to a set of stairs.

After a brief moment, Hudson came in, still laughing. "You don't get out much, do you? I mean, the way you were running from that crab!"

"It's not funny, Hudson." Talia huffed. "We have no access to medical supplies. Any injury out here could prove fatal, given enough time to fester."

"Yeah, but it was just a crab." Hudson finished his laugh and looked back out the window. "So, to the tree?"

"Just a minute." Talia held out her left hand tentatively.

"You can't teleport on this island!" Hudson reminded her.

She used her right hand to shush him and focused on her scribe's powers. With a thought, she turned on her new vision from Kiri, which let her see all recordings in her area. Her vision grew crowded with orbs of varying shades of green. Some were laid out like a radar in the upper corner of her vision, while the closer ones glowed in front of her.

"There are hidden recordings in here," Talia whispered.

"Probably to do with the ceremonies," Hudson said with mild annoyance.

"No." Talia took a step towards the circle of chairs. "These are hidden memories. Like someone didn't want them found. Looks like there are some in the basement."

"The basement?" Hudson raised a skeptical eyebrow. "I don't know if you can see, but those stairs only go up.

Plus I thought you were the one interested in getting in and out of this place."

"Well, getting out is now a problem." Talia said. "We have to find a way off of this island. And I'll bet Pavarti had a secret way of doing that."

"But what about the branch?" Hudson pleaded.

"Well, you check the normal recordings, see if we need to take anything with us to the tree, and I'll take a look at the secret recordings."

"Fine, but let's be quick about it." Hudson walked into the circle of chairs and picked up a book at the center table.

Talia turned from him and headed for the stairs. It didn't make sense to go up, but it was the only way forward. The wood creaked in complaint with every step. She reached the top and found herself in a small hallway with a single door at the end. She tried it, and it was locked.

She tried to teleport through it, but cursed at herself for forgetting again that she couldn't. To calm herself down, she turned back to the stairs and the hallway. The floor was bare, nothing loose. No levers to open a secret passageway.

She turned back to the door and noticed there wasn't a deadbolt on it. Only the handle was locked from rotating. She tried it again, and found it gave a little more. She grunted and put her muscle behind the turn.

This time the knob rotated a quarter turn. With a quick breath she turned again and got the door to wedge open. Dust flew out and choked her.

Once clear, she got a good look on the other side of the door. It was an empty closet. In frustration, she stepped in, knocked on the walls, and jumped on the floor. She listened for any signs that there might be a trap door or something, but there was nothing. Just an empty closet.

After a few minutes of searching, she reluctantly walked back down the stairs. She was halfway down when she saw Hudson was engrossed in a recording. Not knowing how long it would be, she sat down on a step and resigned herself to waiting.

Above the sound of her body slumping to the step, she heard a faint echo from below her. She raised a curious eyebrow and then slapped the step next to her. Again, there was a faint echo. She stomped her feet on the next step down, no echo.

With excitement, she turned around and got on her knees to see the underside of the step she was sitting on. Hidden under the lip was a gold strip of metal with seven tabs sticking out. She pressed all of them and pulled on the step.

Nothing happened. She picked half of the tabs and pressed. Still locked. She started pressing them one at a time, all of them failing to open the latch. Desperate, she went through each combination as systematically as she could. The first two. The first three. The first four. The fist one and then the next two, and so on.

Finally, she tried the two on the left and then every other tab to the right and it popped open. The latch sprung and half of the stair case opened up, revealing a hidden staircase that descended into darkness.

She took another look back at Hudson. He was still in the trance. She shrugged and walked down. Once she was under the surface level of the house, the walls were made of stone, like it was carved into hard earth.

At the bottom it was completely dark. The only thing she could see were the scribe's recordings placed in a pile in front of her and she blindly made her way to them.

A chair was in her path and she almost tripped over it. Before it was lost in the darkness, she grabbed it and wheeled it in front of her to prevent any more tripping.

Eventually, she reached the pile. She still couldn't see, but the memories were stacked on some sort of counter. There were seven of them. She picked one at random.

The memory was calm. Someone was walking up to the house she was already in. This time, the colors were a few shades brighter, and the windows a few shades cleaner.

Whoever made the recording walked into the house and noticed with shock the stairs open with a large tunnel leading down. The scribe looked around the room from left to right, and cautiously made their way to the opening.

When the scribe looked down there were faint lights, mostly in blue hues, reminding Talia of times she went into Miranda's lab late at night. Probably computers.

The scribe took a few steps into the basement and cleared his throat. It was a deep rumble, so at this point Talia assumed it was a man. He reached into his pocket and pulled out a wad of yarn. The object Talia was holding in her hand as she relived this recording.

"Hello?" The man called into the darkness. "Anyone there?"

Someone stuck his head out from the corner. "Aaron, you're early!"

"Thought I would help with the set up, Doctor Pavarti." Aaron took a few more steps down the stairs.

Pavarti sighed. "I told you there would be no need for that. Well, come in, have a seat."

Aaron reached the bottom of the stairs and entered the room. It was a musty room, the floor was made of steel, and the walls were covered with computers. Each monitor showing video recordings of people in the room above, going through the motions of chanting. Right in the middle of the basement, there was a light fixed to the ceiling, but no switch that Talia could see.

"This chair here will do." Pavarti gestured to one in the middle.

There were five chairs in the room. All of them looked normal except the one Pavarti pointed to. It had straps on the arms and some sort of head apparatus hanging to the side.

Without a second thought, Aaron sat down in the chair. He shifted until he was comfortable and then looked back at the monitors.

"So, what is this place?"

Pavarti sat in the chair next to him. "This is where I monitor the progress of our visitors."

"Monitor?" Aaron sat up. "Why?"

Pavarti made a calming motion and pressed Aaron gently back into the chair. Then he started strapping him to the chair. "You know, you're lucky I haven't placed the branch back into the tree just yet."

"The Ancestral Branch had been taken from the tree?" Aaron sat up and jerked against his restraints.

"Relax. It's in this room right now." Pavarti calmly stood up and walked to a locked panel on the side of the wall. He unlocked the panel and it opened, revealing a gun and the Branch. "Because if it wasn't here, then I would have to use the gun. But, with the Branch, I can simply wipe your memory."

Aaron spun the chair around with his feet to face Pavarti. Talia noticed just on the wall of the entrance there was a lightswitch. Pavarti turned and pointed the branch at Aaron. A large, green orb shot from it like a cannonball and slammed into Aaron with a blinding force. When the lights faded, Talia was back out of the memory trance and in the darkness.

Talia grabbed a hold of the chair and rolled it back towards the entrance. There was some light from above, but not much. She fumbled her way to where she saw the light switch in the memory and flipped it on. The halogen light flickered to life, illuminating the room before her.

It was the same room as the memory, only now the computers were shut off. Talia looked around for some sort of button to turn them all on.

"Talia?" Hudson called from above. "Are you down there?"

"Yeah," She shouted back. "Come on down, give me a hand with this."

Hudson plopped down the stairs and stopped in the entrance way. "A monitoring system."

"Yeah, I guessed that." Talia turned back to the system. "I wish I knew how to turn them on. I've only recently had an exposure to computers through my sister."

"I've learned a thing or two about them." Hudson walked to the side panel of one of the stations and flipped a switch. All of the monitors turned on simultaneously. "Let's see what we have here."

Hudson pulled up a chair and sat in front of a keyboard.

"Where'd you learn to use computers?" Talia asked.

"I've spent some time in Cantera Bay and other cities doing research with my father." Hudson typed words into the computer and the screens jumped from image to image. Talia was having a hard time keeping up, not sure what he was doing.

At last, he clicked on a green triangle and a video started playing.

In the video, seventeen people were sitting in the chairs upstairs, talking and conversing. An alarming number of them looked younger than Talia. From the upstairs hallway, Pavarti strolled into the room carrying the Ancestral Branch. The group of people gasped, and then Pavarti turned and pointed the Branch at each person in the group.

Talia watched as one by one, all of the seated people went quiet and still. Their animated faces grew blank. Talia didn't see the orbs shoot out this time, and Talia guessed the camera wasn't picking up everything.

"Talent uploading test batch forty-three." Pavarti said to the room. "The Branch has neutralized seventeen subjects, and are waiting subliminal instructions, and extra enhancements."

He walked to the closest subject, a little girl. He handed her a bottle of purple liquid. "Drink this."

Pavarti handed the drink to everybody in the room and then a few people came in through the doors. They each carried a briefcase and a surgical mask on. They set down their cases, opened them, and pulled out syringes.

"I want blood samples before and after the injections," Pavarti said, walking calmly with his hands behind his back. "Then, I want Kiandoli to work on the left half of the room."

The rest of the video showed them working on the scribes. Hudson fast forwarded it a little towards the end. The assistants moved from scribe to scribe, drawing blood and injecting other substances into the bodies.

After that was done, the assistants placed large goggle-like things over the eyes of half the scribes, and Kiandoli came in and placed her hands on the other half.

Finally, at the end of the video, the scribes started waking up, and Pavarti lead them out the door.

"What do you think that was about?" Hudson asked as the screen went black.

"Something about talent uploading?" Talia scratched her head. "Pavarti wasn't saying much about what they were doing."

"I think he was making snatchers." Hudson clicked excitedly around the file that played the video. "Talking about talent uploading, the notes in this file seem to be experiments to get people to upload talents into their bodies like a computer program."

"Huh." Talia looked around the room. "Anything in that computer about where he keeps the soul jumper interference switch?"

"I'll look."

Hudson clicked around on images on the screen for a while longer and moved on. Then he came across something that said *Cherubim's Schematic*. He clicked on it and a three dimensional image of the island appeared.

"There's two other hidden labs on this island." Hudson pointed at the screen, but Talia couldn't make out how he knew that. "Both on the other side of the island, behind the cliff. One there, just under the water. It has a tunnel that leads up to the second one in the middle of the mountain."

"I'll bet the Branch is in one of these three hideouts, as opposed to the tree." Talia turned to the open and empty panel where she had seen Pavarti take the branch in the memory trance.

"We should check the tree, just in case."

"Right. Let's get going."

*****

The trail to the memorial tree was, at one point, a smooth path of cobblestone and sand surrounded by sturdy hand rails.

In the few years of neglect, nature had seen to making it a little less smooth. Weeds with prickly extensions grew out of the cracks of sand. Vines with itchy oils wove in and around the handrails.

Talia clutched her stomach as they grew closer to the center of the island. Whatever signal was blocking her mists was growing stronger. It felt like the earth was vibrating.

Talia swatted giant flies out of her face as she walked on. Her frustration built and she longed to teleport, to make these inconveniences disappear, but more than the ease of travel, she thought of her sister. With her powers, she could spy on anyone she wanted, just to see if they were alright. Now she couldn't.

"There it is," Hudson exclaimed.

As they passed a thick patch of weeds, they came to the tree. Half of it was black and charred. The other was barren and gray.

The once well-tended field was now home to shoulder height grass. The brick circle surrounding the tree was no longer visible.

"Where would it be?" Talia asked.

"Probably in the trunk of the tree." Hudson waded into the grass with his hands over his head.

Talia took a tentative step to the grass, and then entered the fray.

Sticky grass clung to the skin of her arms and face. The tree itself was not impressive. It was mostly trunk, with one half snapped branch dangling from the side.

Talia looked around the tree for any loose bark or knotted holes to hide anything in. But what was left of the tree was still solid.

"There's nothing here." Talia turned around just as a hand in a black glove closed around her face.

A second hand grabbed her by the arm and something sharp poked her. Already sick from the island, she now was beyond action. Her eyes grew heavy, and her body refused to fight. Blearily, the world went dark.

*****

A wave of water splashed onto Talia's face, waking her up. A man dressed in black tactical gear was wading out in the ocean just offshore, carrying her on his shoulder. Talia fought the urge to panic, but it was too strong. She let out a yelp, and the man gave her a stern squeeze. Then he jumped and they sank underwater.

Talia kicked and thrashed, trying desperately to escape. Her lungs, not prepared with even a small intake of breath, screamed the moment they were underwater.

After a few seconds, her ears popped. Talia tried not to fathom how deep this man was taking her, how far she would have to swim up even if she managed to free herself. The water grew darker. It was as if a lunar eclipse chose that moment to block out the sun.

The tangy salt prevented her from opening her eyes, but she could feel them slow down somewhat. After a second, they landed on something and they stopped altogether. Her captor pushed off of whatever he was standing on and they were rising again.

A small tinge of relief ran over her, but she was still out of air, and didn't know how much longer she could hold her breath.

Then, suddenly the glow of artificial lights beamed on her closed eyelids. A few seconds later, they splashed out of the water and she was tossed onto a wet tile floor.

"She's awake, that one!" The man coughed into the air.

"No matter," another man shouted. "Where's the other one?"

"Broils is on his way down now with him."

Talia managed to open her eyes and calm her breathing. She was in a small spherical room that looked like an indoor pool. Everything was lit with halogen lights, and tiled floor circled around a small watery opening into the ocean.

"Come with me, princess." The new man grabbed her by the arm and dragged her up the long hallway behind him. She took one last look behind her, watching her captor catch his breath for a moment in the water.

Just behind him the wall turned into a dark haze, like a wave of heat was centered on it. Someone stepped out of the portal and started talking to the man who dragged her under the water.

Talia's mind raced at that. *That's how the coalition is moving around so fast. They found portals that don't affect the mind. That must be how Doctor Pavarti moved around as well.* The realization made her dizzy. She had to warn her sister.

They continued to walk up the hallway. The tile gave way to doormat style rug, which gave way to an elegant carpet. The walls went from a bright tan to a dark maroon.

Then they entered what Talia guessed was Pavarti's main lab on Cherubim's' Perch. It wasn't very big. Most of it was filled with monitors, like the room in the ceremony house by the beach.

In this middle of this room, however, was an operating chair, complete with arm straps and spot lights right above.

"Tie one of her arms and one of her legs to the side of the chair. The boy can go on the other side," came a calm voice from behind a chair.

Talia was strapped to the left side of the chair by her right arm and right leg, and then left alone in a slightly dangling position. She swung her free arm to reach and undo the strap, but it wasn't going anywhere.

She looked around the room for anything to use. Behind the chair was a blank wall with nothing but a few discarded books laying on the floor. To her left on the wall was a locked box, just like the one Pavarti pulled the branch from in the memory trance she saw this morning.

Hudson was brought in, still unconscious. They strapped him to a chair while the man behind the chair continued to navigate the computer. He knew what he was doing, just like Hudson. The screen moved too fast for Talia to keep up, but she saw brief glimpses of schematics and blueprints. One of them was for the Ancestral Branch.

After what felt like an hour, the man behind the computer chair swung around and looked at the two of them.

He stood up from the chair with a condescending smile. "Hello there. I'm Donovan. You must be my little teleporter."

Talia froze and the pit of her stomach turned. With great effort, she focused her will and began recording the environment around her. None of the Coalition guards around her would notice the signs. Her goose bumps, already elevated because she was still wet and cold, swayed like trees in the wind. And inside her, a green orb was taking in energy and storing it as a perfect memory.

"How do you know..." she stammered.

"I have satellites in the sky watching everything. I've even watched your battle on the beach with the tetrapaths a few times, just to begin to comprehend how powerful you are." Donovan walked right next to her and knelt down so he was level with her. "I am very impressed."

"How did you know I would be here?" Talia asked.

"I didn't." He shrugged his shoulders nonchalantly. "We were here first, looking at the secrets of the island. One of my men heard you screaming down near the beach on the west side. When we found out it was you, well, I just had to say hello."

"And what if I teleport you off of a cliff right now?" Talia reached and itched her tied arm. It was already starting to feel numb.

"You would have done that already." Donovan stood up. "No, I suspect that your teleports are stopped the way my soul jumping is stopped on this island."

To her right, Hudson was slowly waking up. Donovan looked at him and walked back to the computer.

"Right now, I'm on a deadline." Donovan typed some more commands into the computer and pulled up the schematic of the branch. "So, tell me where this object is."

"What is that?"

"You know what that is."

"You can find plenty of those around here." Talia rolled her eyes.

Donovan gave a fake smile, as if to show his patience was at its limit, but he did not say anything.

"I honestly don't know where it is." Talia tried pushing up on her free foot, but that only swung her into a different awkward position.

"That's a shame." Donovan turned and sat back down in his chair.

With her free hand, she reached down and pulled off her shoe, and then her sock. She pressed the green orb of her recording into the sock and held it above her head. Donovan turned around with some sort of syringe in his hand and then stopped suddenly in confusion of her pose.

The three closest soldiers took a few cautious steps toward her and she started swinging the sock. Flecks of water flew everywhere. Some hit the soldiers on their armor or at least their clothing, but nothing happened.

The soldiers all walked in to subdue her, and then things grew interesting. Close to the edge of her swinging radius, a fine mist of water was gushing out. Talia banked on them rushing in, and inhaling that mist.

Before they could touch her, they fell to the floor in a memory trance. Donovan smiled slightly and walked towards her. She threw the sock at his face. He caught it with his bare hand and kept moving toward her like nothing happened.

"What?" Talia breathed frantically, trying to escape the chair now.

Donovan grabbed her free arm and placed the needle close to the skin. "Last chance."

"Alright!" Talia screamed. "I have an idea where it would be. I think it's in that locked cabinet over there!"

Donovan smiled, and put the syringe back into a pocket on his suit, and walked to the red cabinet bolted to the wall.

"Nice try," Donovan sneered. "But my men and I have already tried opening this thing for hours. I don't think there's anything in there."

"Don't you always put the important stuff in a hard to get to location?" Talia asked. "I saw a video of Pavarti opening another one of these this morning. If you untie me, I think I can do it."

Donovan turned around and considered her. "If you can't?"

"That's up to you." Talia turned to Hudson, and saw that he was under her memory trance as well. "You can have it whereever it is, just let us go."

Donovan walked over and calmly unstrapped her arm and leg. She fell to the floor with a thud, blood returning to her foot and lower leg. The soldiers began stirring awake from the memory trance. As she sat there, she put on her sock and her shoe.

"Now, the puzzle box?" Donovan said impatiently.

Talia half crawled into a better position. As she crouched, she reached into a weapon pocket on the soldier nearest her and pulled out a small stick with a picture of a bright light on it.

Talia stood up and half limped to the box on the wall. It was red like the other one. Hinge on the right side, no handle, no lock. She brought to memory the motion Pavarti used on the other box and stood to press on it. She pressed the left side in, up slightly, and then twisted the right side up. She felt it snap like the other one, and it popped open.

Inside was the ancestral branch. It was a small knot of dark wood with tangled little branches extending out of it.

Donovan walked towards her, and she activated the weapon from the soldier. It exploded in a blinding flash of light, and Talia grabbed the branch while the others were shielding their eyes.

Donovan was unfazed by the flash and continued to advance on her. She ran around the room and Donovan slowly moved to keep her pinned in.

Not sure how the branch worked, she fed it the memory from her sock. The green orb traveled back up her foot and into the knotted wood.

Donovan jumped at her and she fired. The branch blasted an orb right though his body and he fell to the ground.

The soldiers stood up and Talia fired again. This time, half a dozen orbs shot out of each of the little branch tips.

"Wow," Hudson said. "That was amazing!"

Talia ran over to him and unstrapped his restraints. "Yeah. Let's get out of here."

"How are we going to escape?" Hudson asked as his leg was free, and they worked on his arm.

"There's a portal at the end of that hallway." Talia said, pulling at the straps with all of her strength. Her fingers were still damp and slippery.

"I didn't bring my life's memories." Hudson lent his free hand, and together, they tugged the strap open.

"You won't need it with this one," Talia reached back down and picked the branch back off of the floor.

Donovan stirred behind her.

"Come on, let's go!" She shouted and they both hobbled down the hallway.

Talia's leg was more or less working again and she pulled on Hudson's arm, willing him to go faster. Their feet echoed from pounding the tile, and then the concrete. Two soldiers were at the pool, and they turned their guns at them.

Talia was a little faster. She took aim with the branch and fired. This time two green orbs launched out of two of the branches at once and connected with the soldiers. They slumped to the ground and left the portal wide open.

"Are you sure about this?" Hudson yelled.

Talia focused on not slipping on stray puddles of water. "Yes!"

They ran around the pool and jumped into the portal. On the other side, Talia let out a small cheer when she found out she was right.

They were inside a tall building with rows and rows of operating chairs, navigational charts, and scientific equipment.

"We made it!" Hudson shouted beside her.

Nearly fifty soldiers and coalition scientists turned to look at them with surprise.

"Sort of," Hudson amended his previous statement. "Crap."

Talia let out a small smile as she felt the nausea from Cherubim's Perch was gone. Which meant they weren't on that island anymore.

With one shot, seven green orbs blasted from the branch and they all found targets. With her free hand she conjured up a mist on the left side of the room and engulfed a group of soldiers.

On the right side of the room, some of the soldiers started to raise their guns. Talia blasted seven more shots and neutralized the fastest of them. Her other mist appeared above the rest of the soldiers, and all of the people teleported from the first mist fell on top of them.

"Come on." Talia grabbed Hudson by the arm and pulled him along with her.

"Wow," was all Hudson could say, as they looked for a way out of the building.

Talia sent one of her mists through a few walls, and conjured another mist in front of them so she could see where they were going. She still had no idea where they were, and teleporting without a frame of reference was a bit unusual for her.

The mist found a way out of the building for them, and then elevated to the sky for a better look. As the sound of running soldiers came from behind them, her mist in the sky saw where she was.

The Control Center Island. She sighed in relief and teleported to her bedroom back in Naprea.

Hudson was still running and tripped on Talia's bed. "Ow! Bit of a warning would be nice next time."

"Deal with it." Talia smiled and held out her hand to help Hudson up. "I had a lot of enemies to juggle back there."

"Literally." Hudson said as she pulled him up.

The two of them stood there, close together for a moment.

"Yeah." Talia agreed. Her heart was pounding faster now than it was during the chase. She held the branch in her hand. It felt a lot sturdier than it looked. "Go get some rest. Get another grave opener. We'll try for the other two tomorrow."

Hudson stood still, and it looked like he was going to suggest something else.

Talia teleported him back to his house by the library. Then she slumped down on her bed, exhausted from the day.

CHAPTER 15: REINCARNATION

The crowd around the breakfast street vendors was busy and Scott kept his head down. He used a kid to order breakfast, and walked from street corner to street corner, looking for signs of other snatchers.

Scott walked through some of the tighter parts of the crowd, trying his best not to bump into anybody. After several blocks, his left leg began to grow warm, warning him of nearby tetrapath. In panic, he stood up taller, looking for the source.

Several turns into his scan, a small hand grabbed his arm. Scott turned around, ready to fight, but saw Olivia standing there, holding two cups of coffee.

"I saw you only had food." Olivia smiled. "But you look like you could use a wakeup call."

Scott looked at the extra cup of coffee and then back at her. "Olivia, you're up and about. When did that happen?"

"A few days ago," she said.

Scott's leg continued to itch. His eyes darted quickly across the crowd. "Sorry I didn't come to see you. I've been busy."

"No need for that. I wanted to catch up with you and thank you." Olivia handed him the extra cup. "The doctors tell me you saved my life."

Scott accepted the cup and his leg grew even warmer. "This is poisoned. With the tetrapath infection."

"Is it?" She smiled. "I was wondering why it was so black."

Scott looked around the street and contemplated his options.

"Let me do the math for you." Olivia said. "There is nowhere in Naprea you can dump that without worry that someone will eventually be infected. And it will eventually start eating through the cup. The only option right now is to drink it."

"I could feed it to you right now."

"And give away your position?"

"You found me anyway. I'd take my chances."

"You wouldn't kill an innocent person would you?" Olivia looked around the crowd with fake concern. "Risk all of these people getting the infection?"

"Why are you doing this?" Scott asked.

"Because I got a peek at some of the turmoil you go through when snatching, And I don't want you snatching right now."

Scott looked down at the cup, its contents silky smooth in betrayal of the danger lurking inside. With a quick breath he chugged the whole cup, and then quickly followed it with seven pills, emptying another bottle.

"Still taking the placebos, I see." Olivia gestured for them to keep walking in the crowd.

Scott coughed violently into his shirt sleeve and drew back bits of blood. "They'll have to manage until I can steal the real thing."

"Don't worry. Donovan is prepping extra measures to prevent that from happening."

"Is he your master now?"

"Don't be ridiculous." Olivia snorted. "He's my husband."

"Come again?" Scott took several deep breaths to try and stay coherent.

She looked at him with a raised eyebrow. "Oh yes. Proper introductions. My name is Inara, and I've taken over Olivia's body."

"And Donovan is your husband?"

"You *are* listening." Inara stopped at a street corner to admire a collection of flowers for sale. After a moment she turned back around and looked at him like he was a giant spider. "But you don't look so good."

"Why are you telling me this?" Scott shook his head and finally felt his pills taking the edge off the tetrapath infection.

"Because I'm giving Dixon the biggest head start he can get." Inara turned back to the flowers. "He's already killed two of them."

And then his head cleared up. Dixon was hunting the white ghosts in the crowd. His fellow snatchers would stick out of any crowd, no matter how good the disguise. Dixon would spot them easily. And now, with an amped up amount of the tetrapath infection running through his system, Scott couldn't find Dixon and take his powers without risk of finally going over the edge. He would have to wait until the new batch of infection within him passed.

Scott stood still, paralyzed with the need to make a decision. Here Inara was freely giving answers, but only in an effort to stall him. He needed to know what had happened to Dixon, but he needed to keep the other snatchers safe.

He shook his head in frustration and ran down the street, back towards the hospital. It took him several minutes before he made it to the right side of the road to go with the traffic of bodies trying to make it to one spot or the other.

The hospital was the last place he wanted to go, but Olivia's mention of kills brought up the prospect of a filled morgue. There might still be something he could gleam from the bodies of snatchers.

The center of town was less packed than normal, and Scott found an alleyway leading to the back door of the hospital, where the morgue entrance was.

Nearly ten random-looking people were standing in front of the entrance door. Scott could clearly see two guarding the door, but there could have been more amongst the small and dispersed crowd of people in the alleyway.

Frustration started to boil in his chest. He could feel the tetrapath waging war against the lame excuse for a cure he had ingested.

But there was nothing he could do to get in, apart from turning into a monster and killing everyone. He would have to find a new angle.

Scott turned around and ran right into another woman. The seconds worth of contact brought to vision this woman's talents, and he knew straight away who this was. The first woman he soul jumped in the hospital.

"Sorry. I told her we shouldn't be sneaking," the woman said in an annoyed whisper. "Now this is all wrong."

Scott held her at arm's length, unsure of what to do. She was shaking her head, which was level with his. From here, he got his first good look at her. She was maybe in her fifties. Graying blond hair, wrinkles around the eyes and the mouth. Her eyes a faded blue.

She held out her hand. "We're here to help."

Scott took the hand. "Help with what?"

"No." Her eyebrows furrowed in agitation. "We're not here to help. Don't listen to him."

"Sorry, what's going on?" Scott was at a loss for anything else to say.

"Hold on. We're just deciding what we're here for."

Scott looked around the alleyway. "There's just one of you."

"On the outside, maybe," She said."But there's a lot of us packed in here."

"A lot of you?" Scott raised an eyebrow.

"Seventeen." The woman pointed to her chest. "Kiandoli and Doctor Pavarti crammed seventeen life memories into this body."

"I've seen multiple soul jumps into one body before," Scott said tentatively. "Wouldn't having that many people in you kill you?"

The woman smiled and looked around the corner. "Well, it wasn't from a lack of trying on Kiandoli's part. Anyway. We are here to help. Saving others means saving our lives. You have our services."

"Your...services?" Scott asked.

"Yes." The woman nodded to the morgue entrance. "We voted. It was nine to six. Two of us didn't vote, but they never vote, so we don't bother asking anymore."

"What services?" Scott asked.

"We can get you into the morgue and out without detection." Her face frowned. "No, wrong word there. In and out without capture."

"How?"

"We have many talents locked up in here." The woman said. "Just follow us, and everything will work out."

She nodded, darted her eyes between Scott and the door behind them, and then walked calmly to the morgue. Scott scratched his head and walked around the corner after her.

Before they were in view, the guards around the door held their hands up to their eyes. One of them even dropped his gun and covered his whole face.

"Man, that's bright!" the other shouted.

As they walked, the sound of footsteps rounded the corner behind them. But it wasn't just a pair of footsteps. It was thousands. They echoed in Scott's head like rain drops. The sound of gunfire erupted from somewhere, but it was like thousands of guns were firing from every direction. The pedestrians around them were screaming and holding their heads, and the screams were as if millions of people were burning alive.

And then it stopped. Scott stood up tentatively and looked around.

"Sorry," the woman said. "The six who lost the vote are a bit upset about going back to the hospital. They chose to use our powers against you to stop this from happening. Be ready. I can't promise it won't happen again."

Scott contemplated running away, but the woman was already opening the door and he needed to at least get her to safety. The guards at the door were still holding their heads and screaming as Scott followed the woman into the morgue.

Inside, everybody was clutching their eyes or their ears, or some body part and wincing in pain.

"We can amplify people's sensitivity to anything." The woman said, this time with a calm, maternal tone. "That is what you experienced in the street back there."

Scott wasted no time trying to figure out what that meant. He walked through the lobby and into the storage facility.

The room was not overly big, but it was cold. Metall everywhere. Two bodies were on tables in the middle, and two morticians were clutching their heads and rolling on the ground.

Scott knew the fresh corpses were two of the snatchers. He ran up to see if there was anything that he could learn about them.

His hand hesitated above the closest corpse. The tetrapath was already raging inside of him. What would happen if he snatched from a dead snatcher?

"I can't." Scott said.

"See? Worthless!" The woman shouted and threw her hands up into the air. "Why are we risking our lives again?"

Scott grabbed her by the arm and ran back out of the morgue. He was about to lead them back into town, but the woman started to run for the space ship.

"Hey!" Scott shouted after her. "Where are you going?"

The woman turned around. "If you're going to help us all, you need a base of operations. I know of one that has not been in use for some time."

She slapped the top of her hand. "He's not going to help us. Did you see how scared he was of a little snatching? He'll be fine. He just needs training is all."

She slapped her other hand and turned around and walked quickly to the space ship in the center of town.

"I don't like her," Inara shouted behind him. "She creeps me out."

"Have you been following me?"

"Constantly." She looked over him towards the woman. "You better hurry. You're about to lose her."

Scott turned around, trying to catch up to her, to call for her attention.

"So," Scott said as he finally caught up. "What do I call you?"

"We have many names in here." The woman put her finger to her lips in concentration. "We've been trying to find a fair compromise, but to be honest, there's been no need for a group name in a long time."

"There is now." Scott smiled a little as they made their way to the center of the city. "But first, we need to lose a tail."

"I suppose you may call me Clarity." She turned to them. "And I don't have a tail."

"No, I mean, somebody is following us."

"Who?"

"That blond woman over there." Scott pointed to Inara.

A second later, Inara dropped to her knees and screamed in pain.

"Okay. That's done." Clarity nodded firmly. "On we go."

"Uh, where are we going?"

"The submerged part of the ship."

"Submerged?" Scott asked. "It's not underwater."

"Oh yes. Sorry. Buried. The buried part." Clarity waved her hand dismissively. "It's underground."

*****

They reached the back side of the ship, opposite the main entrance where Scott and Miranda would normally enter. On this side, there were no guards, no hint that anybody was watching or looking for them.

Clarity placed her hands against the side of the ship, and her face was twisted in concentration.

"It's on the other side of the ship!" she snarled. Every sentence was spoken with a different cadence and rhythm. Like a young woman rehearsing for multiple parts in a play. "No, I'm positive it is close to here. I alone have navigated these sections. Your memory is wrong! You may have been the one here, but we can all see your memories too. Your own memory betrays you."

"Um," Scott started.

"Shh!" Clarity closed her eyes and started feeling out the contours of the ship with her hands. "They don't know what they're talking about. It's right here."

Her fingers grabbed onto a section of metal and pulled. A panel opened and fell to the ground. Inside the exposed square of the ship, there was a circle with a handle laid flush into a groove. She flipped the handle out, twisted it clockwise ninety degrees, and pulled.

A tube pulled out of the ship. Clarity kept pulling until she revealed a small nook, barely big enough to hold a person.

"What is that?" Scott asked.

"A remote access tube." Clarity waived her hands along the tube like it was appliance she was selling. "They used it when this ship was in space. If a technician needed to repair something on the surface, he or she would come out of this and be magnetically attached to the side of the ship. Now, in with you."

Scott pulled himself up and laid in the small groove in the center of the tube. Clarity got to the end of it and gave a bit of a grunt as she pushed it into the space ship.

Scott tensed up as he was squeezed through the opening. His shoulders and arms brushed gently against the walls, until he came out the other side. The tube stopped, and then rotated. Scott flung his arms as he was dumped out of the tube and onto the floor.

He grunted and pushed himself up as the tube rotated back and was pulled out of the ship. He got a look around the room. Nothing major. Just a square room with a thick door on one end. The door was currently open, and the hallway beyond was dark.

After a moment, there was a faint knocking from the outside of the ship. Scott looked back town the hallow tube, and realized there was no one to push clarity in. He looked around the room, sure there would be a control panel or something to activate the return of the tube.

But there was nothing. Nothing but a blank room. Clarity sped up her knocking. On the far wall, there was a small, thin panel. Scott walked over and pushed on it. It opened, revealing a long, wooden stick with a hook on the top end.

He pulled it from the panel and went back to the tube. Crouched down so he could see all the way to the end, he could just make out a latch. He extended the stick, hooked the latch, and then pulled the tube into the ship.

Clarity rolled herself out of the tube, and she dusted herself off. "Ok, so we're inside. Now what?"

"I thought you knew?" Scott asked.

"Now, we descend." Clarity clapped her hand on his shoulder and walked into the hallway.

Scott followed her at a small distance, half groping where he was going in the dark.

"Here it is." Clarity stopped in front of him. "The elevator. And it looks like it still has power! Good, that means we don't have to climb down."

They stepped inside and waited. Clarity knelt down at the floor and pressed a few buttons on a panel, slightly unsure of herself. After a few attempts, the elevator doors shut, and they were descending.

"Technically, this was a lateral transport when the ship was in space." Clarity said. Then she corrected herself. "You don't know that. Yes I do. Look at how low to the ground the controls are. When she was in space, the artificial gravity held them sideways. No, the artificial gravity adjusted to whatever way the ship needed it to. That's why the rooms are still right side up even when the ship is sticking straight up and down in the mountain. This elevator goes up and down. Yeah, well, we're still heading to the front of the ship."

The elevator came to a stop and the doors opened. Outside was complete darkness. Scott could smell tiny bits of dust, stirred for the first time in a long time.

Clarity stepped out and lights turned on automatically. The room was a huge corridor. Heavy looking doors lined the walls on the ground floor. A set of stairs led to a catwalk where more heavy doors lined the walls.

"What is this place?" Scott asked.

"This is our Genesis," Clarity gestured around, "Where Doctor Pavarti got the bodies he needed to populate Cova."

"Populate?" Scott asked, trying to keep his mouth closed from the dust.

"This planet was originally uninhabited by humans," Clarity said. "In Earth's far future, Doctor Pavarti steals this ship and crashes it here. Then he begins his experiments."

"So, these doors hold..." Scott started.

"Cryogenically frozen humans," Clarity confirmed.

"Wait." Scott stepped in front of Clarity. "Earth's far future?"

"Yes." Clarity stepped around him and kept walking. "Don't ask us how it works. But Pavarti called this planet Cova for a reason. Short for *covalent bond*. He believed Cova and Earth had some connection that tie our two galaxies and solar systems together. None of us were ever able to find out what that was. But, with Pavarti dead at the moment, I suppose we can start our work again."

"Our work?" Scott asked.

"Each of the memories in this body have one thing in common." Clarity pointed to herself. "We all knew too much. We were all close to exposing Pavarti for who he really was."

"How?" Scott asked.

Clarity pointed around the room. "After Pavarti learned to control memories, he killed off everyone who knew what this ship was originally for. Then he woke people up from the cryo-sleep with planted memories. Forged his own history of the planet. After the planet was populated enough to build his many empires, he kept the rest of the bodies in here, and used them for himself."

"Himself?" Scott asked.

"Yes." Clarity stopped at a control panel and started pressing buttons. "For a long time, the most confusing aspect of Pavarti's reign was his longevity. We have no way of knowing, but our best guess puts the date this ship crashed here close to two thousand years ago. And the evidence that he's been manipulating everything is at least that old as well. But, now that we're all together in this body, we have the complete picture. On the eve of his death, he comes here, to this room. He has one of the Scribes take his entire life memory and plant it into the next body he awakes from Cryo-sleep."

"So, because he died away from this room, he's done now?" Scott asked.

"So far." Clarity shrugged. "People in the city keep talking about bringing him back, like they're aware he's been reincarnated, but no one knows how he did it. We think he is gone for good."

"So, what are you doing then?"

"First, we need the other snatchers." Clarity walked around an old computer monitor station and fiddled with the keyboard and mouse. "I will train you to find them, and then we will pool all of our knowledge to unearth all of Pavarti's secrets and spread the truth to Naprea."

Scott took one more look around the room. "And you'll be fine while I'm gone?"

"Better. We will be productive." Clarity smiled. And then she stared into his eyes with calculated evaluation. "But before you go, we need to work on your snatching skills and etiquette."

Scott felt his insides tense up. "I don't have time for lessons, Clarity."

"You have never received lessons from a snatcher. You'll need all of our lessons if you want to catch any of the others. Also, it looks like you need a while to calm down from the tetrapath infection."

"How did you..." Scott started, his mouth open slightly.

"Like we said." She pointed to her head. "Many talents."

CHAPTER 16: UNLIMITED MEMORY

Miranda placed her left hand on another pile of archive memories in the shelves of the Archive Hall. She was about a hundred yards deep into the hallway, from the entrance to the temple. Thousands of memories, mostly in small stones, were collected on the shelves that lined the wall.

Each stone she touched lit up with their green glowing orbs and shot up her hand and into her archive stone. She lifted her hand and repeated the process. More stones shot more orbs into her bracelet.

It was an almost giddy feeling. She had thought her archive stone would be nearly limitless in its capacity to store recorded memories, but she never thought she would give it this kind of test.

Each of the stones on shelves held memories that lasted hours. Some even longer than a day. She had already transferred several thousand memories and there was no sign that her archive stone even had a limit.

[The portal will soon be opening.]

Miranda pulled her hand back from another set of stones and walked back to the entrance.

"How do I look?" Miranda asked her suit.

[Replication is complete. You will resemble Councilor Blake under the strictest scrutiny.]

"Perfect."

She stepped up to the arch made of stones that looked like petrified water. After a moment, they emitted a glow and the inside of the arch grew hazy, like it was hot.

She stepped through and back into the lab.

"Councilor Blake, where is your escort?" the security tech asked.

Miranda turned to her right to face him. "She is loading more of the stones. Said she wanted to finish a few more of them. I have her radio, she'll buzz me when she needs to return. You can turn off the portal."

The security tech nodded and Miranda turned to the contraption to her left.

"I'll just be a moment; I must have a better look at this interface," she was saying, but the security tech wasn't paying attention. He was already helping the next group get to their destination.

She took in a slow breath and the hairs on her arms swayed like trees in the wind. In the center of her body, a small green orb pulsated in rhythm with her heart.

Her senses were heightened and she began her perfect recording of the environment.

The portals were monitored and controlled by two large replicas of Cova, Earth, and the surrounding solar systems. The replicas were stationed inside aquariums.

Cova and Earth were covered in small light bulbs. Some were red, and others were blue. The security tech turned on the portal again, and a blue light lit up right where they would be on the map. A second light lit up somewhere near the Coalition headquarters in Cantera Bay.

People walked through the hazy portal and then both lights turned off. Blue lights indicated the new portals, red lights indicated the old portals.

Miranda let out a small breath and the green orb traveled to the archive stone on her wrist. Her next move was to look for a computer. She needed all the files the Coalition had on these portals.

"There you are!" Lester said from behind her. "I've been looking all over for you! We just got a shipment of tetrapath sent in and we are ready to start the experiments."

"Experiments?" Miranda turned to face Lester, whom she had never met, but Councilor Blake was quite fond of him. Green clouds danced around her bracelet as she accessed Councilor Blake's memories, only slightly slower than she would have recalled her own memories.

"Yes. To see how the tetrapath go through any portal without getting memory wiped."

"Right!" Miranda said as the memory brought her new knowledge. "The Earthbound portal experiments."

The weight of what she just said quickly registered in her mind. They had working portals that lead to earth.

"Yes." Lester put a hand on her shoulder. "Look, I know we've all been losing sleep over this, but we have a chance to make history here! Reaching out to an alien world!"

"By sending tetrapath to infect them?"

"We're starting with the cured ones first." Lester said, defensively. "But we have to see if the portals are safe to cross. So, unless you want to volunteer yourself, we need to send them over. And if they have problems, we do have orders to send an infected tetrapath over."

A vile sickness rose in her stomach.

"Marc has the portals lined up," Lester said. "Better get a move on. We have a quota to fill."

She walked around a large work station table and through a few operating chairs towards the back of the room. Here, the recently cured tetrapath were strapped to gurneys on wheels. Most of them were sedated, but a few close to the walls were awake and moaning.

"Help," one said softly. "Help. Where am I?"

"How cured are these tetrapath?" Miranda asked.

Lester raised his eyebrow again. "What's gotten into you? They're cured. But physically unstable. Just like all the others. Now, can we please begin the procedure?"

"Alright." Marc clapped his hands. "First portal test. Subject is a female. Probably in her early twenties. We will be sending her fully conscious, into a remote corner of Africa. Judging by the map, this location is hundreds of years into Earth's past."

As soon as Marc was done talking, Lester grabbed a corner of a gurney and looked at Miranda expectantly. She grabbed the other end and waited. The portal turned on, and this one was closer to what she was used to. Dark red, with clouds of purple. They pushed the woman through the portal. Marc pulled up a video feed of the other side, and they watched the subject.

The cured tetrapath rattled against her restraints for a few moments, and then went still.

"Pull her back in," Lester said as he grabbed the rope.

Miranda grabbed the rope and helped him pull the woman back into the room. She shook again for a moment, and Marc ran a diagnostic MRI scan on her brain.

"She's a vegetable," Marc said.

"Send in a few more." Lester moved the first subject out of the way and readied another. "We need to be sure that they can't make the trip before we send in a fully fledged tetrapath."

Miranda groaned on the inside. It was hard for her to stomach watching someone convulse like that. But if she didn't act the part, she would be found out as an imposter.

Silently, she flicked through the menus on her suit. Eventually, she found her program for uploading a virus wirelessly to another computer. She started the program and aimed it at Marc's computer.

The upload time said it would take five minutes. Miranda sighed and grabbed the other end of another gurney with Lester. Together, they pushed through another subject and watched as he shook uncontrollably. They repeated the process three more times.

"Okay, that's enough." Marc said. "Obviously, the cured ones can't make it through. Let's send an infected one."

"We can't send a tetrapath into Earth." Miranda protested. The virus upload progress bar showed she still had a minute before it was uploaded. "Especially at that period of earth's history. That one tetrapath will infect the whole earth!"

"We have our orders," Lester said, grabbing the handles of a glass cage. "We need to see what it takes to make it to Earth. You never used to care about these things. What's gotten into you?"

"I just need to get some fresh air before we do this." Miranda scratched her head. "All these portal trips are making me see things."

"See things?" Mark asked, holding up a portable MRI scanner. "Like what?"

"Nothing." Miranda played it down. "It's just-"

At that moment, the virus finished uploading and Marc's computer crashed. A few seconds later, all the other computers in the room crashed.

"What the-" Marc turned around and looked at the garbled screen on his data station. He hit it and swore. "It looks like Miranda hit us with a virus."

"She's here?" Lester asked as his eyes grew wide. "I heard rumors about the ship attack."

"Yeah, me too," Marc said. "I heard she took out dozens of guards on her way to plant the bombs on the ship's guns."

Miranda smiled a little. "I heard she created her own portals and just rolled the bombs through them and into the ship. And that her friends can control tetrapath monsters."

"That's bad news if she is around." Lester said. "I hope they catch her before she does anymore damage."

"At any rate, we better not try any more of the experiment until we get the system back up and running." Miranda took her hand off of the tetrapath cage.

"Right," Mark said as he tried to compose himself. "We wouldn't want to do this without instruments to record possible data. "

Miranda turned from them and walked back to their station, where she breathed a sigh of relief. When the other two walked off, Miranda placed her hand on the computer and began to pull all the information she could about the portal to Earth. They weren't marked on the previous model, but they were everywhere. And they were scattered around the earth in space and in time, some of them back as the origins of man.

"Remarkable," Miranda said under her breath.

She scanned a few more files, until she found one marked *Naprea*. She opened that one quickly and found a few schematics of the village and the ship. The display showed the ship buried in earth, but most of the bottom was still intact. There were a few fault lines and a few locations marked for explosives, but the plans didn't call for enough explosives to sink Naprea, just shake up the dust a little bit.

She noticed the top rim of the crater was marked with portal energy, and it looked like Donovan was planning on destroying that.

Miranda blinked and the display went away. She had seen enough. Donovan intended to destroy Naprea, and she couldn't let that happen.

CHAPTER 17: SWING VOTE

Inara held her head tightly, trying to stop the pounding. Moments ago, she was assaulted by thunderous noises of all kinds. When she was finally able to stand, Scott and the crazy woman were gone.

"Donovan, are you there?" she asked.

[Yes. The tracker in the poison worked. I am following Scott's movements now. They are heading to the space ship.] The words flashed across the contacts in her eyes.

"I'm on it." Inara scrunched her eyes and rubbed her temples.

[Are you ok?]

"Fine," Inara lied as she stood up and continued to follow Scott's trail. "All this mountain air. Or lack thereof. I'll be fine once I come home to you."

[I can't wait.]

Inara quickened her pace and passed an elderly couple in the road. "What of the teleporter?"

[Not sure at the exact moment. She moves fast.]

"We need to keep the pressure on her." Inara approached the library. "If she discovers what we are doing, everything will be ruined."

[You overestimate her.]

"She can teleport!" Inara rounded the green grass and walked towards the back of the ship. "Not even an army of tetrapath at the control of Azurand was a match for her."

She stopped, her voice cut off by the sight of some long tube slipping into the side of the ship. Inara knelt down, fearing she might be seen. After a few moments, however, she discovered that caution was no longer necessary. Neither of them were around.

She stood back up and walked to the wall of the ship. The metal glistened in the sun and she rubbed her hands along the wall.

"To think, this ship has traveled the stars."

[They're descending, deep into the mountain. The ship is more massive than I thought.]

"Another secret lab of Pavarti's?" Inara asked as she twisted the handle in the wall and pulled the tube out.

[Possibly.]

The tube hung out of the wall, inert.

"It doesn't look like I'll be able to get inside today." Inara pushed it back in. "I'll have to get Silas or somebody to give me a hand with it once we know Scott's gone."

[Pull out your portal ring; I have a few gifts for you]

She pulled the ring off of her finger and expanded it. The portal opened and she reached her hand in, feeling several small drones.

[Place those inside. They will scan the inside of the ship. They can even create portals.]

"Perfect! One step closer," She said as she pulled out 30 robots and placed them in the tube. She closed the tube and started heading back to the library. "All we have to do now is figure out how to disable the rim portal."

[Now that you mention it, it looks like that portal above you is acting up again. You should seek shelter.]

Inara looked up and saw a small, swirling vortex in the center of the crater hole, floating above her.

"Have you found out what's causing it?"

[It is definitely the activists doing something from Earth. I think there are a few protocols in Pavarti's defensive systems. It can rain different memories into people depending on his need. If he wants an army, all of the raining memories are related to terrorist attacks that galvanize the people to defend themselves. The activists must have found out a way to control it on the Earth.]

By the time Inara rounded the hospital, the first drips of rain splattered on the ground. People looked heavenward and cried out in fear.

"Take cover!"

"Run!"

Inara pulled her shirt up to cover her head and broke into a run to shelter at the library. She passed one man who had dropped to his knees and stretched his arms straight out to his side.

"I am ready, Lord." The man said. "Show me your wisdom!"

"Fool," Inara muttered as she hopped up the stairs and into the library.

Inside, the library was lit up and packed with people. Men and women were huddled around tables with maps. Others were trying to catch a glimpse of what was happening outside.

The rim around the city sparked like it was short circuiting. The light drops turned into heavy rain.

The man who kneeled to embrace the rain fell to the ground, shaking. There weren't many people still out there, but those that were did the same thing during the entire rainstorm.

After it was over, the man on the ground pushed himself up and ran head first into the library door. The man fell down, and then got back up and did it again.

A smudge of blood was left on the door, and the man did not get back up.

The crowd in the library let out surprised yells at each impact. When the man lay unconscious at the doorstep, the crowd murmured nervously.

"Let me solve the mystery for you," Inara said over the low mumble of the crowd. Many people turned to look at her. "We are losing our portals. We can no longer move to the islands. We can no longer leave this town for fear of the outside world."

She paused and then stood up on the closest table.

"The rains are getting worse. This town is no longer safe." She pointed to the ceiling, and made a wide circle with her finger, indicating the portal attached to the rim of the crater. "The heavens are no longer kept at bay by the protective shield of the portals. It will only be a matter of days before the coalition can come flying up the mountain and lay waste to us the way they laid waste to the island villages."

"What do we do?"someone shouted.

Inara turned to face Silas and motioned for him to join her.

"We elect somebody that knows how to solve all the problems."

Silas stepped up on top of the table and she raised his hand.

"Somebody that knows how to repair the portals, and knows how to purify our people."

The crowd erupted into a small round of applause.

"Our town has many problems, and Silas knows how to address them all."

"But he wants to kill people," someone in the back shouted. "I can't condone that, no matter the crime!"

Inara pulled a sock from her pocket. Silas put his hand to hers, trying to stop her, but she shook her head and continued.

"I have here, a memory, stolen by me. It is a memory that belonged to Scott Orr." Inara dropped it onto the edge of the table. "It's from the day Pavarti died. The day the tetrapath overran the soul jumpers and their island. Scott was there, in the thick of it with his brother, Azurand. Dixon and Miranda were there too. They were responsible for Pavarti's death, and as such, their continued presence here is preventing the reincarnation of Pavarti."

Silas stood and smiled beside her. But Inara kept going.

"The storm is passing, but anyone who wants to examine the memory is free to do so," Inara said. "We need a leader willing to take the right action. A leader who knows how to fix our society."

She stepped off the table to another round of applause. Silas followed her with a heavy step. The crowd slowly began to disperse as the skies cleared up.

"That was a wonderful speech," Silas said quietly from behind her.

"Whatever it takes." Inara turned to face him. "I think this will push you over the top when the voting takes place."

[You are brilliant, dear.] Donovan typed on the screen on her contacts. [This town is as good as ours.]

CHAPTER 18: MIRANDA'S DISCOVERY

Miranda idly tapped at her datapad while sipping on a cup of coffee. Others walked by, barely grunting out a good morning. While no one was looking, she pulled out her EMP chip and readied the portal on her thigh that held the gun.

On the far wall, another portal was popping up. One that Donovan was about to come through.

When he arrived, Miranda would power down his suit with the EMP chip, take him hostage, sabotage the new portal network just as she escaped to the Helix Cascade and wait for Talia to show back up. At least, that was the plan.

Miranda stood up from her desk and made her way to the portal. Her knuckles clenched as she prepared herself for what she was about to do.

"Councilor?" Lester called from behind her. "I could use your help with this."

She didn't even turn around. "Not now, Lester."

Three soldiers stepped through the portal and into the room. Then, Donovan stepped out behind them. He was taller than she remembered, and her stomach tensed up like it used to when he would check up on her work.

Lester's hand grabbed her shoulder and he tried to pull her around. Miranda threw the EMP disk, but it hit the glass case surrounding the models of Cova and Earth. It fizzled feebly.

She fought the impulse to swing around and punch Lester, but just barely.

"What is it, Lester?" Miranda said through clenched teeth.

"Whoa." Lester held up his arms. "Just wanted you to take a look at some of the tetrapath. Get your clinical expertise."

"Yeah. Well, I have something I have to do right now." Miranda turned back around.

Donovan was just stepping back through another portal on the wall leading somewhere else. Miranda shook off Lester's arm and made her way to the security tech controlling the portals.

"Where did Lord Donovan just go?" Miranda asked the tech.

The tech shrugged. "One of the other islands."

"Which one?"

"I can't tell you that, councilor."

"Can you tell me when he'll be back through here?"

"He gave no specifics. He said he will be in touch when it is time to come home."

The tech stood up and pointed at the sparking EMP disk. "What's that?"

Miranda brushed the tech's cheek with her archive stone and he fell to the ground. Quickly, she pulled the disk off of the glass and put it back in a portal. Then she sat on the chair and tried to find which portals were activated last. She had to find Donovan.

"Councilor Blake?" Lester asked from behind. "What did you do the tech?"

Miranda didn't turn around, but knew Lester was kneeling next to the tech on the ground.

"He'll be fine, Lester." Miranda said with a tone of annoyance. "Come over here and help me."

She moved her arm to touch his head with her archive stone, but he backed up. "No. Something's not right with you."

He ran backwards for a few steps, fear in his wide eyes. He almost tripped, and then he turned around and ran.

Miranda turned back to the monitor and tried to find where Donovan traveled.

A strong hand grabbed her on the shoulder. "Councilor Blake, please come with me for questioning."

"Questioning for what?" Miranda stood up and walked with the soldier for a few strides.

"They didn't say." The soldier lead her to the quarantine room.

Miranda panicked and slowed her steps. "There must be some mistake."

"No mistake, Councilor." The soldier reached back to grab her arm.

She flung it and smacked the soldier across the chin, connecting with her archive stone.

He dropped to the floor and she ran back for the terminal. A gunshot rang out and something slammed into her rib cage. Her body convulsed and she fell to the ground while a taser bullet electrocuted her.

The suit took a little time to react, but it finally expelled some corrosive acid onto the bullets, dislodging them.

Her chest felt like it was burning and suffocating at the same time. Her body refused to move even as soldiers surrounded her.

[Suit integrity damaged. Suit skin modification no longer possible in all areas.]

"It's Miranda Whitlock!" One of the soldiers shouted.

Miranda cursed with what little breath she had. Apparently her suit was no longer displaying councilor Blake's face.

"Pull her up." Another soldier ordered. "We need to get her into custody."

Two hands grabbed her by the shoulders and half carried, half dragged her to the quarantine cell. Miranda took a deep breath, trying to force herself to fight free, but her body was still in shock.

She pulled up the menu on her HUD and navigated to the health and safety section.

An adrenaline shot was injected into her blood stream, along with some pain killers and other amping chemicals. Her heart rate jumped, and her body convulsed as if she had received a shot from a defibrillator.

The guard on her right tugged her hard and she twisted her hand to dig into his glove. She made contact with skin and sent him into a memory trance.

The guard on her left tugged back, and she twisted and slapped him in the face with her free hand. Another green orb lodged into her victim's brain and both of them lay at her feet.

Another soldier ran at her. She reached under her lab coat and pulled out a memory pouch. She tossed it at him and it exploded in a cloud of dust.

"Open fire!"

Miranda ducked and rolled behind a lab counter as gunshots zoomed everywhere. Chunks of the counter top rained over her. They were using real bullets. No stunning this time.

Miranda quickly crawled to the other end of the lab counter and made her way around the room behind the guards.

She peeked around the corner and saw Lester, cowering in the fetal position in front of the tetrapath cages. There were other scientists there, but no other soldiers. They were all on the other end, shooting their guns.

A portal pocket on her thigh opened up and she pulled out a small cylinder. She set it on the floor and slid it across the room to the crowd of scientists.

More memory gas escaped and the scientists fell asleep. She made a break for it and ran for Lester's computer. There, she unlocked the tetrapath gates.

Her shoulder rang out in pain and she fell to the ground. Blood spilled onto the floor in front of her, and her suit injected her with blood clots.

She rolled to the side and more gunfire was sent her way, but not for long. She rolled out of the way just as a pack of tetrapath roared in anger and charged the group of soldiers.

Screams of panic were only topped by the cacophony of gunfire. Tetrapath monsters sliced and smashed their way through the soldiers. Soldiers unloaded their full arsenal of flammable shotgun rounds, helium hammers, grappling hooks and high density bullets.

Miranda pushed herself up, clutching her shoulder. With all of them focused on killing each other, Miranda was able to grab three more memory pouches and throw them casually into the mix.

They exploded, engulfing soldier and monster in memory dust. One by one they fell to the ground, dreaming in inter-spliced memories.

Miranda stepped over the sleeping bodies, and made her way to the portal control panel.

A heavy breathing sound came from behind her. A soldier in a gas mask was pushing himself up with his left hand, and holding a hand gun in his right. He saw her, dropped back to the floor and took aim.

Miranda jumped behind a counter just as the gun was fired. Sparks flew on the control panel and the portal system switched off.

She opened her thigh pocket portal and pulled out the hand gun. She stood up and the solider was right there. In surprise, she swung the gun at him. He grabbed her arm and twisted the gun out of her hand. Miranda threw a punch and told her suit to harden the left arm to form a club.

[Command not available. Suit integrity compromised in that area.]

A display of compromised areas of the suit popped up in her vision.

The soldier blocked her punch, kicked her in the stomach and aimed his gun again. She dropped to the floor, but tossed a pouch of memories at the soldier.

He rolled left to avoid the blast. Miranda pushed herself up and towards him. She sent out a command to harden the right arm.

[Calculating.]

Before the soldier could get back up from his roll, Miranda kicked the gun out of his hand. The soldier stood up and threw a few punches. Miranda blocked the first one and slapped the soldier in the mask.

As she went to block the second one, her right arm hardened in a bent position, and now she had no flexibility or range. She missed the block and got hit in the face.

The blow was hard. She dropped to the ground, little spots dancing in her vision. The soldier pulled out another gun, and shot her in the leg.

She cried out in pain, but didn't fall down. The soldier calmly walked over to her and rested the gun barrel on her head.

"Surrender!" the soldier warned.

Miranda sent an order for her suit to send out an electric shock suit wide.

[Warning: suit integrity compromised. Cannot guarantee safety of the wearer.]

Miranda confirmed, and then convulsed as the suit sent out a mild voltage shock. The soldier fell back screaming and fired the gun wildly into the air.

Her breaths were sharp and painful, and she felt like she was going to pass out. She touched her face, and her fingers were coated in blood.

With a grunt, she pushed herself up, willing her legs to work before the other soldiers arose. Her right leg clenched when she put weight on it. The pain almost made her fall over. She held onto the closest counter and pushed herself along towards the portal control panel.

On the way, she picked up a hand grenade from a fallen soldier. She primed it and turned on the portal leading to her island.

It opened and she limped through it, dropping the grenade on the control panel on the way. She made it through the portal and fell down. Instants later, the portal turned off, she hoped for good.

She collapsed on the spot. She tried to get back up, but her body wasn't responding. Her eyes grew heavy, and her arms refused to budge. Tired of fighting, she closed her eyes, and drifted out of consciousness.

****

"Miranda!" came a shout. Something shook her good shoulder violently.

Miranda opened her eyes, and bleary person was kneeling over her.

"Are you okay?" the blurry one asked.

Miranda blinked a few times and looked at the source of the voice. A tall woman, young, with brown hair. This time chopped hastily. Miranda couldn't believe it. The last time she had seen this woman, she was dying on a beach as Terrance murdered scribe after scribe.

"Brea?" Miranda asked. "How?"

Brea smiled the way she used to while she was training Miranda. "Terrence thought I was dying. So did everybody. After you guys left in the submersibles, I saw to my wounds and laid low."

"If I thought you were alive... I would have..." Miranda struggled to keep breathing.

"No, don't worry about me." Brea said. "What happened to you?"

"Coalition is after me." Miranda panted and looked at the temple floor. "They may be sending more soldiers to the island now."

Brea kneeled, looked around, and then examined her. "Can you move your leg? There's a lot of bleeding there."

"No. A few too many hits with a shotgun, a couple of knife scrapes, and I got electrocuted. Twice." Miranda let out a cough. "I don't blame the leg for taking a strike. The new suit's not holding up so well either."

Miranda brought up the suit because Brea helped her reverse engineer the Coalition suits in the beginning.

"Wow." Brea raised an eyebrow and pulled on the tattered fabric of Miranda's suit. "You're lucky you didn't die. I take it this suit was the prototype copying the Coalition's?"

"Yeah." Miranda let out a grunt as she tried to sit up. "It still has a few bugs to work out."

"I can see that." Brea laughed. "Look, I'm not sure how long it will take those soldiers to get to the island, but my hiding hole isn't too far from here. Let's get you over there and patch you up."

Miranda nodded, and with Brea's help she stood back up. Brea stood underneath her arm and acted as a crutch the whole way there.

The path was uneven, and most of the terrain posed a challenge for Miranda's leg. After some rough navigating, they made it to a small cave with a patch of wood covering most of the hole. Brea moved the wood aside and they went into the cave.

Brea lit a torch and revealed the refuge. There was a deformed mattress on one end of the floor, a half of a table leaned up against the far wall, and various weapons strewn around. Most of them looked like they were broken.

"Don't mind the mess," Brea said. "I had to scrounge for anything I could find in the village. They didn't leave much intact."

"No, they didn't." Miranda gritted her teeth, trying to block out the pain in her leg.

"Here, lie down on the mattress," Brea insisted. Miranda was in no shape to argue.

The mattress welcomed her with a creaky protest, but she felt comfortable. Brea brought her a small pouch of water and she drank it up.

"Thank you," Miranda said.

Brea nodded and started tending to her wounds. "You forgot to mention the grenade. Your leg has just a few bits of shrapnel in it. Not enough to damage your leg, but I'll have to pull them out before they fester."

Brea walked off somewhere and Miranda felt her body relax. She tried to fight it, knowing she was probably in shock, but everything was so peaceful. Her eyelids grew heavy and shut.

She dreamed frantically. Mice and other rodents were eating her leg, people were shouting at her. Scott was off in a corner somewhere kissing Olivia. Donovan laughed while dangling Olivia on puppet strings.

The smell of steamed vegetables woke her up. Brea had her back turned while she was tending to the pot. A small pouch next to Miranda was filled with water.

She drank, closing her eyes and reliving the intense images of her dreams.

"Oh, you're awake. Perfect timing." Brea brought over a small bowl of soup. "Eat this; it will make you feel better."

"Thank you." Miranda gingerly took the bowl and sat up to eat it.

"So, where's Scott?"

"Huh?" Miranda rubbed her head.

"He's pretty set on taking out the Coalition." She returned to her chair. "Doesn't seem like him to sit out a mission like this. That and the two of you looked inseparable the last time I saw you."

Miranda looked down at her leg, wrapped in bandages. "He stayed behind."

"Why?" Brea persisted.

"Because he's pursuing other interests," Miranda said tensely.

Brea looked like she was going to drop the subject, but she kept going. "Romantic troubles?"

"We were never romantic." Miranda took another chug of water. "Never a real couple. We were sort of in an arranged marriage as kids, and to appease my dad we took engagement rings from him."

"Then why are you still wearing the ring?" Brea asked.

Miranda fiddled with the ring, she had almost forgotten she still had it. "I couldn't see the point of letting it go."

"Does Scott still wear his?"

"I... think so." Miranda said.

"See there?" Brea said. "I'm not sure what's going on, but I can tell you're mad at him. And I think you're mad at him because you love him."

"I don't..." Miranda thought of Scott and Olivia kissing.

"It's okay." Brea stood up from her chair and collected Miranda's bowl of water. "You'll figure it out soon enough."

There was a long silence while Brea refilled the bowl. Miranda's thoughts wandered on different tangents, all of them coming back to Scott. Did she love him? She never stopped working long enough to ask herself that.

"So, how's Naprea holding up?" Brea pulled up a chair and sat next to her.

"Not well," Miranda admitted. "There seems to be a sort of holy war starting over Scott, Dixon and me."

"Why?"

Miranda hesitated. "We sort of blew up the controls to the Archway Portal."

Brea merely nodded, urging Miranda to continue.

"And now, Silas and others think we're the reason Pavarti isn't coming back."

"Pavarti isn't coming back because he's dead." Brea insisted.

"Yeah, but the rest of the town puts a lot of stock around religious prophecies." Miranda took a drink of water. "Especially when it relates to Doctor Pavarti."

Brea reached out and touched Miranda's head. Green orbs of energy flowed between them and eventually filled the room.

"Prophecies are complicated things," Brea said.

"You don't believe them, do you?"

"I believe some of us were meant for great things." Brea conceded. "But that is only because they are driven to greatness. You, for example. You are the first person in a century to place more than one memory into a single object. And that power is setting you on a path. One that will bring you lots of pain. But one that will ultimately save us all."

Around the room, misty water gathered on the floor. The walls went dark. Kiri's face appeared above them.

"Kiri's death memory?" Miranda asked.

"Just as Kiri said, you've sent your sister along the path to finding her mother. For now, that is enough. Rest on."

Brea and the room faded into bleary smoke, leaving Miranda alone in the dark, sleeping on a small island the size of a train car.

CHAPTER 19:
THE SHIELD OF ASCENDANCE

Evening came too soon for Talia's liking. She rubbed at her head and blinked her eyes awake. She was in her room, but something felt wrong. She sat up slowly and took a look around. There were several people in there with her. All adults, all men.

"Now, before you try any funny business," the man closest to her said as he put up his arms. "I just want you to hear me out."

With a blink Talia teleported all of them to the top of the space ship. The man who started talking was right in front of her, while she placed the others at the four corners. They started running towards them.

"Tell them to stop, and I'll consider listening." Talia said.

The man made a stopping gesture to his men. "You may remember me. I'm Silas Stanton."

"Go on," Talia didn't want to acknowledge Silas.

"You may know that your sister and your friends and I don't really see eye to eye on everything."

"Get to the point. On a bit of a schedule today."

Silas smirked a little bit. "Alright then. I want you to tell me where your sister is."

"And why would I do that?"

"Because it's for the good of the city," Silas said calmly. "And because if you don't, others in this city might kill her if they find her."

"They won't find her," Talia said curtly. "Not possible."

"You know, some of them want to kill you, too."

"Most little girls might be afraid of that threat." Talia teleported the other men off of the space ship. "But there's nothing in this town I'm afraid of."

Silas pulled a gun out of his pocket. "Can you stop a bullet, little one? I'll give you one last chance. Tell me where your sister is so we can cleanse this city."

"Anyone can stop a bullet." Talia smiled. "I wouldn't recommend it though. Leaves a nasty scar."

"Do you not fear death?" Silas asked. The gun trembling slightly in his hands.

"I'm not dying today." Talia said calmly. "Are you going to shoot me or what?"

Silas clenched his jaw. "Well, it has to be done some time."

He pulled the trigger, but the bullet never left the gun. Talia had made a small portal inside the barrel, and the bullet went through it. It came out of a portal to the side of Silas and slammed into his lower leg.

"Ah!" Silas screamed and fell to the ground, where Talia stood over him.

"There, you see? Even you can stop a bullet!" She teleported the gun into the ocean. "Lots of blood though, I told you there'd be scarring."

With another thought, she teleported him to the hospital, and herself to the catalyst fountain on the Helix Cascade. With her powers on mute most of the previous day, her body was left with a dull headache, and even controlling those little gusts of mists had already drained her.

As she drank, she teleported the Ancestral Branch into her hand. She held onto it by the cattle-bell like handle at the end and rested the extended branches in her other hand. With a twist, a green orb shot into the Catalyst Fountain and rested there.

She teleported back to Naprea and shot several more orbs into buildings, rocks, and trees. She teleported to the Control Center island, and shot more orbs into any object she could find.

Satisfied she had all of her bases covered, she teleported back to the meeting place with Hudson. It was a currently empty playground, a long ways from the center of Naprea.

Hudson was sitting on a swing, reading a book.

"This place is creepy without any children here," Talia said as she stepped over bits of softened bark.

"Which could change any minute." Hudson closed his book, and then did a double take when he looked up at her. "Wha-"

"What?" Talia asked.

"You've grown." Hudson said. "Overnight."

"What do you mean, I've grown?" She opened a portal in front of her and used her other portal to get a good look at herself.

She did look taller. And there were a few more noticeable curves. Her hair was even more curly, but longer despite it. Almost to her waist.

"You look older than me now," Hudson said as he stood up from the swing. The way he was looking at her gave her a weird sensation. She could feel her cheeks growing warm.

"So, which relic are we after next?" Talia said, trying to change the subject.

Hudson nodded his understanding and pulled another grave opener out of his pocket. "Time to go grave digging."

Equal parts excitement and dread filled her chest. She would finally hear her mother's voice today, but she would have to brave the army of tetrapath that stood in her way.

"Great." Talia nodded over her shoulder and teleported a backpack there. "This time, I'm prepared, just in case."

"I don't think that will be a problem, seeing as how the island use to be the home for a nation of soul jumpers."

"It never hurts to be prepared."

"Right," Hudson agreed. "You do know what's on the island now, though?"

"The tetrapath infection." Talia pursed her lips. "Maybe you should sit this one out."

"Why?" Hudson looked angry. "You need my help. You need me to open the grave."

A young family and their children rounded a corner and started to approach the park. Talia's eyes darted between them and Hudson.

"Stay right behind me." Talia almost whispered. "Don't warn me about dangers, because it will break my concentration."

She blinked, and they were teleported to the condemned island of the Nebulous Reef. They stood at the shore, with their backs to the ocean. A tuft of mist hovered above and behind them, giving her additional eyes for any predators that might want to pounce.

"Charming place." Hudson said behind her.

"A lot of death has happened here." Talia slung the backpack over her shoulder. "Let's get moving. Where is the shield?"

"Pavarti had a secret lab here too." Hudson said. "This one is inside the temple."

Talia teleported them to the base of the temple. A giant stone pillar stood next to a crumpled stump of a pillar in front of the entrance to the cave. The entrance was carved into the side of a hill, and was now surrounded by grass up to Talia's shoulders.

A rustling in the grass came from her right. Without thinking, she sent her portals to the sound. A tetrapath leapt at her and she teleported it to the ocean.

A chorus of high pitched shrills filled the air. Dozens of tetrapath leapt of from the grass and charged them. She could hear more running up the cave of the temple.

With a few waves of her hand she swooped her mist around, sucking them up and throwing them at high velocity into rocks, trees, and each other.

"Into the cave!" Talia shouted and she ran.

With a mist in front of her, they plowed their way into the temple. The stairs descended rapidly, and there was a lot of loose gravel. Talia almost stumbled a few times on her way down.

They reached the bottom of the stairs and came to the proper ceremony room. It looked much like her temple, but this one was in ruins. None of the seats remained, none of the structures in the center stage remained standing. There was rubble all over the ground, and there were tetrapaths everywhere.

Talia conjured a portal the size of a great whale. It swooped around the room, eating the tetrapath before they could move.

Once they were clear, Talia put up a wall of mists on the front and back entrance to the temple, meaning if any tetrapath tried getting in through those paths, they would run through one and come out the other.

"We don't have much time," Talia said. "If this is anything like my temple, there are probably more than two entrances, and I can only cover two."

Hudson pulled a book out of his backpack spilled the rest of the contents. He hesitated over what he spilled, and then fumbled through the book in his hands. "The lab is probably in here. Near the stage."

He looked around with furrowed brows. He held up the book, looked at a page, and then put it down again. "It should be here."

"What?" Talia asked. Her question came out tense, but that was from the strain of creating such a large portals, and then holding the two portals for so long. Dozens of tetrapath ran in and out of her mists with a bloodthirsty frenzy.

"A statue." Hudson said. "There should be a statue around here with a spiral staircase underneath."

"Have you seen this place?" Talia asked. "Rubble everywhere. The statue was probably knocked down. Check the floors."

Hudson ran off and started kicking rocks and dust everywhere. Talia looked up towards the temple ceiling, where several tetrapaths were creeping in through another entrance.

"Hudson, we have company!" Talia shouted. "Hurry up!"

"I'm going as fast as I can!" Hudson shouted back.

Talia abandoned her portals at the entrances and swept up the tetrapath again with her whale like portal. Her only move at the moment was to send them tumbling into the various hard rocks, or the ocean.

They started coming in from the sides now, dozens descending into the temple for a fresh meal. Talia moved her hands furiously around, trying to send as many of them out of the temple as possible. And it was hurting. She could feel another blackout coming. Her backpack dropped to the floor, multiple water bottles splashing around inside.

"I've found it!" Hudson yelled from behind her. "But its locked or something. I can't get it open."

Talia ran for him, still sweeping the tetrapaths away like ants caught in a water hose. She knelt down next to him and started to press on the cover. She tried to conjure a portal into the room beneath them, but they weren't working.

Her portals exploded in a bright shower of lightning and engulfed the entire island. She could see every tetrapath collected in her portal vision. Everything went white, and then colors faded back in.

They were outside, on some beach Talia had never been to. It was secluded, with a small hut about fifty yards from shore. There, a pregnant woman was laying on the ground screaming. About a dozen men were advancing on her.

Tetrapath and debris fell over the water and rained over the beach. Talia tried to get up, tried to stop them, but her body was shutting down.

"Talia!" Hudson shouted. He was standing laying on the beach next to her. "We have to move."

She shook her head. She was nearly too weak to talk. "Backpack."

Hudson's face grew pained and worried. "I'll be right back."

He pushed himself off the ground and ran towards the mist. It was sweeping along the shoreline, right for them.

"No!" Talia managed a weak whisper.

But it was too late. He jumped through the mist and was gone. Three tetrapath were sucked up in the portal as well. Others from the water jumped onto shore and charged.

The group surrounding the pregnant woman saw what was happening and ran into the jungle in fear. The pregnant woman was bleeding, crying and looked over at the approaching monsters in terror.

Her portal mist cracked with a bright flash of lightning, and Hudson fell out of it screaming. Before he landed, he tossed the backpack towards her. It landed five feet away.

She crawled, forcing herself to make it there before the tetrapath reached her. She fumbled with the zipper for a moment and then pulled out a water bottle.

The liquid rushed down her throat and her mind cleared. Her mists erupted in another flash of lightning and there was a split. She had three mists. One back in the temple, and two on the beach. And they felt stronger.

One mist flew high into the sky and kept going. Her other mist expanded and sucked up all the tetrapath in the water, in the jungle, the whole island. Her portal back in the temple sucked in the three that made it back there.

Once all of them were gathered, she sent them to the portal in the sky. But now it was in space. Halfway to the moon. Nearly three hundred tetrapath taken out.

Her portal in space fizzled and was lost. Just her two remained.

Talia ran to the pregnant woman, who was crying.

The woman held up her hand, beckoning her closer. Talia dropped to her knees and put a hand on the woman's belly.

"What were those men doing?" Talia asked.

"Inducing me into labor."

"We need to get you to a hospital." Talia brought her mist back. But the mist in the temple wouldn't leave the amphitheater.

The woman shook her head and smiled. "It'll be ok."

"You're bleeding," Talia insisted. "If we don't get you to help, you'll die."

"That was going to happen when the baby came anyway," the woman assured her. "But you're here, so everything will turn out fine."

"There was a rustling in the bushes behind the hut.

"Honey!" Someone shouted.

"My husband is coming," the woman said. "Don't worry about me."

Her mist on the beach swooped over Hudson, Talia and the woman and she took them all back to the temple. But the woman did not come with them.

"What?" Talia sent her portal back to the island, but there she could only see a burned down hut and an empty beach. The woman was gone.

Hudson was kneeling next to the secret lab entrance, trying to pry it open.

"Do you think that woman will make it?" Talia asked.

"She said she was going to die during childbirth," Hudson said with a grunt as he pushed on a lever. "But I think you saved her child."

"Yeah, I kind of did." Talia smiled to herself and pulled the last water bottle out of her backpack. Then she turned to Hudson, who was pushing on a lever, trying to pry open the manhole. "I can teleport us down there in a minute."

"No, thank you." Hudson said. His hands were shaking.

"Are you ok?" Talia asked.

"First things first," Hudson stopped pushing on the lever and turned to her. "What happened to you?"

"Oh, it was nothing," Talia lied. "I experienced a near blackout. Almost lost control of my portals."

"Lost control?" Hudson looked into her eyes with deep concern. "You didn't tell me there were limits to the endurance of your power."

"I didn't think they would be tested," Talia admitted.

"Didn't think they would be tested?" Hudson interrupted. "Not while teleporting a whole island worth of tetrapath around?"

"I've... never pushed myself this hard before." Talia took another drink. "And admittedly I need this stuff more often than I have in the past."

Hudson ran his hands through his hair. "So in other words, they're growing more dangerous."

"No," Talia insisted. She finished her water and shook the bottle in front of him. "I just need to drink more. And when we've got what we came for, I don't ever have to push myself this hard again. I can control them."

"I wish I could believe you." Hudson looked away from her and back at the entrance door to the underground lab.

"Then let me show you," Talia said. "Let me show you how wonderful they are."

"You're not going to lose control of them?" Hudson asked.

Talia shook her head and smiled as a thick patch of mist materialized on the floor. "I'll have more than enough energy for this."

They fell through the mist and into the sky. Hudson screamed, and flailed in circles.

"Calm down, you big baby!" Talia shouted.

She cupped her arms close to her body and glided towards him. He was spinning in a tight circle and she had to time her reach, but she managed to grab his hand.

" Relax!" She shouted. "Spread your arms out, and hold on!"

Hudson stabilized, and they fell down together.

"Uh, the ground's coming up fast!" Hudson shouted.

"That's what happens when you're falling!"

A large cloud of mist appeared on the ground and they fell through it. Talia angled the next portal so they were shot out of it parallel to the ground.

"Whoa!" Hudson shouted, a smile on his face.

Talia tucked her body in so that she could reach his other hand, putting them in a pose like they were dancing. She swung her legs a little bit and they spun slowly around as they raced across the ocean surface towards an island.

Talia stared at Hudson and he stared back. The wind was whipping their hair violently, but everything else was peaceful.

When they started to lose momentum, Talia teleported them up high to fall again. They nosedived and Talia pushed away from Hudson with a playful smile.

Hudson looked at her with alarm for a minute, but then tucked his arms into his body and flew after her.

"Whahoo!" he shouted.

"I know, right?" Talia shouted back.

Hudson almost caught her as they approached the ocean again. She teleported them, this time, they were shot high into the air.

Talia angled the portals just right, bringing their trajectories gently together. As they raced higher, Talia glided gently into Hudson.

He caught her with a laugh, and the hug lingered.

"See?" Talia blew a strand of hair out of her face. "Not all bad, is it?"

"No, it's not." Hudson leaned in and kissed her.

Talia's lips grew warm and she grabbed the back of his head. They were slowing down, so Talia teleported them back into the soul jumper's temple just as their momentum ran out.

Hudson stumbled for a minute, and the kiss broke as he fell onto what was left of a front bench in the temple. His smile covered his entire face.

"I was going to ask how you stopped falling without killing yourself." Hudson leaned on the bench. "But I didn't want it to stop. The flying I mean."

Talia returned the smile and sat next to him, taking his hand in hers. "I don't want this to stop either."

His cheeks grew red and he laughed a little again. "Then it doesn't have to."

"While we're here, why don't I send you down to get the shield and play with Pavarti's computer?" Talia leaned her head into his shoulder. "I need to go refill my water bottles and get another drink. When we're done, we can visit my mother's grave and then, I don't know. Spend some time together away from all of this?"

"Sounds like a plan to me." Hudson let go of her hand and wrapped his arm around her shoulders. "Oh, my mom is going to kill me when she finds out about this."

"We'll cross that rickety bridge when we get to it." Talia kissed him on the cheek and stood up. "For now, go get that shield. I'll be back in 10 minutes, tops."

Hudson nodded and she teleported him under the ground and into the secret lab. She picked up her backpack and teleported back to the Catalyst Fountain.

The bottles shot up bubbles as she refilled them one by one and drank from the mug. Her body grew sharper and her portals more in control.

But more than anything, her lips tingled. Her hands still felt warm from where he held them. She smiled and put the bottles back in her back pack.

A small moaning sound came from behind her. Talia turned around quickly, ready to teleport any threats.

Her blood drained from her face when she saw Miranda, laying on the ground near the center of the temple, bleeding out.

Talia ran for her and tried to see what was wrong. Her leg and shoulder were bleeding, there were burn marks on her chest and her face was covered with a sickly sweat, but her heart was still beating.

She slung the backpack over her shoulder and teleported herself and Miranda to the hospital in Naprea.

They came through in an empty room with several beds. Miranda landed on one of the beds and Talia pushed it through the doors and into the hall.

Several nurses spotted her.

"What happened?"

"I don't know," Talia tried to hold in the sobs she didn't even know were coming until she tried to speak. "I just... just found her. Please help!"

A tall nurse took the handles of the bed and they ran to an operation room. A doctor stood up and touched Miranda in the face.

Everyone was quiet while green strands of memories flowed from Miranda's mind to the doctor's.

And then the memory transfer was over. The doctor knew everything that caused the injuries.

"Bullet wounds to the right hamstring and left shoulder. Electric burns along the torso. Team, let's get to work."

Talia put her hand to her mouth, shock and fear pouring through her, tears now pouring down her face.

"Young miss?" A nurse put a hand on her shoulder. "You'll have to wait outside."

"I'll stand right here. Won't get in the way." Talia shot her a stern look and the nurse backed off.

There was nothing she could do except watch and hope.

CHAPTER 20: HALF SPEED

Scott's head was numb. He adjusted his posture by moving a few inches on the floor, and sitting up straighter.

Clarity sat directly across from him, holding her hands out. She nodded her head to her hands and he took them.

Hundreds of orbs of all colors filled her body. Most of them were white or gray, but there was a large green one as well. The only missing color was red.

The most dominant among them was Clarity's snatching power. Small stats floated next to that white orb. Clarity could snatch as many as 30 talents at once, and she could even make stolen talents her permanent talents. But not powers. A soul jumper's power was only hers for a limited time.

A few of his talent orbs shot out of his body and into hers.

"OK, now let's train." Clarity said as she withdrew her hands and stood up.

"I thought that's what we were doing?" Scott asked.

"We haven't even begun." Clarity raised a single finger and pointed it into the air. "We need to apply your observations of our talents in combat."

"Combat?" Scott asked as he stood up.

"Yes. Don't worry," Clarity assured. "We'll go half speed. All you have to do is make contact and steal as many talents as you can"

Scott nodded. She swung her arm in a wide and gentle arc to strike him in the throat. At half speed, he caught her arm and a catalog of talents flashed over his vision.

Before he could see what was happening, Clarity slapped him in the face with full force.

"Hey!" Scott backed up. "What was that for?"

"Sorry." Clarity shrugged. "Some of us in here are still on the fence about helping you. They pick the wrong time to protest. Well, we aren't given a proper platform to complain are we?"

"Do you need a minute?" Scott asked.

"No, we're fine." Clarity shook her head. "Did you take anything?"

Scott clenched his jaw and shook his leg to keep it from cramping up. "No. You have too many talents. I couldn't pick one."

"You have to be quick." Clarity shook her head. "We are only going at half speed, but you will likely never face a foe with as many talents as we do. Now, let's try again. Only block our attacks, and on each contact, you are to take at least one talent. We don't stop until you have five locked in that head of yours."

She swung her arm wide again and Scott extended his to block it. This time, he pulled out a star mapping talent. A dull gray orb floating around in her mind. It floated to his mind and be began thinking of constellations.

She swung her leg in a sweeping kick, Scott extended both arms and pushed himself back. This time he took whistling.

"You're going for the easy ones!" Clarity shouted as she closed the distance. "Push yourself."

Another wide swing, and he blocked it. A white orb sailed though his chest and shot out of his foot before he could even tell what it did.

She swung her knee up at him. He used both arms to block the knee. On this contact, he brought in another gray orb. Her talent for kicking.

His head rang with pain and he felt all orbs he was carrying shoot out of him. He fell to the ground, barely missing Clarity's knee as it was coming up for another hit.

Scott grabbed his throbbing head and rolled away from Clarity. Stars rang in the darkened vision of his closed eyes.

"Get up, Scott. We need to try again. There is little time to waste." Clarity said from behind him. "No, he is tired, let him recover. There is no time. He won't learn anything this way!"

"Why can't I just take your talent for talent taking?" Scott asked as he pushed himself off of the floor. "I did it with my dad, and he's dead."

"Talent snatchers are not very patient." Clarity said. "They never have to work to craft a unique skill. They merely have to borrow from others. The one skill they do need to craft is how to better steal other's talents. This talent cannot be stolen from another snatcher. It must be earned. Tonight, you are beginning to earn yours."

"It came pretty easy to me when I was fighting against my brother."

"Stress and adrenaline can heighten your abilities." Clarity rubbed some hair out from her face. "You may notice that when you take Dixon's ability to soul jump, you have no issues assimilating that power."

"Apart from nearly turning into a monster." Scott corrected.

"Precisely!" Clarity almost shouted with her excitement. "The tetrapath infection provides the adrenaline needed to easily take and absorb talents. But adrenaline alone cannot sustain those powers."

"But I had my dad's powers for weeks after the event!" Scott scratched the back of his head, almost pacing, trying to remember what that felt like. "And then it was just, gone."

"Your dad specifically left that for you as an inheritance." Clarity said matter-of-factly. "You were in possession of a sort of death memory, and he wanted to give his talents to you as a passing gift. But your powers were still too young to hold it forever. You'll have to visit his grave again sometime, after you have mastered your gifts. But for now we need to focus on your training. So, here we come again."

They practiced for hours. Towards the end, he managed to take four easy talents in one contact. Whistling, knitting, cooking, and astronomy. Holding all of them at once felt liberating. But it was still too easy for Clarity's taste, so they pushed him further.

He took bigger talents related to snatching. An hour later, he was taking up to ten big talents without even getting dizzy. An hour after that, he was able to take multiple talents with one contact.

"We think it is time to go to the field and reclaim the others." Clarity leaned back against the control panel and let out a tired breath. She looked a little pale. "You are as prepared as can be considering the current circumstance."

"Thank you, Clarity."

"You're welcome." Clarity turned around and pulled out two bracelets. "These will block your ghost from the soul jumper's vision. Now remember, Dixon will see the others until you give them these. It would be wise to use his powers against him to aid you in the hunt."

Scott nodded and put on the bracelets, but his heart raced in adrenaline just thinking about unleashing the tetrapath infection again. Taking regular talents was fine, but taking a soul jumper's power? A scribe's power?

"One more thing." Clarity said behind him as he hit the elevator button.

Something warm and loud hit his mind.

[We're coming with you!] The voice of a man rang in his ears.

Scott grabbed his head and looked around for who was speaking.

[It is us, Clarity] came yet another unfamiliar voice. [We are connected in your mind, but we can't read your thoughts. You have to think about speaking to us to get our attention.]

"Don't you already have too many voices in your head?" Scott asked.

"One more can't hurt," Clarity said. "Now go, and save as many as you can!"

On the way up the elevator, he opened the next bottle of pills. He took five, closed the bottle and stuffed it back in his pocket.

The sun was now on its way down on the horizon, and the streets were crowded again. He gladly accepted the cover and started making his way to the outskirts of town. If Clarity wanted nothing to do with the hospital, the other snatchers were sure to be as far away from it as well.

After walking up and down a few streets, his legs grew sore. He searched food courts, alleyways, he even went into a few buildings. But he didn't see anybody acting weird. Towards the edge of the city where the business section gave way to the residential, Scott came across a tall building that overlooked a large section of the valley.

He passed a crowd of people at the door, and everyone got out of his way. The stairs were right at the entrance, and they lead to a latch for the roof. He climbed through it and was greeted by the beautiful view of the city.

He cupped his hands to his eyes and scanned the city for anything out of place. It didn't take long for Scott to spot Dixon running across rooftops.

[Scott, have you seen anyone?] This voice was male, almost uptight. [The others are curious.]

"Maybe." Scott shuffled to the other side of the roof to keep Dixon in view. "Can you guys see what I see?"

[No. We can just hear what you think.]

Scott focused as Dixon leapt down to a road and caught an elderly man in the crowd. Within a few seconds, the man was limp in Dixon's arms. A group of people walked up to Dixon and took the man. As soon as the man left his hands, Dixon was running off into the crowd again.

"Donovan's just killed another one." Scott concentrated, hoping Clarity would hear.

[Hurry, you need to snatch what you can from him.]

"I'm on it," Scott mumbled as he ran down the stairs and back out the door.

He rounded the corner and found the street was now empty, except for two men hauling the corpse away. Dixon was not around.

The men spotted Scott at the same time, and dropped the corpse.

"He's here!" One of them shouted.

Scott ran to close the distance. The two men both threw rocks softly at him. He had to fight every instinct to catch them. He managed to dodge the rocks and reached the first man. He was tall, with thinning hair and a leather jacket.

The man slashed out with a knife. Scott took a slight step back to avoid the blade, and then grabbed the back of his arm. The other man came charging with a knife of his own and Scott swung the tall man into him and they fell to the ground.

He ran around them and quickly slapped the fallen snatcher's head. Everything slowed down while Scott looked at the catalog of talents.

Dozens of talents appeared in his vision, and Scott zoomed in on a few he thought would be handy. The red orb of Dixon's soul jumping power tempted him for a moment, but he scrolled past that and found some easier ones to take.

A bright pink orb floated to the front. A talent for blocking and locking soul jumps. Scott took that one.

A deeper pink, almost red orb floated by next. It was the talent to snatch more talents through soul jumps. Scott didn't anticipate taking a soul jumping power anytime soon, but decided he would take it any way.

And finally a faded white talent. This one brought up an enhanced vision, where Scott could see the talents of people without contact, much like the talent his father gave him on the beach while he was fighting Azurand.

The contact was over and the three orbs floated into his body. He spun around to stare down the two men, but they were keeping their distance, looking between him and the fallen snatcher's corpse.

"Back up, he's dangerous and he's mine," came a shout from a roof to Scott's left.

Scott turned around just as Dixon slid down the side of a building and landed gracefully in the street. The pink orb in Scott's arsenal of stolen talents pulsed with energy, and one of Dixon's ghosts appeared in his vision. It sailed with tremendous speed and slammed into Scott's chest.

Scott and Dixon let out a grunt at the same time, but the soul jump was not complete. Dixon had no power over him. The bright pink orb pulsed again and clamped down on Dixon's ghost, trapping it in his body.

With a mixture of surprise and fury on his face, Dixon sent out the rest of his ghosts. They bounced harmlessly off of Scott's body.

Scott had blocked Dixon's soul jump, and not only that, one of Dixon's souls was trapped in Scott's body.

Dixon let out another agitated grunt and ran after Scott. Scott stood his ground, and a catalog of Dixon's powers appeared.

Again, the prominent red orb hung in the air, tempting Scott even more. But instead of taking that, he moved to the orbs in the gray section and took his fighting and climbing skills.

At the last second, Scott used the pink orb to squeeze even more on Dixon's ghost and Dixon drew his arms in to clutch his chest in pain.

Dixon fell down to his knees and Scott swung his leg in a full roundhouse to Dixon's head. Dixon fell to the ground and Scott ran around him and to the nearest building. He scaled it with ease and was leaping to the next roof top without thinking about it.

[I'll kill you!] Dixon shouted from behind him. But it wasn't a verbal shout. It was still through the soul jump. [Just like I've been killing your friends.]

Scott reversed the soul jump and began reading Dixon's thoughts. Seven snatchers, dead by Dixon's hand. A sick fury filled his stomach and he desperately wanted to return and fight Dixon. But Dixon was not himself. His mind was altered.

[Scott, don't forget to take Dixon's power if you can.] Another one of Clarity's voices said. [You'll need it to find three snatchers left.]

Scott thought about it one more time. He was several blocks away now, but still holding on to Dixon's soul. As long as he had contact with that soul, his new talents allowed him to steal more talents through the soul jump.

Instead, he read Dixon's mind further. Four more snatchers remained. Clarity was one of them. Scott had three more to save before Dixon killed them all.

CHAPTER 21: THE DOMINION ROD

Talia sniffled and rubbed her eyes. The only light in the recovery room was LED, meaning there was no way to tell the time.

Miranda was still unconscious. Her heart rate monitor chirped along rhythmically and fluids were draining into her. She looked peaceful, at least. The color was almost restored to her face.

A lone nurse checked the vital signs and fiddled with some of the knobs on the health equipment.

After a moment, the nurse turned to Talia. "Your sister is stabilizing, but we have no idea when she's going to wake up. You should probably go home and get some rest."

Talia nodded, but had no intention of moving. Most of the town wanted her sister eliminated. She couldn't risk leaving her sister unguarded and defenseless. Still, her eyes were heavy, and the thought of laying in a comfortable bed was tempting.

The nurse left and Talia considered her options. She could stay here and never sleep until Miranda woke up. She could teleport away, but keep a cloud of mist here at all times. Or she could bring in some help.

The last item appeared the most sensible thing to do. She conjured a portal in front of her and opened it so she could see out of the other portal.

That portal materialized over the city and flew over it, searching for Scott. She started near the hospital and swooped it out around to the outer limits of the town.

Finally, she found him. He was near the edge of the city on the south side, slinking between a few trees scrunching his eyes like he was trying to see something far away in the dark.

She teleported him to the hospital room and he fell to the ground.

"Ow!" He yelled.

"Sorry," Talia whispered and put a finger to her mouth. "I should have warned you. But I need your help."

"With what?" Scott asked as he stood up and rubbed his shoulder.

Talia pointed to Miranda on the bed. The color drained from his face slightly.

"Is she..." His lips kept moving, but he couldn't put the breath behind his words.

"They say she'll be fine," Talia said.

Scott took a few slow steps until he was standing over Miranda. His left hand reached out and touched Miranda's gently.

"But we can't leave her here." Talia said. "This town wants her dead. She's vulnerable."

"I have a place." Scott's voice cracked a little bit and he cleared his throat. "Clarity, we have someone recovering from injuries in a hospital. Are any of you a nurse?"

"Who's Clarity?" Talia asked.

Scott held out one hand with his index finger up, indicating to give him a minute. The other hand was on his temple, like he was listening to a sound piece in his ear.

Talia leaned slightly to get a look at the ear. It was empty. Scott was going crazy.

She was just about to say something when he looked sharply out of the room and took a few tentative steps.

He turned back to Talia. "Can you teleport all of this equipment, keeping her stable?"

"Yes, but I don't..."

"Good." Scott interrupted. "I need to go snatch a talent. Be right back."

Scott walked out of the room, and Talia turned back to her sister. "Don't worry. We'll get through this."

Her confidence was not overwhelming.

After a minute, Scott came back in, panting.

"Have you been running?" She looked at him with concern. Was he going to have a tetrapath outbreak?

"Not exactly." Scott nodded to Miranda and the equipment around her. "Okay, it all needs to come with us. And it needs to be connected to a power source quickly, or we could lose Miranda."

"Um... Where are we going?" Talia asked.

"Oh, right." Scott laughed a little. "New secret base. Can you take my memories, or do I have to tell you?"

"I can't take people's memories."

"In the spaceship. Underground. There are lots of memories in the room we have to go to."

Talia sent a portal out of the hospital and plunging into the earth, parallel to the space ship Naprea. After a minute, she came on the room.

"There's someone else there," Talia said tentatively.

"She's with me," Scott said. "Her name is Clarity."

She teleported them and the equipment to the room deep in the ship. The machines shut down and Scott scrambled to hook them up to power sources along the walls and power stations in the edge of the room.

His hands raced through cords and entered commands, willing machines to turn back on and resume monitoring and keeping Miranda alive.

"Remarkable," Clarity said behind Talia. "You were the one she talked about. The one who saved her."

Talia turned to face the woman. She was tall, and elderly, but she wasn't frail. She had a resilience to her.

"Who talked about?" Talia tilted her head.

Clarity scratched her head. "We can't remember. But she talked about her own daughter saving her. We found this strange because the woman was still pregnant."

"What..." Talia fumbled around for words for a moment.

Then Scott walked over to Clarity and they clasped hands. Scott tried to give her a nod of understanding, but Clarity was scrunching her nose a little bit.

"We would like to make it clear that some of us feel like we may not have time to watch this woman." Clarity said. "We may have other duties that should come first."

"Reprioritize," Scott said. "This woman is important, to... she's important. She's on our side, and she will be helpful to us."

Clarity nodded her understanding and Scott turned to Talia. He put his arm around her shoulder and guided her to the stairs that lead to a second level catwalk.

"What happened to her?" Scott asked.

"I don't know," Talia said. "I found her lying in my home temple, bleeding out and unconscious."

"It's getting too dangerous out there." Scott clenched his jaw slightly. "We need to stick together whenever we are outside of this base. No more wandering around in temples on your own."

"Sure." Talia said. "Together."

And then Talia swore. Hudson was still trapped in the soul jumper's temple.

"What is it?"

"I sort of left somebody stranded on an island." Talia said as her portals started to appear.

"Who?"

"No one," Talia lied. "I'll be right back. I'll just go get him."

"I think I should come along." Scott stepped closer and tried to keep himself in the mists.

"Scott, I'll be fine. Hudson will be too intimidated if I bring you along."

"Hudson?" Scott asked. "That boy who helped with the grave?"

Talia nodded and teleported to the soul jumper's temple without Scott. From there, she teleported down into Pavarti's secret lab.

Hudson was typing away on the computer monitor, going through files, oblivious to her presence.

"Hudson?"

"Gnah!" He shouted and spun around in his chair. His eyes were wide, his arms extended as shields. His chest pumped in and out rapidly. "Don't do that!"

"Sorry."

"Sorry?" Hudson replied curtly. "You leave me here for two days and all you have to say is sorry?"

"Two?" Talia paused, trying to account for her time spent in that hospital. "My sister was hurt. I know that's no excuse, and I could have teleported you out of here at anytime, but my mind was sucked in. I couldn't think of anything other than making sure my sister was taken care of."

Hudson chewed on the corner of his mouth, and then sat back in his chair. "Fine. Let's just move on then. We need one more relic."

"What about my mother's memory?" Talia asked. "We were going to visit her grave while we were here."

"Your leave of absence has shortened our time table." Hudson sneered a little bit.

"Why?" Talia's blood warmed. Hudson had a right to be angry, but this passive aggressive nonsense was helping no one.

"Because we have a slim window of opportunity to get the dominion rod."

Talia sat in a chair next to him. "Explain it."

"The Dominion Rod is kept on a island called Solomon's Porch," Hudson began. "It's a long island with a manmade lake encased in a rock. It's the tallest island of the bunch, and the lake is near the summit. The rod is kept in the center of the lake, under an artificial flooring built by Pavarti. The lake is full of water and the flooring can't be lifted. Except about once every year."

"What happens once a year?"

"The Geyser."

"There's a geyser on the island?"

"No. I'm talking about the lunar geyser."

"What?" Talia tried to put two and two together. "That geyser on the moon that can affect weather patterns here on Cova?"

"Yes." Hudson said. "And Solomon's porch has the tallest mountain of all the islands. Once a year, when the moon is at its closest point to earth, the geyser goes off right above the half lake. When the steam from the geyser hits the lake, something happens to the density and the flooring can float, exposing the chest containing the Dominion Rod."

"And today is that once-a-year deal?" Talia asked.

"No, that's not for another four months." Hudson pulled out the map and pointed to Solomon's Porch. "But later today the moon will be close. Anybody standing on the mountain will be able to see the geyser's burst fall harmlessly to the ocean, maybe causing a tropical storm."

"What good does that do us?"

"Well," Hudson hesitated, clenched his jaw and looked away for just a second. "I was hoping you would be up to teleporting that burst into the pool."

Talia bit her lip. "I'm going to need another drink. How long until the geyser goes off?"

"According to my calculations, about three hours." Hudson traced his finger along the map.

"Okay," Talia said. "I need to refill all of my water bottles, and drink as much as I can between now and then. Do you want to come with me this time?"

"No," Hudson did not look up, and the word came out short and tense. "I need to be alone with my thoughts."

"Oh." Talia stammered. "Can I look at the shield while I'm gone?"

Hudson tossed it to her and then she teleported to her mother's grave. If she had the time anyway, she might as well use it.

She held the shield in her hand and examined it for a moment. A curved piece of metal, forming a blunt spike at the bottom. On the inside, the handle swiveled, allowing for different holding positions. There were also three orbs that looked like they were made of faded amber. These were probably the storage orbs for talents. She teleported it back to the lab next to Hudson.

Talia focused on the dirt around the grave and conjured a mist. It seeped into the ground and then disappeared. The hole in the ground now revealed her mother's casket.

She snuck a portal back into the secret lab Hudson was in and teleported the grave opening disk onto the casket. It hummed and clicked, and then the grave popped open with a hiss.

The stench of death was overpowering. Talia put her hand to her mouth and stood back.

Talia closed her eyes and focused on her memory-spotting talent. A few green orbs lit up over the landscape. One in particular resided in the casket. Talia teleported it out, not wanting to reach her hand in.

It fell to the ground with a gentle crunch in the sand. It was packaged in airtight plastic. With trepidation she knelt down in front of it and unwrapped it. Inside the package was a black cloak with red fabric on the underside.

Inside the cloak, was a small, bound diary. The green orb was floating along the spine of the book.

The memory trance instantly took her to a familiar looking, secluded hut on a beach. Her mother was walking along the outside, her toes digging in the sand. The air was crispy, a slight breeze stirring it up further.

Her mother paused at the door of the hut, turned, and took one last look at the ocean. Talia's father was out swimming and climbing on a jetty. He hadn't noticed her arrival. She sighed and then went inside.

The house was clean, but lived in. Shoes were piled against the wall, clothes hung on the furniture. She walked up the stairs to her right and into a bathroom.

Talia got a good look of her mother there, as she stared into a wide mirror. Her eyes were bloodshot and puffy. Her jaw was tight with worry.

This was the same pregnant woman Talia saved while battling the tetrapath.

"Talia," she began with a few sobs. "I... I just found out. I just had my check up, and they say I'm not going to make it. They say that it isn't going to work this time. Our generation wasn't marked for cross-breeding. You, however, they can save. You will be the first person born of parents from two different tribes. Me a soul jumper, and your father a scribe."

She sobbed and sat down on the edge of the tub. "Your father. How is he going to handle losing another wife?"

She shook her head and kept going. "I don't know who you'll look like the most, or what talents the gods have in store for you, but I want you to know that I love you. And I will always be there for you. I don't have much to leave you, but I want to give you my ceremonial cloak, in the hopes that when you wear it, you will feel my embrace."

A small trickle of blood ran down her nose. She wiped it, and it smeared all over her hand. She let out a moan and ran her hand under the sink.

"Doctor, I'm done now." She shouted to no one in particular. "You can turn the memory off now."

More blood rushed out of her nose, and her mother's vision went in and out of focus. She walked back out of the bathroom and half stumbled down the stairs.

Out on the beach, her father was walking out of the ocean. A group of people were gathered around, trying to deliver the bad news. He wasn't taking it well. She let out a scream of pain and collapsed on the sand.

"It's happening!" she shouted. "Turn off the memory! I don't want Talia to see this."

She looked up at her father, pleading for him to understand. At that moment, one of the doctors pulled out the ancestral branch and pointed it at her. A green orb shot at her just as a purple mist appeared in the distance. The memory ended before Talia could see what it was. She was back in the present, kneeling over her mother's grave.

She shook the cloak and dusted it off. Once satisfied it was clean, she slung it over her shoulders and tied the ends together. Then she reached behind her head and pulled the hood up.

The smell brought more tears to her eyes, it must have been what her mother smelled like. It fit her perfectly.

She felt a warmth and an energy emanating from the robes that overwhelmed her. She dropped to her knees again, the tail of the cloak covering her calves.

The journal was still in the sand. Using the sleeve as a makeshift glove, she picked up the book and put it in her pocket, grateful for the tiny glimpse of her mother.

This new memory brought up old questions. Was her mother rebelling against Doctor Pavarti by entering the interracial marriage? Her father told her that they knew that Pavarti had not sanctioned anyone from their generation to intermingle to that degree, that they weren't ready for it. Only the next generation would be. So why did they do it? She must have known she was facing death. Or maybe she didn't believe, as the others did, and decided the risks were made up?

As she pondered these questions, she teleported back to the Catalyst Fountain and filled up her bottles, preparing herself to create the biggest portal of her life.

*****

Tufts of mist slowly materialized around Talia and Hudson. She took her time, drawing energy and reducing dizziness. In a few moments, she switched portals and they were greeted with a stiff breeze blowing up the mountain.

They stood on top of the burnt red, rocky slab shaped like a large water basin. It resembled a dinosaur rib cage stuck at the top of the mountain. A jumbled collection of curved beams were attached together by the slab itself.

The water was clear, but against the red rocks and green moss, it looked like a faded, murky mess. Talia could see to the bottom, and she quickly spotted the platform guarding the chest.

"We don't need to wait for the moon," Talia said.

With a wave of her hand, she conjured a mist at the bottom of the lake. Or at least she tried to. Nothing happened. She tried again, this time above the water. A thick cloud of purple materialized and she sent it into the water. But the surface was like a shield to her mists.

"What's going on?" Talia asked. "I've teleported water all the time."

"That's not regular water," Hudson pointed out. "Pavarti wanted to make sure none of his experiments could get their hands on this. The legend has it, that if a soul jumped person fell in there, the soul jump would be broken. Memory trances are blocked. Nothing happens in there that the good old Doctor Pavarti didn't want."

Talia turned from the mountain and looked at the moon in the sky.

"How long do we have to wait?" Talia sat on the ledge of the rock formation, her feet dangling over the edge of the cliff.

"Maybe an hour." Hudson sat down next to her and pulled out a sandwich. "Have you told anybody about our quest?"

"No. And I hope you haven't either."

"Not a soul," Hudson said. "Especially not him."

"What are you telling your dad you are doing all this time?"

"He's been too busy to notice I'm even gone." Hudson laughed. "Trying to fight some sort of holy war."

Talia sat up a little straighter. "He tried to shoot me, under the pretense of that war."

"Shoot you?" Hudson shouted incredulously. "See, that's why he and I fight all the time. He just takes things too far."

"So, what are you going to do after this?" Talia leaned back and closed her eyes, absorbing the sun. "When we have all three relics, I mean."

"I don't know. I don't want to talk about it." He put his hand over his eyes and looked up at the moon. "Looks like it's starting."

Talia stood up with her hand over her eyes to block the sun. The moon's surface had changed. A ripple of water and dust burst out in a circle on the moon's surface.

"Are you ready for this?" Hudson asked.

Talia chugged the rest of the water bottle and put it in the backpack. Then she closed her eyes and began to focus.

"You'll need it to be high. Almost out of the atmosphere," Hudson said.

"I know." Talia clenched her teeth, her words came out angry. "I just need to concentrate."

Hudson took a few cautious steps backwards and Talia opened her eyes again. She reached both arms high towards the sky and they started shaking.

A large portal opened miles above the ocean, achingly close to the outer atmosphere. She widened her hands and the portal cloud expanded out for miles. She felt the gushing water hit her cloud, and she turned one hand behind her and raised another misty, purple cloud over the pool behind them.

Like a torrential waterfall, the geyser's blast poured out of the mist and into the pool. The water in the pool bubbled and rippled, like some intense chemical reaction. Water spilled over the edge and threatened to push them over.

"That's enough!" Hudson shouted behind her. "The panel is lifting!"

Talia let her portals drop and about collapsed on the edge. Hudson grabbed her by the arm, and held her just enough, but she could even feel his feet giving way on the slippery stone.

"Hold on there. I have you." He set her down gently on the ground.

She took in a few deep breaths and laid down on the cool stone. At some point Hudson handed her another water bottle.

"Drink up," He said as he took off his shirt. "I'll go get the chest while it's up."

Hudson walked away, and Talia laid still, too tired to argue. She took sips from her bottle and tried to calm her breathing. In the distance, she saw the remaining blast from the geyser steaming into clouds in the sky. The clouds were darkening quickly and twirling rapidly.

Hudson let out a grunt behind her, but she couldn't even turn around to see what he was doing. So instead, she kept drinking to be sure she would be ready for the trip home.

In the distance, the rest of the geyser burst was entering the atmosphere and turning into a storm. The winds were already picking up when Hudson sat down next to her on the stone edge. He panted for a moment and then he shivered.

"That's a brisk breeze now!" he declared.

"Yeah," Talia said. "We should probably be going."

"You should rest a little longer," Hudson said. "I don't want to risk you teleporting until you've had more of your drink."

Talia nodded and chugged the remains of her water bottle.

"Also, I want to test this thing out." Hudson held the Dominion Rod in his hands.

It was long and metallic, but shaped like it was carved of wood. Thinner on the ends and slightly thicker towards the top. A few rings were clasped around the sides.

"Test it?" Talia asked. "There aren't any soul jumpers around."

He twisted it slightly, and the rings around the rod lit up with a deep red light. "There's always you."

Before Talia could say a word, a red orb of energy shot out of the rod and slammed her in her chest. She didn't feel anything from the impact, but the instant it was in her body, her head started hurting like when she was on Cherubim's Perch.

"Ouch, that hurts." Talia said. "Turn it off."

"Can you teleport?" Hudson asked.

"I don't know. Give me a minute. And turn that thing off!"

"I want to know first," Hudson insisted. "Can you teleport?"

Talia grimaced. She held out her hand and tried to conjure a portal. Nothing.

"No, I can't," she admitted. "Now, will you turn that stupid thing off! This is really hurting!"

"I wouldn't call it stupid," a voice said from behind her.

Talia turned and saw that they were surrounded by Coalition soldiers on the ground just below. All of their guns were trained on her. From the crowd, Donovan stepped up towards her.

"It's a wonderful tool, actually," Donovan said as it started to rain. "Keeps people like you in line."

Hudson tossed the rod and the shield to Donovan, who caught it with a smile. Hudson let out a small grunt from behind her and he fell to his knees.

"Talia, I'm so sorry," Hudson sobbed. "He had me in a soul jump."

"Donovan did?" Talia shouted. "You expect me to believe that? He doesn't have powers."

"But I do have a lot of resources," Donovan sneered. "With those resources I have discovered nearly all of Pavarti's secrets, including this gift you just got for me."

The rain was starting to come down harder. Thunder crackled in the distance. "How long have you had him in the soul jump?"

"Since you left him in the secret lab almost two days ago." Donovan looked to the sky. "Now, let's get you out of this storm before it gets really bad."

"I'm not going anywhere with you."

Donovan turned and the rest of the soldiers followed. After a few moments, Talia felt a strong pull in her chest. She fell off the ledge and landed in a pile of dirt. Her chest felt like something was pushing its way out, like there was a string between her chest and the Dominion Rod pulling her with them.

"She's not cooperating," one of the soldiers said.

"Tranquilize her and carry her," Donovan said nonchalantly.

"Leave her alone!" Hudson shouted from the ledge of the lake. He threw a rock at the closest soldier. It bounced off his armor like a plastic ball.

He jumped off of the edge of the lake basin and fell hard on the ground. He screamed in pain, but got back up and tried to chase Talia down.

Donovan simply nodded to the soldier who got hit with the rock. The soldier turned and fired a rifle. A stream of red exploded from his chest and Hudson collapsed onto the ground.

"No!" Talia screamed. She reached her arms out in futility, trying to catch him, to teleport him back home, or to the hospital, or something. Anything. Her portals would not work, and she could not reach him.

Something pricked her in the back of the neck and she fell to the ground.

*****

Talia awoke in a bright, rectangular box about the size of two train cars welded together. She touched the smooth sides, guessing it was some sort of glass. It wasn't clear; nothing could be distinguished on the outside. All she could make out were shapes.

There was a bandage on her right elbow. She pulled it off and found a small puncture mark where blood had been drawn.

She pressed her head against the glass to try to see better, but it was still too blurry. She turned back in to look at what she had. A bed on the left wall, a refrigerator on the right, a microwave next to that, a table and chair set surrounded by medium-sized house plants, and an enclosed bathroom.

They were going to keep her here a while.

After several minutes, the glass cleared up, revealing the room outside of her space. It was a large empty box, with no roof. Outside of the room was a large cave. In the distance, Talia could make out what looked like people walking on thin air, near the roof of the cave.

Donovan stepped in, swinging the Dominion Rod casually. He nodded to several of his assistants and they got to work on computers around Talia's cage.

"In the early days," Donovan began. "Pavarti would use this rod to teach new students what it felt like to soul jump. He would make them dance and help them learn how to use the gifts he gave them."

"I've already got the basics down, thanks," Talia sneered.

"Yes, but that's not all it can do." He pressed a button and the red rings lit up again. "I need to study your unique gifts. See what makes it work. But in order to do that, I need to pull a few mists out of your body."

Talia snorted.

"But if I do, that unleashes your portals, and no matter the weaknesses of them, they are still formidable enough for your escape and quite possibly the destruction of my lab."

"So you can't study me. Just let me go."

"Ah, but I can." Donovan smiled.

He twisted one of the rings on the Dominion Rod. He then flicked it, and against her will, two portals shot out of her chest and hung in the air for a few seconds. She reached out with her hands, trying to bring them back. But, one at a time, Donovan conducted them with his wand into one small tree each.

Talia tried to call them back, but they were latched to the trees.

"By now you will realize that controlling your portal clouds is impossible." Donovan stood up from his chair and opened a data screen on the wall of the cage she was in. "The prison prevents soul jumping while in it, just like your first island excursion, but the Dominion Rod is above those containments."

As he spoke, two small portals opened on the floor under the plants that held her mists. The plants fell through the portals and into the outer room where Donovan stood.

"And right now, we are starting to collect the preliminary data to find out what your portals can really do." He tapped a few commands on his screen. "How fast can they go? How far away? How big? How many people at once? How much mass? Some of the answers I got from you while soul jumping poor Hudson, but what if I manufactured it? Would that change these answers?"

"When I get out of here, I'm going to kill you," Talia mumbled.

"Well, until then, I want to thank you for this gift. Your portals truly are remarkable."

Donovan turned to walk out of the room.

"No!" Talia shouted and ran for the glass. She pounded the walls with her hands, screaming, losing her mind with the futility of her position.

The glass faded again, blurring the veiw of everything on the outside.

Talia curled up into the fetal position, tears rolling down her cheeks. She had failed her sister, Hudson, and everyone else she cared about.

CHAPTER 22: SNATCHER CATCHER

Scott slipped into a gathering crowd, unnoticed. They were standing outside the library, which now had a permanent platform for Silas to preach and campaign. Silas was doing that more often. But today was different. Today was the eve of voting day.

Time was rushing on now. Miranda was slowly recuperating, but still unconscious. And there was still no sign of Talia. She never returned after dropping off her sister almost three weeks ago.

[Clarity. Has Talia come back yet?] Scott asked.

[No. We'll tell you when she does.] The response came nearly a minute later.

Meanwhile, he was no closer to finding the last of the scribes. The good news was that Dixon was still looking for them as well, meaning they were still alive, for now.

The day was gloomy, as were most days in Naprea lately. People wore thicker layers, not because of the cold, but because of the rain.

The portal around the rim of Naprea was showering the town with memory-laced rain at least twice a day at random intervals. Scott's hooded jacket fit right in with the crowd.

Upfront, the library doors opened and Silas stepped out, Inara right behind him. The crowd cheered and Silas waved his hand with a smile.

"Thank you for braving the potentially stormy weather today!" Silas shouted and pointed to the sky. "A menace, I assure you, that will be fixed once I am elected as the next elder of the circle."

The crowd clapped again. Scott clapped with them and kept scanning. It wasn't likely the three scribes were here, this close to the hospital, but he was running out of places to look.

"In a few short hours, I will debate my opponents for the last time," Silas continued. "They have their plans, and I have mine. And mine is the only path that will restore this holy city to its rightful glory."

The crowd cheered more enthusiastically than ever at that line. Silas let the cheers die down before continuing.

"But this is going to take the whole town. United. There can't be anything holding us back. And that means transparency on my part." Silas's smile faded and he looked at the crowd, with a little worry in his eyes. "It is in that capacity that I want to bring something to the attention of the public. I have just discovered that there are more dangerous scribes living among us. Yes, it's true. Calm down. I know how serious this is. These scribes were locked in captivity by Doctor Pavarti and his followers. But Scott Orr has freed them. We are fairly certain there are three of them."

The noise of the crowd grew again, and Silas waited patiently for order.

"I know what you are thinking." Silas nodded, regaining control of the crowd. "My concerns are yours. Snatchers can blend in, a wolf among the hens, as they say. This is where you come in. If you come across anyone you don't recognize, inform us. We will capture them again."

"What about the other twelve you killed?" Scott shouted, his head down in the crowd. "Or should I say Peter Dixon killed, because you let him out of his cell?"

Scott shuffled a few rows to the left, trying to avoid the gaze of the people around him. From his new spot, he saw a woman in a black dress walk up on stage.

A guard put his hand up to stop her. She touched the man on the shoulder, and a faint flash of white sparked like static electricity from her hand. The guard's eyes twisted up and he sat down on the side of the stage, crying.

[Clarity, I see one. She's making a move on Silas.]

[Go get her!] Three of Clarity's voices shouted at once.

Scott pushed his way through the crowd in a hurry, and Silas spotted him. Inara too, and they were both pointing and shouting, trying to be heard over the crowd, which was now in a slight panic.

The snatcher woman touched Silas's shoulder. His face went from angry and tense to sad and teary in a second. He too sat down on the edge of the platform and cried.

By the time Inara turned to look at Silas, it was too late. The woman in black was around the corner and running towards the capitol building.

Scott pushed his way through the crowd, trying to go after the woman himself. But the people were packed in tight, and not willing to move.

"Rain!" Scott shouted on a whim.

Several in the crowd screamed in panic and that got them moving. Scott moved his legs quickly and navigated the crowd like a rushing river, letting the current of people do the work, but positioning himself away from the trees and other obstacles.

About a hundred yards ahead of him, the snatcher woman ran up the marble steps of the capitol building and through the front door.

The people in front of Scott were clearing and thinning, and he reached the door.

[Can you tell who it is yet?] Clarity asked.

[I don't know. She's little shorter than me. Black hair. Makes grown men cry by touching them.]

[Reina. Make sure you identify yourself before engaging.]

[I'll keep that in mind.]

Scott opened the door, and then felt a light memory trance tingle up the back of his head. He didn't go unconscious, and he was still aware of his surroundings.

"This is Silas. My assistant Olivia has a positive ID on one of the snatchers. She used her powers on me just moments ago. Here is a memory, recording the snatcher."

A brief visual of Reina subduing Silas with depression, and then rushing into the front door of the capitol building flashed over Scott's vision.

Scott looked around the area, trying to find the source of the memory transfer. There was nothing he touched with a memory.

[How is that possible?] Scott asked Clarity.

One of the older male voices came on. [How is what possible?]

[Silas just hit me with a memory trance from half a block away. It wasn't a full trance, I was awake for the whole thing.]

[He must have connectionless memory transfer abilities, much like a soul jumper can latch onto another's soul without contact. Very few scribes have ever had this ability.]

[Great.] Scott walked into the building and stopped at the enormity of it.

Two large stair cases rose in wide, arcing spirals to his right and his left. They met in front of him as a balcony, one level up. A bird's eye view of the stairs would show the outlines of a circle between them.

Directly in front of him, on the other side of a glass table with a flower bowl, a hallway led to an open door. Through the open door was a large room with a stage and hundreds of chairs set up.

Someone ran down the staircase on Scott's left, not watching where he was going. Scott ran to his right, around the right staircase.

On the other side of the staircase was a small hallway lined with a pair of bathrooms and tables with flowers on them. At the end of the hallway, another door lead to the conference room in the back.

The front door to the capitol building opened just as Scott rounded the corner and hid behind the staircase. The man running from upstairs began shouting hysterically.

"Silas!" The man was panting from his running. "Your image worked. I found the snatcher, and I have her in a five minute memory trance right now."

"Good work," Silas said. "But I heard Scott Orr in the crowd, and someone says he came running in here just moments ago. Seal everything. We'll all barricade ourselves in the room you have the snatcher in. And out here, the capitol guards will try to take him out."

"Send out the guards!" the man shouted. "Lock this place down!"

Scott ran into the woman's restroom before someone spotted him. Outside, people were shouting and taking positions. Inside, it was quiet for now.

Scott waited behind the door as quietly as he could. He focused his new vision of talent spotting, and the whole building was lit up with floating talents. Floating orbs of color became markers where all of the guards were.

A pair of guards walked his way, and after a moment, the bathroom door swung open and two women walked in, their backs now to him.

They were standing side by side, each holding a wadded up ball of tissue paper, their green orbs of talent in full use as they loaded fresh memory trances into tissue.

Scott snuck up and grabbed both of them by the arms and forced them to hit each other with their memory orbs. They fell down, unconscious, and Scott kneeled down and touched one of them in the face.

The instant the contact was established, two grey orbs floated into his mind.

He now had the schematics of the whole building and the layout of each patrol.

A dozen timers were now counting in his head. The paths of each of the guards were mapped out, thanks to the scribe's diligence in learning them.

Another guard would round the stairs and check the men's bathroom in half a minute. Right now, it was clear.

He double checked with his talent vision, to make sure no one was off course, and it checked out clear as well. He walked out of the bathroom and towards the door that lead to the conference room.

He waited at the door, as the counters ticked to zero and people turned in the opposite direction.

The door opened quietly and he snuck into the conference room. Three scribes were on stage, one looking at the main entrance, one looking at the opposite entrance, and the other turned the other way, looking at a back entrance.

Three more scribes were walking the isles, but all of the close ones were walking the other way.

He ducked below the line of chairs and half ran towards the main entrance.

Another big clock in his head flashed red. The main guard he was worried about would be facing the other way, walking towards the entrance for the next fifteen seconds.

He made it to the conference room entrance door and slipped through.

On the other side, a guard was walking casually towards the main entrance, around the glass table with flowers on it. Two other guards would have just walked around the other side of the staircase.

Scott ran and jumped on the table. Using a technique he snatched from Dixon, Scott pivoted his feet and jumped straight up.

His arms grabbed the edge of the balcony and he did a half pull up. His right leg swung out and caught the ledge. Using his leg strength, he pulled himself up to the ledge, and then quickly climbed over the hand rail.

Two guards were now going down either stair case, and two more were on their way from separate hallways to his left and right.

There was a small clearing and that led to the main office door. Scott walked up to it and stopped. Based on his talent vision, four people were in the room, including the other snatcher.

Scott's hand rested on the handle ready to attack. He had 10 seconds until a guard came around the corner and spotted him.

Silas would subdue him in seconds if he charged in with no remorse. He needed more firepower.

With five seconds left, he turned back to the staircase and took inventory of every talent the guards had. Most of them had significant fighting skills, crafted around their memory talents.

With two seconds left, he found a talent he could use, a talent that blocked memory trances. The orb was currently floating in a guard walking around the glass table with flowers just below the balcony, the one guard he didn't want to confront.

Scott sprinted and used his hands to push himself over the handrail. He slid down the pillars and let himself down silently onto the table.

The guard was still walking towards the conference room door. Scott slowly got off the table and closed the distance between him and the guard.

Scott was fully in the hallway when the guard turned around. He was about to scream for help, but instead pulled out his weapon. A paper mace. It looked more like a whip with frayed bits of paper at the end, but the effect was the same: something big to swing at your opponent. Instead of a heavy spike ball, this was a mass of paper laden with memories.

The guard swung it for a moment and then threw it out. Scott shrunk up against the wall to avoid the hit of the mace. A slight breeze tickled his face as the paper tassels swung passed him.

The guard pulled sharp on the rope, pulling the mace back. Scott ran and lunged for the guard's ankles.

The guard picked up his foot and Scott missed. His momentum was wearing out, and he pushed himself into a roll and leapt for the conference room door. He smashed through the other side and crashed into the back row of chairs.

All of the guards in the room ran for him. They were far away enough that Scott could gather his bearings and deal with the paper mace guard for a moment.

The guard came through the doors and swung the mace. Scott picked up a chair and blocked the mace, tangling it up.

With a quick tug, Scott pulled the rope in and the guard toppled forward a little bit.

That was enough for Scott to close the gap and slap the guard in the face. On contact, the bluish green orb floated into Scott's mind and he had the ability to block memory trances.

Scott ran through the door and made his way to the stairs. One guard was on the stairs and threw a wadded up piece of paper at him.

Scott caught it, and no memory trance washed over him. The guard backed up in shock, and Scott made his way to the head office where Silas was keeping the snatcher prisoner.

Only now, he could see at least one more snatcher, but he wagered there were two more in there. The last three.

Scott opened the door and Silas shot a memory trance at him over the air, but trance washed over him.

Silas smiled a little, "You are a resourceful one."

"I just want to collect the snatchers and leave." Scott held up his arms. "I have no stake in the battle for Naprea's soul. Just let me take her, and I'll never set foot in this town again."

"That's not good enough, Scott." Silas pulled out a gun and aimed it at him. "I'm a fair man, but nothing gets between me and my town."

Scott held his hands up, and improvised. "How about the Coalition?"

Inara's eyes grew wide.

Silas merely scoffed. "They can't get in here."

"They already are." Scott took a small step towards them. "Hiding in plain sight."

Inara stood up, and edged closer to the gun. "What are you waiting for Silas? Shoot him!"

"Afraid he might figure it out, Inara?" Scott asked.

"Inara?" Silas turned his head to her. "Who's-"

That second of hesitation was enough. Scott kicked the gun, and it shot into the ceiling. As his foot came down, Scott leaped onto Silas and put him in a choke hold.

Inara pulled out a Coalition issued pistol and was aiming it at Scott, but Scott was using Silas as a human shield.

"See there?" Scott asked as Silas tried to break free of the hold. "Your own campaign manager. It's just a matter of time before she decides to shoot you because you're expendable. The question is, who's going to shoot first?"

Silas stopped struggling and aimed his gun at Inara.

"He's lying." Inara's hands were shaking.

Scott loosened his grip slightly so Silas could talk.

"Where did you get the gun, Olivia?"

Inara stammered for a moment. "Smuggled it, when I escaped."

"Then put it down and let me have a bit of your memories to prove your innocence."

Inara dropped the gun, and fell to the floor crying. Reina, the captive snatcher stood up behind her and took the gun.

Scott twisted on Silas, to keep him from shooting Reina. Silas reached out with his free hand to shoot another memory trance into her.

Scott grabbed that hand and pulled it away. Reina walked causally up to Silas and put a hand gently on his cheek. Silas relaxed and dropped the gun.

"You should have let us walk away," Scott said as he picked the gun up and stood up.

"You're right." Silas put his hand to his mouth. There was a slight tremor in his voice. "I'm such an idiot."

"Come, the hunter will be here any minute," Reina said. "We must find the others and hide."

"You're with the other two snatchers?" Scott asked, as they both walked out the door. A dozen guards were spaced out along the balcony.

"That's it. We're doomed." Reina's shoulders dropped.

Scott held out the gun. "Out of the way!"

The guards all put up their hands and opened a path for Reina and Scott. They slowly made their way down the stairs.

"Where are the others?" Scott asked.

"They hide," Reina said. "They have a talent for cloaking their appearance while motionless."

"Out of the way!" Inara shouted from atop the stairs.

Scott turned his gun, but Inara reached the balcony and fired.

A flash of white faded next to him, and an elderly man jumped in front of Scott. The bullet hit the man and he disintegrated.

Scott fired three shots at Inara and she ducked behind the balcony. Reina was on her knees above the ashes of a fallen scribe.

"We have to go." Scott said to her.

"No!" Reina shouted.

Scott grabbed Reina by the arm, and felt all hope drain from his body. Any chance of escaping now seemed impossible. And even if they did? Inara would find the hideout in the ship pretty soon anyway.

[Scott?] Clarity asked. [What's happened? Everything okay?]

Inara shot another elderly man at the top of the stairs, and Scott dropped his gun, convinced he was next.

Reina slapped him in the face, and everything came back into focus, just as Inara stopped on the stairs and took aim again.

Scott scooped up the gun and fired. He hit her leg and she fired back a few rounds. Sections of the wall disintegrated around him.

He pushed himself up and ran out of the building with Reina.

"After them!" Inara shouted from inside. "They've killed Silas!"

CHAPTER 23: THE DUEL

Talia's stomach turned as the microwave beeped again, telling her the food was ready. It had taken her a while to figure out how it worked. Plastic wrappers burned and stuck to the food on her first attempts.

She sat at the table, inside her glass prison, oblivious to the world outside, and indifferent to the cooling food. The pain of losing Hudson was too much.

"Variety is the spice of life," She told herself unenthusiastically, forcing herself to the microwave.

Talia forced herself to eat the different meals provided as way for her to count the days she had been trapped there. Twelve meal options, and she had cycled through them three times. Thirty six days and counting.

And it had been a lonely thirty six days. Even when people entered the room, they were fuzzy through her glass cage.

As soon as Talia finished her meal, she put the plate and the food box in the garbage and walked over to the bed.

Just as she was sitting down, the doors opened and Donovan walked in, a few assistants in his wake.

"I've done it!" Donovan shouted. "Talia, I've done it!"

Talia closed her eyes and did not respond.

"Oh, this is perfect." He clasped his hands together and finally stopped at the entrance door to her fishbowl cell. "I've manufactured them!"

"Manufactured.. what?" Talia hesitated.

Donovan put his hands to the glass cover and everything came into focus. "Your mists."

With a small push, the door to her cage opened. A small breeze from the overhead air conditioning came wafting through. It wasn't much, but Talia's skin tingled at the sensation. She closed her eyes and let the skin of her face enjoy the small moment.

When she opened them, the assistants were wheeling in two small aquariums, filled with her mists. Every few seconds, a noiseless flash of lightning erupted within.

"These are yours," Donovan said dismissively. "You can have them back. I can't bend them to my will as I have done with mine."

"Yours?" Talia ran her hands along the top of the closest aquarium. "You can teleport like I can, now?"

Donovan gave a conceding nod. "I'm limited by the technology I have, but eventually, that won't be an issue."

"What are you going to do now?"

"Weaponize it." Donovan held out a hand and the lids to the aquariums popped open. "You two clear out. I don't want any collateral damage."

The assistants walked out as fast as they could and Talia's mists seeped out of the aquariums slowly. But they still wouldn't listen to her.

"Oh. Well, it looks like you'll have to be out of the room to control them." Donovan stood to the side of the door and gestured his hand in a bow to show he was clearing the way for her.

"Why are you doing this?" Talia asked. "You know I'll burn this place to the ground."

"I need to stress test my creations," Donovan said. "See where I am lacking and make improvements."

Talia took a step out of the glass box and the mists followed her out, but then they started darting around wildly.

Reflexively, she pulled the mists into her to keep herself from getting hurt. They felt like a familiar, warm blanket.

Then she turned to Donovan. A small purple mist covered his hand, teleporting the Dominion Rod there. Before Talia could react, Donovan shot her again with a red orb, trapping her mists inside her.

"Come along, little one." Donovan said as he walked outside of the door. The Dominion Rod pulled on her like she was caught with a fishing hook. "We need to take this outside."

They walked outside of the cubicle lab and into another one. Here, a large cement block was in the middle of a blank white room. One side of the block looked like it was smoking. Wavy heat lines ran up and down it.

Then she realized it was a portal. Donovan gestured for her to go through. Reluctantly, she obeyed.

The other side was the scene of Hudson's death. They were on the hill just under the large basin where the

Dominion Rod was recovered. The wind was kicking up in her face again. She had to squint her eyes at the sudden influx of light.

Just up the hill, under the basin, she spotted her green backpack, the one containing water from the Catalyst Fountain. She took a few steps towards it when Donovan stepped through the portal behind her.

"Now, don't go easy on me," Donovan said as his heavy boots crunched through the grass. He pointed the dominion rod at her. "I need to know how far I have truly come."

The Dominion Rod released her, and she instantly teleported herself to the catalyst fountain, because it was a trip her portals found the easiest to obey. But Donovan was already there, standing between her and the fountain.

"Poor, predicable, Talia," Donovan said.

She swiped her hand and a portal mist engulfed him. She opened the other portal over the ocean, almost out of the atmosphere.

But Donovan was still standing in front of her. He smiled as she dropped to her knees, a sick pit of pain in her stomach. She still needed a drink. Clouds of purple flashed in and out of existence with intense burst of light.

"You could have teleported anywhere in the world." Donovan pulled out a grenade and threw it at her. "Instead you run to your comfort zone, and your death."

The grenade exploded in a flash of purple, and Talia was back under the basin. She teleported herself back to the fountain and Donovan wasn't there. She ran for the fountain, but a rocket zoomed past her and hit the fountain. The explosion knocked her back, and she saw the fountain crumbling in shrapnel and liquid.

She teleported somewhere soft for the landing and then right back to catch as much of the water as she could in her portal. It wasn't much, but with a little bit of effort, she opened the second portal inside of her.

It was more than she usually drank, and the effect was immediate. Her body shook violently and she fell to the floor. There were still chunks of debris despite her best efforts, and it was tearing up her body.

"You didn't do what I think you just did?" Donovan asked from behind her. He shot her with the Dominion rod and twisted it. All of the water and debris that Talia caught with her mists fell back out of the mist and onto the floor. She felt a little bit of relief, but she was still winded.

A grenade landed next to her and another explosion of purple teleported her. This time, she was standing on the pool on Solomon's Porch, just above where Hudson died. He was still laying on the ground, lifeless.

Donovan materialized several feet from her with a few grenades in hand. "Stop running! Here I am. Fight me!"

Talia grunted and opened a portal over a patch of trees on the other side of the island. She didn't have proper control of the mists, but she didn't care. She owed this man a death. The portal shot lighting and set several trees on fire. With another sweep, she detached them from the ground and teleported them high above Cova. The fell pointy end down, building up speed.

"Looks like my work is done here." Donovan put the grenades away and then he extended his hand. A small puff of mist materialized and a gun was teleported right to his grip. "Thank you for all your help in my research."

Before he pulled the trigger, she opened a portal to his right. Talia targeted him with fiery trees like she was handling a machine gun. At the last second, a purple mist engulfed Donovan, and he teleported away.

The mountain side erupted with fire and splinters. Talia jumped into the water of the lake, to hide from her own fury. The sounds of trees crashing were muted under the water, even when some of the trees crashed into the lake.

When everything calmed back down, Talia resurfaced and swam to shore. Donovan was nowhere to be found.

"That was for Hudson." Talia choked and pulled herself up on the concrete slab holding in the manmade lake. Outside of the water nearly the entire landscape was on fire.

With every ounce of energy she had, she teleported her and the backpack back to Cantera Bay, in the old abandoned theater, the one place Donovan wouldn't look for her.

The sun was setting, and there were several streaks of red clouds on the horizon. A chill from the wind enveloped her wet body as she shivered and cried.

CHAPTER 24: NAPREA

Inara stepped up to the doors of the morgue. Two scribes standing guard let her in, and she walked the lonely hallway to the room where Silas's body was kept.

"I'm not sure I can do this," Inara panted. "Kiandoli will find out. She might already know I shot him. She might even know about the shield."

[Stop here. I have your suit ready. It's time to push our plan into action now.]

"So why bother dealing with the loose ends here?" Inara stopped and pulled off her ring. "This place will probably be toppled over soon anyways."

[Because we need Kiandoli's power to complete the set.]

She rubbed the ring in her fingers, activating the portal, and then stretched it out to be big enough to pull out two black boxes. She opened the first one and pulled out a slim piece of fabric. It fit her a little loosely and then it pulled itself snug.

Her HUD came to life, showing her menus and cataloging things she was seeing.

"You've made some upgrades," she purred with excitement.

"Welcome to the new Coalition armory," Donovan said in her ear.

"Oh, I've missed your voice." She scrolled through the menu to familiarize herself with the new functions. "Now, let's go get that last power."

She opened the second box and pulled out the shield of ascendance.

"Thanks for holding onto this for me," Inara said. "It looks like it still has Silas's power."

She put her ring back on under the suit and walked to the room where Silas's memory extraction was taking place. The top orb of the shield was glowing green. She held it with one hand and stood at the doorway.

In the room, Kiandoli was standing with three doctors around Silas's body.

"You're sure it was her?" Kiandoli asked. "Olivia shot Silas?"

"Yes, professor. Once everyone was clear of the room, she shot him. That is the last thing he saw before he died."

Inara slowly entered the room and the green orb in the shield flowed into her. The shield had taken Silas's powers just before death.

The three morticians fell to the ground in memory trances that Inara fed them through the air.

Kiandoli turned around.

"I like this shield," Inara said as she stepped over an unconscious mortician. "Your turn."

More memories shot into Kiandoli and she fell to the ground.

Inara knelt down and brushed the side of the shield against Kiandoli's face gently. Another orb on the back of the shield lit up.

"Thanks for your powers." Inara smiled and exited the library. "Are the soldiers in position?"

"Yes." Donovan said. "Just waiting on you now."

Inara walked outside, put the guards in a memory trance, and opened a portal on the side of her suit leg. With only a slight twisting, she pulled out a bazooka. She took aim at the entrance rim of the crater and let fire. As the rocket sailed to the rim, a small grenade fell out of the back of the bazooka. It puffed out a purple teleporting mist that enveloped her. The rocket exploded on the rim in a cloud of purple. There was a quick flash, and she was teleported from the mist enveloping her, to the mist where the rocket exploded. She was now on the top of the rim.

"That is so cool," Inara said as she tucked the bazooka back into her leg.

Then she pulled the shield back around and touched the two glowing orbs. Silas's power for sending memories over the air and Kiandoli's power for manipulating images in recordings saturated her.

A few of the rim guards came running from opposite directions.

"Olivia, are you okay?" One of them shouted.

"Never better." Inara used her new powers to shoot memory trances into the guards. Green waves of energy washed over them. Inara weaved false images into their minds, a convincing tale to get them to open up the gates and let in an small contingency of Coalitions generals.

The guards calmly walked back to their stations and opened the gates. A select few soldiers entered and took out the guards.

"What are your orders?" a general asked her.

"Take out the rest of the guards around the rim. Place charges as you go and blow it up. Once the portal is down, we can enter with floatpods. From there, just cause chaos, but leave that giant spaceship in the center alone. That's where I'll be."

She looked back down at the ship and pulled her bazooka back out. The rocket streaked across the sky and hit the base of the ship.

Once she teleported to the ship, she pulled out the entrance tube, laid in it, and was pulled in by one of the robotic droids.

"Ok, Donovan, I'm in," Inara said as she walked into the dark corridor. "Time to do a portal check."

"Seismic charges are fully operational." Donovan said on the other end of the line. "Beginning Helium Seven transport now. Oh, and set a portal grenade to frequency F-Seventeen."

Inara pulled out the grenade and dropped it. The mist exploded, and she walked through it to the Underlabs.

"Welcome home," Donovan said with a smile.

CHAPTER 25: MIRANDA

The lights flickered on and off for a moment and Miranda stirred awake. She was strapped to a bed with all kinds of medical equipment hooked up to her.

The room was large and the walls were lined with rows and rows of heavy duty doors.

A woman was throwing stuff around to her right. "No. Wrong. Not relevant. It's not here!"

Each sentence was said with a different cadence and inflection.

"Who's there?" Miranda asked.

Something crashed to the floor. "Miranda?"

The woman walked over to her and put a hand on her head. The woman was middle aged, with graying blond hair, and a few wrinkles around her eyes.

"It's okay. We are called Clarity, and we are friends of Scott." Clarity said, patting Miranda gently.

"Scott? Where is he?" Miranda asked, trying to sit up. There was surprisingly little pain, but it made her feel dizzy.

Clarity pushed her back down, removed tubes and needles from her. "He's on his way right now. He should be here any minute with Reina."

"Reina?" Miranda closed her eyes and tried to ignore the tugging and pulling on her body.

"Yes. Reina. Another snatcher. Did Scott tell you about the snatchers?" A machine beeped and Clarity hit it. "Of course he didn't! She's been unconscious since he found out about us. Okay, you're all unplugged dear."

Miranda cautiously sat up. "Are you talking to me, still?"

"Of course we are." Clarity dropped all the tubes and power cords in a pile on the floor. "It's just that some of us don't consider it rude to interrupt. We all have to have a turn speaking our mind."

Miranda opened her mouth, thinking of something to say, when a door on the opposite side of the room opened.

Scott walked in with a slender woman in a long, black dress. She had shiny black hair to match.

"Miranda!" Scott ran up the to bed and held his hands out over her body, like they had eyes and were checking to see if she was real. "You're awake. How do you feel?"

Miranda put a hand on Scott's face. It was a little scruffy. In the moment of contact, Miranda absorbed his memories. Watched them unfold at lightning speed.

"I feel fine," Miranda said as she checked for any memories with Olivia. Nothing in there about them kissing.

"You know, I can tell when you're reading my memories."

"Just catching up. We have a lot to talk about."

Scott smiled a little and put a hand on hers, holding it to his face. "Yes we do, but first we need to get out of Naprea."

"Why?" Clarity asked.

"Because I tipped Naprea to the fact Olivia is a spy from the Coalition. Whatever plans they have, I just pushed up the time table."

"I found a diagram of explosives in the Coalition database." Miranda said. "There were markers showing hundreds of precise explosives down deep in the ground under Naprea."

"That could be problematic for us specifically," Scott said.

"Why?" Miranda attempted standing up. Her body went slightly woozy, but she stood firm.

"Because we're somewhere buried in the middle of the mountain, at the base of the Naprean spaceship." Clarity threw a small box over her shoulder and scraps of paper fell everywhere. "But we can't leave yet."

"Clarity, they'll be no one left in Naprea to convince once those charges are blown!" Scott said.

"We can't just leave them here." Clarity insisted. "Maybe we can get everybody to Ascendance Rim, the snatcher's island. That was a pretty big island."

"No one will listen to any of us," Reina said, pulling her hair over her face. "And even if we ran now, we probably won't make it."

"We have to try," Scott pleaded with the group. "I don't want to be buried alive down-"

The whole room shook and rumbled. Scott caught Miranda as she fell, but a second later he fell too. Just at that moment, the lights went out.

CHAPTER 26: A CITY IN THE DUST

Talia finished the last of the water bottles and threw it into an old garbage can. Her mists were hers again, for now. But now, someone else could do what she did. Someone bad.

Before she felt invincible. Now, she felt vulnerable, alone, scared. Another tear ran down her face. She stood up, trying to get more oxygen in her breath. She put her hand in the pockets of her cloak and felt her mother's diary.

Gingerly, she pulled it out and flipped through the pages. Most of them were blank. Some of them had drawings. She blinked another tear out of her eye, and her recording vision turned on. The death memory, created by the Ancestral Branch, illuminated the book, but now there was a second memory, one attached to a single page. She flipped to it and touched the memory eagerly.

The green orb shot up to her mind, and her vision went black, replaced again by a little hut on the sandy beach. Her mother was still looking at the mirror.

"Talia. There isn't much time." She was breathing heavy. "The contractions have started. I didn't really have permission to make the recording in this diary. There are some who are very insistent on keeping Pavarti's reign alive and are doing so by violent means."

She let out a groan and clutched her stomach. Then she sat up and looked behind her for a moment.

"They should be here soon." She wiped a strand of hair out of her head. "Pavarti was using us. Experimenting on us. You are one of the reasons he didn't want the tribes intermingling. He needed to control us. Somehow... somehow having you grow inside me has done things to me. Allowed me to see things. See the future. I saw you just the other day, sailing on a purple cloud."

She shook her head. "They are coming. The other memory will probably be altered. Nothing was wrong with me. They are going to kill me when I give birth to you. Please, Talia, you have to stop this. I have seen what you can do. When you grow old, there will be no stopping you! You have to stop this from happening ever again!"

Shouts came from outside the hut. She took one last breath and picked up the ancestral branch and pointed it at the mirror. Or, Talia looked closely, it wasn't the mirror at all. She was looking at her mom from somewhere on the desk. The memory was being recorded through the page, courtesy of the branch.

She awoke from the trance. Rage filled her chest. Her fists clenched and she pulled the cloak's hood over her head.

She took a deep breath and tried to think about what Donovan could really do. Her mind wandered over the fight, contemplating what weaknesses Donovan had, if any.

It was a pretty uneven fight, but she stood up, resolved by the fact that she wasn't beaten at her best.

She was beaten at her worst. Well, now she was at her best. And that had to count for something.

She walked over to one of the theater chairs and reached under it. There she pulled out the Ancestral Branch. Then, with a quick thought, she teleported to Naprea to check on her sister.

On the other side of her mists, Naprea was in chaos. Coalition float pods filled the air like pesky bugs, blasting buildings down and shooting people struggling to get away.

Fires were covering half of the city, and the other half was caved in. Talia scanned the skyline, with the feeling that something else was off. And then she spotted it. The spaceship in the middle of the city was gone. A gaping hole in its place.

Talia closed her eyes and raised a mist over the entire floor of the city. All of the rubble, debris, and loose chunks of blunt objects fell through the floor of purple. Another, larger portal opened up in the sky.

"You know the drill, girls." Talia whispered to her mists. "Let's rain on their parade."

One portal caught the falling rocks, and the other spat them out on unsuspecting float pods.

She swooped it over the hospital and found a pack of seven float pods cornering civilians. Rocks spat out of the mists in a steady stream, crushing the float pods with ease.

It only took five minutes to wipe them all out. Her mists were fast, and she was well practiced. Towards the end, she was using great balls of fire to knock out some of the more persistent ones.

After she was sure that the soldiers were gone, she teleported to the big hole in the middle of the city. With a bit of trepidation, she sent down a mist looking for the spaceship.

The mist fell to the bottom, but nothing was there. Was the ship vaporized? She turned back around to the city and turned on her fog of war vision.

In addition to the thousands of recordings Naprea usually harbored, there were hundreds of new death memories scattered everywhere. She teleported them all to her feet.

One by one, she picked them up and threw them back when they wouldn't let her into the trance. These were meant for loved ones only. After nearly three dozen memories, she found one that made the hairs on her arms stand up.

She closed her eyes and she was in the mind of a woman who had her leg smashed in. The woman was crawling through rubble, cries of agony and pain rang all around her. The ground was shaking. The ship was shaking.

Cracks of earth sunk into the mountain as the ship steadily rose out of the ground. The woman got a good look, and saw Dixon, with Kiandoli on his back, climbing up the side of the ship and trying to open a hatch on the side.

A float pod flew over the woman and blasted her with a laser to the face. Talia blinked, and the memory was over. She teleported to the top of the mountain.

The ship was hovering, completely intact, towards Cantera Bay. It was almost there. Talia conjured two huge mists. One she sent flying towards the ship, the other towards space.

The lower mist engulfed the ship and she teleported it to outer space. Once it was there, she teleported to the cryo-chamber room.

People were floating everywhere. Miranda was caught on the railing of a catwalk, Scott was in mid air, losing blood, and Dixon was anchored to a desk. Kiandoli was there as well, tumbling aimlessly in the air in a fight with Clarity.

She teleported over to Scott and slapped him in the face. "Scott! Wake up!"

Scott gently touched her and she could feel a green orb of energy leave her. He let out a grunt and pushed her away. He floated back and cried out in pain again. His blood started turning dark.

Dixon pushed off of his ledge and floated towards them. Talia extended her hand and the Ancestral Branch appeared. She shot Dixon, Kiandoli and another woman in a long black dress.

"Miranda!" Talia shouted and teleported Dixon next to Miranda. "I've erased all of Dixon's memories. Restore what you have in your archive stone!"

Miranda nodded and touched her archive stone to Dixon's cheek.

Scott let out another scream of pain. The blood was starting the thicken. Talia shot him with a memory trance orb and teleported next to Miranda.

"Ok sis. I'm going to give Scott his pills." Talia said as she floated next to them. "You need to take a fresh life memory of everybody here. We may need it with Kiandoli on the ship."

"Why don't you just wipe her memories?" Miranda asked as she touched Talia's hand with a smile. A small green river flowed between them.

"Good point." Talia reached into Scott's pocket and pulled out the bottle of pills. She opened the cap and the pills went spilling out everywhere. She let out a curse and then conjured another portal to sweep them up from their floating trajectories. "One thing at a time. Do you know how many pills he takes for this?"

Miranda shrugged her shoulders and patted Dixon on the back as he woke up from the memory transfer. "It seems like he takes more and more all the time."

Concentrating very hard, she opened a small portal inside Scott's stomach. Slowly, she deposited all of the pills inside.

"He never kissed her," Miranda whispered behind her.

"Who kissed who now?" Talia asked.

"Nothing." Miranda said, as Dixon started to wake up. "It's just that I must have seen something wrong is all."

After a moment, Scott snapped awake and looked around the room. "Are we dead?"

"Something I ask myself more frequently these days," Dixon laughed behind them. "Seriously, what's going on?"

"Yeah, why are we floating?" Miranda asked.

"That's my doing." Talia said, and then she gestured to the wide expanse of the room. "Donovan stole this ship, and I wanted to take it back, so I teleported it to space."

The group of friends looked at her with shock.

"I... didn't know you could do that." Scott said slowly.

"So, what do we do now?" Miranda asked.

Talia teleported Kiandoli, Clarity, and the girl in the black dress to the beds she saw in the back. Then she teleported inside next to them and strapped them to the beds.

After she was sure they were secure, she teleported her friends to the abandoned theater. "Now, we plan. And then we finish this."

CHAPTER 27: THE GATHERING

"How do you know about this place?" Miranda asked the question she knew the other two were thinking. This was the place it all started for them: The building that Miranda experienced her first memory trance, where Scott was infected, and where Dixon's sister was paralyzed.

"Nevermind that." Talia waved her arms dismissively. "We need to sit down and work out what each of us knows. We need to figure out what he's planning to do with that ship."

"Everybody sit down, here in a circle." Miranda gestured to the floor and sat cross-legged. "I have a way of speeding that up. And I may even pick up on a few details you missed."

The four of them sat cross-legged next to her in a circle, Talia to her left, Scott to her right, and Dixon across from her. She took Scott and Talia's hands and they did the same with Dixon.

"Okay. I'm going to pull and play all of our memories from the last few months over again." Miranda took in a breath. "Don't resist it. By the time I'm done, we should all know what everybody else knows."

The other three nodded in agreement. She took another breath, closed her eyes and concentrated on the memories between the four of them.

Green rivers of energy flowed between their arms and then spilled over into the middle of their circle. They formed a massive orb, and hundreds of memories flashed across the surface.

Dixon's memories were light. She saw him chase down someone Donovan had soul jumped, the attempted break out, and Silas' deal with Olivia to brainwash him with Kiandoli. After that, it was a blank.

Scott was all over the place. Saving Olivia, and then finding out she was Inara, someone Miranda was sure was dead. Then, the discovery of other scribes, and a glimpse of their knowledge of Pavarti's experiments.

Miranda's memories flashed next. The constant hiding and infiltration, the plot to kill Donovan, stopping the coalition from sending tetrapath to earth, and eventually, they saw how she got her new scars.

Talia's memories came last. Miranda's heart sank multiple times as she saw what Talia went through. Her mists growing out of control and possibly bending the concept of time, the thrill of love, the agony of loss, the three relics, and finally, the weeks of isolation while her mists were manufactured.

The rest blurred together, and the four of them snapped out of the trance, fresh tears were running down Miranda's face. She didn't know how to react to Talia, and while she was relieved to find that Scott had not been with Olivia, she felt guilty of the treatment she had given him.

The others had already started talking before she could catch up.

"Donovan and Inara can teleport like you now?" Dixon asked.

"He's trying to restart Pavarti's experiments." Talia snapped her fingers. "That's why he wanted the relics! Perfect control over his subjects."

"He'll kill hundreds of people." Dixon insisted. "He'll hunt us all down."

Talia was the first to stand up. "I'm done watching people suffer at the hand of Pavarti and his followers. We're putting a stop to this now."

"How?" Miranda asked.

"I'm going to teleport something really heavy on top of the Illurium building. Maybe a mountain." Talia bushed a strand of hair out of her face. Miranda noticed her hair was a lot longer. Last she remembered it, Talia's hair was shoulder length. Behind the cloak she was wearing, it looked like it could be down to her waist now. "Oh wait! I have a massive space ship! I could drop that on them!"

"Talia, there are some innocent people in that building," Miranda protested.

"Well, first we have to make sure he doesn't get that ship." Scott said. "He was able to pull it out of the ground. My guess is, he'll be able to bring it back down from space."

"It's already back in the atmosphere," Talia said, her eyes darting about like she was in a vivid dream. "A few thousand miles away, but he's guiding it with rockets."

"So what do we do with it?"

"Can you crash it into a moon or something?" Dixon asked.

"I've never used a portal outside of the atmosphere." Talia said. "And I'd have to get some massive momentum out of it. It is moving pretty slow right now."

"Talia, can you see if Donovan is there, on the ship?" Scott asked. "Maybe we can teleport the ship to space one more time and force him out of an airlock or something."

"We'd have to disable his portals first." Talia said. "That guy can move around like I can."

"Not quite." Miranda corrected. "I watched that duel he had with you. He was playing you. He can only teleport to preset locations. If he doesn't have a receiver mist, he can't go there."

Talia smiled a little bit. "Just checked. He's on the bridge. Somebody is giving him reports on super Helium being teleported from a moon."

"That's how he did it!" Miranda shook her hand, which had one finger pointing to the ceiling. It should have been obvious from the start. "He filled the hull with super helium, strapped a few rockets to the hull for guidance, and pulled it out of the loose soil. Talia, can you get me to his helium portals?"

"Yes." Talia lifted her arms.

"Wait!" Scott held up his hands. "Before you go splitting us up, there is something we need to do."

Scott closed his eyes, and Miranda felt something warm and enter her mind.

[Can you all hear me?] Scott's voice echoed through her head.

"Yes." They all said aloud.

[Picked it up from Clarity. Now, if we need to split up, we can still talk to each other.]

"Perfect." Miranda said. "Talia, I'm ready. Teleport me to my old lab on the ship first."

A cloud of purple washed over her and she was teleported to the ship. Gravity was mostly back in effect, the ship had descended quite a bit during their planning. Her lab was practically untouched. There were a few things that fell of the counters during the takeoff, but nothing was missing or destroyed.

She rounded the counter and opened her hidden cabinet. All of her supplies were still there. The handgun, the EMP disks, and even a few frequency scanners. She pulled all of these out and put them in her pockets.

Miranda concentrated really hard on her thoughts. [OK, send me to the hull. I need to find those helium portals.]

Another portal washed over her and she was in another part of the ship. This was a huge, lopsided room, not intended for people, but as an air pocket in case the ship needed to land in water. The floor was lined with active portals, and the air smelled like gas.

Miranda took shallow breaths as she knelt down and put her frequency scanner on the closest portal to her. It clicked a few times, and she picked it back up.

[Done. Ready to come back now.]

"It looks like he is piping the helium in from one of the moons." Miranda said when she was teleported back to the old theater. Her voice was a little high pitched. "Talia, if you teleport the ship back into space, he'll just keep bringing it back into the atmosphere. But if we can fill that with enough of the Helium that no rocket blast could bring it down, we could keep it stuck up there."

Talia looked hesitant. "If he cuts the portal with my mist on the other side, I could lose it forever."

"It's not a perfect plan, but it's what I've got." Miranda said. "Any other ideas?"

Dixon shook his head. "We'll keep Donovan distracted while you do it."

"We've got to go now." Miranda handed her handgun to Dixon. "The ship's already in the atmosphere."

They were teleported back to Miranda's lab. Everything was still quiet. The ship was swaying gently in the sky as it descended back to the surface.

"No." Scott shook his head. "Donovan would look here first. Take us somewhere random. Somewhere easier to defend."

Another mist washed over them and they were in a dining hall. It was a large room with nothing but cafeteria tables, and a few pillars. Some of the cafeteria tables were overturned, but most of them were still lined up in neat rows.

"This will work." Scott shrugged his shoulders.

"Okay." Talia sat cross legged on the floor. "One mist through the portals, and the other ready to bring helium."

"Flip these tables to make a perimeter." Dixon said, pointing in a circle around Talia.

The tables were pushed around with loud grinding noises until there was a fence of tables around Talia. Miranda was about to suggest a second layer when she turned around and saw a purple mist on the other side of the room.

[We've got company.] Miranda thought in her head.

Scott and Dixon turned to face the mists.

"Welcome aboard the Naprea!" Donovan shouted as he walked out of the mist with twelve soldiers. Inara was standing next to him with a smug smile on her face. "This truly is an impressive ship!"

Miranda activated her frequency scanner and pointed it at the mist. "I'm surprised you didn't rip it in half with your little stunt. "

"I know." Donovan smiled. "Like I said, impressive. I can't wait to put it to use again. Just think of all the achievements I could reach. Cova will be perfected, and then we go to Earth!"

The scanner beeped and showed her the location of Donovan's portal mist. The Underlabs.

"What I really wanted to show you though, was my new tetrapath infection." Donovan and Inara took a small step back and the soldiers stepped forward.

In an instant, the soldiers' armor burst off as they grew taller than a normal tetrapath. Their skin crackled open and it was replaced with new, thicker skin. Their hands distorted into pristine shapes of weapons. Battle axes, swords, spiked clubs, and one even looked like it had a spinning propeller.

"Bigger, smarter." Donovan held up his hands. "And easier to control."

The beasts all charged at once. One came right at Miranda and she moved to put a pillar between herself and it. It sliced through the pillar like it was butter and kept charging her.

She ran backwards, hopping over and under tables, trying to shake the monster. From this close, it resembled a bear more than any of the tetrapath she had encountered before.

She ducked under a swiping blow and rolled past the monster as it brought the axe arm smashing down through a table next to her.

[I can't soul jump them!] Dixon shouted in her mind.

[I'm hit!] Scott shouted next. [Dixon, let me borrow your powers!]

From behind her, she could see Scott slapping Dixon's head and charging into a cluster of tetrapath. The tetrapath infection inside him was already aiding his strength.

[This is different.] Scott said as he jumped on the back of a tetrapath and snapped his neck. He fell to the ground and screamed. [I might not make this one.]

The monster chasing Miranda hooked his axe into a table and picked it up like it was made of paper. He then spun and threw it at her.

She rolled on the ground and it flew right over her back, crashing into one of the barricade tables around Talia.

[I won't be able to hold this much longer!] Talia shouted.

[Those mists behind Donovan lead to the Underlabs.] Miranda said as she pushed herself up and ran. [Scott, I can get you the cure, and maybe I can stop more of these things from coming through.]

[Do it.] Came the response from all three of her friends.

Miranda leaped over a table just as it was smashed in half by another tetrapath. She hit the ground and with a few more steps, she was through the mist.

On the other side, there was a small platoon of soldiers, waiting as backup. Miranda slapped the closest one with her archive stone, and pulled out a grenade from his belt. She primed it and ran right at the group of soldiers.

They cleared the way, trying to avoid the impending blast. It was only a few short steps to the cubicle exit and the door was already open.

"Stop her!" Inara yelled from behind her.

Miranda turned at the door and threw her grenade at the portal generator. The room exploded, and one connection to the ship was severed.

She took a brief moment to reorient herself. The cubicle labs were still laid out in the easy to navigate grid system. The overlook room of glass on the ceiling marked her target. Behind that room was the tetrapath cure.

Inara charged out of the cubicle lab and gave chase. Miranda darted around several cubicles, trying to keep her guessing about directions.

"Do you even know where you're going?" Inara called out behind her.

Miranda turned the corner and ran into a research assistant. She stumbled over him and hit the metallic floor hard. She pushed herself up using his face, and took a few bits of his life memory in the process.

A gun shot rang out, and Miranda could almost feel the wind of the bullet screaming past her leg. She jumped around the corner of the cubicle to her right, and then darted immediately left around the next cubicle. She was glad the cubicle labs were tall and could conceal her direction.

"Give it up," Inara said. "The camera feeds are on my HUD. I can see which way you're going."

Miranda scanned through the stolen memory for anything she could use. Portals, tetrapath enhancements. Inara took another shot. This time, it felt like the bullet grazed her cheek.

Miranda backpedaled and ran into the cubicle door she was close to. This was another empty portal room, and it wasn't activated. She ran behind the door and waited for Inara to come through. When she did, Miranda tripped her and ran back out the door.

Something in the room exploded, and Miranda turned back to look. A giant ball of purple was sucking everything in the room into it with tremendous force.

"They created a portal with a vacuum on the other side?" Miranda asked in disbelief.

Two soldiers grabbed her arms. The soldier on her left held her wrist, and she twisted it to make contact with the archive stone. That soldier fell down, and Miranda pushed into the soldier on her right.

He tripped and flew through the door to the lab and through the portal in the middle of the room. Miranda slid slightly closer to the door and leapt out of the way of the vacuum.

Miranda knelt down and picked up the other soldier's helmet, datapad, and a few grenades. The portal in the lab shut off and Miranda made her way up the stairs to the control room.

[Miranda, we need a new plan!] Talia shouted in her head. [Donovan's cut off the helium portals! Dixon and I are trying to hold off the tetrapath, but Scott's shaking on the floor!]

[I'm trying to get the cure. That's the best I can do right now.]

She reached the lab and more bullets hit the glass walls as she entered. Inara was now on the stairs and running up.

On the other side of the control room, Miranda reached the hallway that lead to the exit elevator. It also had a few doors on the side. The first door on the left was where Donovan kept the cure to the tetrapath infection.

She took that door, ran to the back rack and grabbed a few vials of the cure. Her fingers fumbled with the stolen helmet, but she was able to use it to set the frequency of her stolen grenades. One to open near Donovan, and another to teleport to a space satellite.

The grenade portal to Donovan opened.

[Cure is coming to you! Portal on Donovan's arm!] Miranda thought as she reached her arm through the mist and threw several jars of the cure through portal on Donovan's arm.

The mist disappeared and Inara stepped through the door.

"Time's up." Inara took a few steps into the room and swung the pistol to aim for Miranda's head.

Miranda switched the frequency scanner to a frequency jammer and activated it. Inara looked confused for a second. "What good is turning off my portals?"

All at once, Inara's suit portals deposited everything inside of them on to the floor between them. And then they shut off.

"Wouldn't want you running away." Miranda shouted as she leapt for the handgun that fell out of Inara's leg.

Miranda scooped up the gun and shot Inara over and over again.

Inara smiled while her suit hardened and became bullet proof. "Unless you have a magic EMP machine, you'll never breach the suit with bullets."

Miranda kept firing. As long as the suit was in bullet proof mode, it couldn't move. But with the portal disabled in the gun as well, the bullets would run out.

As she fired the gun, she moved around the room, picking up other guns and grenades. The Shield of Ascendance lay on the ground. Miranda picked that up and slung it over her shoulder.

The first gun emptied. She dropped it and Inara charged. But the suit hardened again when Miranda resumed shooting her with a new gun. She spaced out the timing of each shot to keep Inara still while conserving bullets to a degree.

"You never did figure out this problem, did you?" Miranda shouted as she hit Inara with round after round.

"Your friend Dixon was able to make it work."

"Yeah. By melting his way through the floor." Miranda changed guns again. "Go ahead. See how far down into the crust of Cova you'll reach before getting stuck."

"You'll run out of bullets sometime."

"Pretty soon, actually." Miranda primed several grenades and put her back to the door. "

She opened the door and slammed it back on Inara. Dozens of explosions thundered in the room and Miranda dropped the frequency blocker on the ground in the hallway.

She ran as fast as she could back to the glass enclosure control room. The room itself was impervious to the frequency blocker. She programmed a portal grenade for a satellite in space and rolled it to the edge.

She ran out the other door and slammed it shut. There she waited and hoped Inara would make a tactical mistake.

The portal grenade exploded and inside that room the vacuum of space was total.

Inara pushed through the exit door, and the look of terror did not even have the time to register on Inara's face. Her suit, not longer connected to its power source via portal, was out of power. And while normally, her suit would become adhesive and keep her rooted to the ground, it couldn't do that now. She was sucked into the vortex in an instant.

Miranda let out a sigh of relief, waited for the portal to dissipate, and then entered the control room, ready to cause chaos.

CHAPTER 28: CRUISE LINER

Another table was smashed to the side like rotted wood. Talia let out a shrill squeak as the guttural sounds of attacking tetrapath drew nearer. From somewhere behind her, Dixon shouted.

"What's the matter, Talia? All out of portals?" Donovan taunted her.

Talia concentrated on a message for her sister. [Miranda, we can't hold here. I can't let my friends die. I'm doing something about this.]

Message sent, Talia stood up and faced Donovan. He smiled his crooked smile and two tetrapath rushed her.

Talia brought her closer portal back into the room and swept it over them, but they did not budge. The mists rolled over them like a regular cloud.

"New feature," Donovan said as if he were describing a computer instead of a death monster. "Your mists wash right over them. Is that my super helium coming out of your mists?"

There was an odd flash in Talia's eyes. Donovan's helium portals were no longer working. Her other mist was on the other side of those portals. One of the more distant moons of Cova. She tried to summon it, but it only moved so fast.

She fell to the ground and shrieked. It felt like someone had ripped her ribs out of her chest. A tetrapath leapt at her and she opened her portal instinctively.

The vacuum of space filled the room. Her other portal was floating between a moon and Cova, and the other was set in the room.

Several tables lifted off the ground and the tetrapath in front of her shot through the mist. Talia flew off the ground as well. She closed the portal and fell onto the ground, rolling.

A table crashed to her right, the tetrapath slammed into the ceiling behind her and fell to the ground.

[Cure is coming to you! Portal on Donovan's arm!] Miranda shouted.

A puff of purple mist flashed on Donovan's arm. Talia opened her portal in the center of the room, the vacuum of space pulled everything there.

She closed the portal and leapt into the air. The small container Miranda had teleported was flying right towards her. She caught it and tossed it to Dixon. He caught it and made his way to Scott.

"That's a nice trick," Donovan said. "I have one just like it. Have a look."

He threw a grenade into the air and a puff of purple erupted. Once again, the vacuum of space filled the room. Talia was pulled off the ground, and went tumbling towards the open portal. Scott and Dixon were both tumbling as well.

Talia closed her eyes and focused on her portals.

[Close your eyes, you two!] Talia shouted to them. [And Dixon, hang on to that cure!]

She swept her mist over them, and they were sucked into space. They stopped spinning around and Talia swept the space mist over them, sending them to another part of the ship.

She landed hard on the ground, but she was hurting more from the extreme cold. Dixon coughed next to her, and shook as he force fed the cure to Scott.

"Don't ever do that again." Dixon said.

"Sorry," Talia said as both mists returned to her in the room. "Had to improvise. But now I'm whole again."

"Good." Dixon sat back against a wall as Scott's breathing calmed down. "Because we're going to need you at your best right now."

"Donovan knows all of my tricks." Talia said. "His tetrapath can't be teleported, he knows I'm running out of power..."

"Talia, he's no match for you. He's been controlling the terms of the fight from the beginning. And in those terms he can corner you. You have to break the rickety box he has you trapped in and show him that he is no match for you."

Talia reached in her pocket and felt her mother's diary. "Let's sink it." Talia said.

"What?" Dixon asked.

"I can't keep it in orbit forever. Let's crash it into the bottom of the ocean." Talia made sure to concentrate on that last thought so Miranda could hear as well.

[Good idea!] Miranda responded.

Scott moaned a little and tried to sit up.

"When he's up, you guys need to go make sure all of Donovan's helium portals stay offline." Talia closed her eyes and swept the soul jumper's island with her teleporting mist. Seconds later, several dead tetrapath were teleported onto the ground next to Dixon. "You should be able to soul jump these. Use them to fight off whatever Donovan throws at you."

"What are you going to do?"

Talia teleported a space suit into her arms. "Take out the rockets he has attached to the side of the ship."

She put on the suit over her cloak and teleported outside to the surface of the ship. The entire skin was covered with small portals. Each one would spit out flames periodically, keeping the ship steady in the air.

Two portals were conjured, letting out all of the stored helium in the ship. There was a noticeable dip in their altitude, but the ship remained stable, making its way slowly to the Underlabs.

She brought her portals close to her, and used them as a spy glass to see what was directly below them. Ocean.

[Talia, you should flood the Underlabs.] Miranda said.

[Aren't you in the Underlabs?]

[I have a way out. Just warn me when it's about to hit.]

Talia took a breath and teleported back into the cafeteria. Donovan was standing there, with more tetrapath at his command.

"Nice suit. Are you going to send us back to space again? Or have you come back for another duel?" A mist appeared in Donovan's hand. Talia knew what it was before the mist was done forming. The Dominion Rod. "Looks like your sister managed to take over my Underlabs, but these tetrapath should be enough to kill you."

"You have no idea what it takes to kill me."

The entire floor was engulfed with mist. Talia and the tables fell through it and into free fall under the ship. She spun around to look at the ship again and teleported it closer to space. With another thought, she teleported back to the top of the ship.

After she was sure the tables were going fast enough, she opened another portal under them, and a portal on the underside of the ship.

The tables shot out of the second portal, slamming into the rockets Donovan had attached to the hull. The ship quickly tipped over so the front nose was pointing down, and it fell.

As the tables bounced off of the hull, Talia teleported them back, slamming them into more of the rockets. The ship was falling at a faster and faster rate.

The ship was in free fall for a good minute when tetrapath came crawling out of the side of the ship in little maintenance tubes. Donovan stepped out with them.

Talia smiled and teleported left over shrapnel from the tables to strike the tubes with force. They exploded, and most of the tetrapath were launched off the hull.

The rest jumped out of the way and popped out wings. They were now flying down with her.

Talia held out her hands in the free fall, swerving between two dead tetrapath. She was now about twenty feet away from the hull, and falling straight down with the ship. From here, she could see the destination. The Illurium building. The idea of crushing it was still tempting.

Three tetrapath swooped towards her. Two with axes for hands, and a third that looked like it had a beehive network attached to its shoulders. Talia conjured a large portal along the side of the ship, gathering the fire from all of the remaining rockets attached to it.

Another portal was conjured and it spat out a hot beam of fire at the tetrapath. She swept her mist over two of them, melting them like insects.

The final tetrapath swerved to her left to avoid the blast. Talia's portal followed, but the tetrapath proved too elusive. It spun and shot something out of its beehive holes.

Talia tried to swerve out of the way, but one of the blasts hit her on the shoulder, tearing her space suit. Her shoulder burned, and she spun out of control.

The tetrapath fired again, this time missing her and hitting the ship. The world was spinning too fast. Her stomach grew nauseous, and she was having a hard time concentrating.

She could hear the sound of the tetrapath shooting over and over again.

Talia teleported to the side of the ship and clung on for dear life. That stopped the spinning. But her body still felt the effects.

The tetrapath swooped down and landed on the ship and slowly crawled to her. The beehive like holes widened and made clicking sounds.

Talia closed her eyes and conjured a portal right over the tetrapath.

The mists thickened and lightning struck. Fire incinerated the monster in seconds.

Donovan pulled out a gun and shot at her. Her mist formed a shield, and she teleported the bullets to the rockets, taking them out one by one.

"Looks like you forgot to make your bullets portal proof!" She shouted into the wind. It wasn't likely that he heard her, but she felt good nonetheless.

She teleported back out so she was falling parallel with the ship again. Here, she could see how far they were from the ground. They were getting close, and they were falling faster than she had ever fallen in her life. He shoulder burned from the sheer speed pummeled it through the suit.

She brought her arms in and conjured a large portal. It covered the entire ship, and extended down almost to the top of the Illurium building.

[Sis, if you're still in the Underlabs, now is a good time to get out.]

[I have a way out. Do it now, the tunnel gates are open.]

Talia took a quick look at Cantera Bay below them while Donovan shot blindly at her. The Illurium building was still right under them. Just to the east was the crescent bay that held her broken down theater. On the other side of the theater was a naval dock, complete with a tunnel that led to the Underlabs.

[Scott, Dixon. Hang on.]

They were inches from crashing into the Underlabs when she teleported the ship out over the middle of the ocean. The ship crashed with a thunderous explosion. Talia teleported herself back to Cantera Bay, and used her momentum to shoot back into the sky.

She opened another portal over the splash in the shape of a giant dome. The water entered the portal with explosive force. She opened another portal right over the supply entrance tunnel of the underlabs. Water rushed down the tunnel and slammed into labs.

[What was that?] Miranda screamed her thoughts. [Oh. It was Donovan. He just crashed through his own lab! Looks like his suit wasn't strong enough to handle that! Talia, I've got the Dominion Rod and the Shield!]

[What are you still doing there? The wave is coming!]

Talia desperately shot both of her portals down to the labs, but they bounced out, useless. She was running out of momentum. She would start falling soon.

[I have a way ou-]

Miranda's voice was cut from her mind with a piercing silence.

[Sis? Sis!] Talia shouted the words over and over in her head.

[Talia!] Scott shouted. [Help! We're sinking!]

Talia reached the tip of her flight, and hung in the air for nearly a second. Before she started falling, she teleported back to the Cryogenics lab on the ship.

She wobbled for a moment, and then fell to the ground. The room was spinning. Her mist appeared unbidden with a thunderous crack.

"That'll do nicely," Came the cooing voice of the Phantom Queen. "Now we're ready to bring our attack to them."

The mist disappeared and Talia fell to the ground, All of the energy sapped out of her.

[Dixon. Cyo-] That was the most she could do. Thinking hurt too much.

CHAPTER 29:
ANOTHER WHITLOCK DEATH MEMORY

Scott and Dixon came running into the room and picked Talia up. Her arms were limp, and her head was ringing. The walls shook and made crumpling metal noises. They were sinking into the depths of the ocean.

"Talia!" Scott's voice came to her as an echo, like her ears were damaged. "Talia, we need to get out of here. Teleport us out!"

Talia shook her head, feebly. "They're gone. They won't come back."

She couldn't even lift her arms to show them. Her mind slowly turned around the realities. They were stuck in a sinking ship. She couldn't save her friends, and her sister was already dead. Clarity lay motionless on the floor next to her. Talia had a vague recollection of her portals electrocuting Clarity.

"I killed her," Talia said. That truth hurt the worst of all. "I should have lifted the ship higher again. Given her more time to get out of the Underlabs."

Scott gave her a look like he wanted to console her, but his patience with the situation was running out.

"Miranda made her own choice," Dixon said. "She told you to sink it then. We'll have time to mourn her loss. Right now, we need to get out of here."

Slowly, memories from Miranda came into her view. Infiltrating the coalition, hating and then loving Scott for his actions with Olivia, and discovering Doctor Pavarti's secret portals.

Scott pulled the space helmet and suit off her. She didn't fight it. Her hands flopped uselessly to her sides and hit her mother's diary.

"Miranda will have a death memory!" Talia shouted, the realization making her sit up right. "We need to go get it! Oh Scott, it could be for you!"

"We need to get out of here first," Scott picked her up. "Are you sure your portals are gone?"

"Yes. They killed Clarity!" Talia shook off Scott's arm, and pointed to Clarity on the floor.

Scott checked her pulse. "No, she's alive."

"For now," Talia said.

Scott picked Clarity up and put her on his shoulders. "We will save her."

Talia shook her head. "There's no time. But, there is another way out of here."

"What's that?" Scott asked.

"Miranda discovered what Donovan was using to island hop." Talia looked between the two men, their faces were scrunched in confusion. "The hidden portal system! Pavarti's hidden portal system! That extends here! We need to activate it and it will take us anywhere on Cova we want to go!"

"Brilliant!" Dixon said. "But how do we get there?"

Talia closed her eyes and focused on the details Miranda had painstakingly recorded. The hidden portal system was a complex maze. Finally she found what she was looking for.

"In the engine room, there's a switch," Talia began.

"It turns on all of the portals! And there is even a portal in that room!" Dixon completed the thought.

The ship groaned and shook. Gravity gave way just a little bit, indicating they were sinking faster.

"Let's get going," Scott said.

"What about those people Talia tied to beds back there?" Dixon asked.

Talia rubbed her head and looked around the room with her new vision for planted memories. She found a recorded memory glowing a very dull green behind a panel by the stairs. "Broken panel by the stairs. I mean... I checked them. They're all dead." Talia shook her head and grew worried at the worried looks Scott and Dixon were giving her. "What?"

"Are you okay?" Dixon put an arm around her shoulder.

"I'm fine." Talia shook her head and pointed to the exit. "Let's go."

They left the room and got in the elevator, followed behind by three very badly tattered tetrapath under the control of Dixon's soul jump. Scott pushed on the controls and the elevator sped along towards the back of the ship.

Talia kept revisiting Miranda's memories, trying to remember all of the portal connection points, how to work the controls to help her pick the right destination through the portal. Anything but the death of her sister.

The elevator stopped and opened right to the engine room. It was more massive than she was expecting. Catwalks, large pipes and tubes, giant boxes and control grids were laid out in another complicated maze.

A thin layer of water lapped at her ankles, and the sound of rushing water could be heard nearby. The three looked at each other and began sloshing through the engine room in search of the switch.

After several minutes of searching, the water was up to her knees. They turned a corner and found it almost at the same time. A small control panel with a hidden latch, revealing another control panel.

Talia ran towards it and lifted the panel. Without thinking, she activated all of the portals in the ship. They hummed to life, at the same time a pair of shrill shrieks rang out behind them. Five tetrapath were charging through the water towards them.

They already looked beat up, cut and smashed.

"I thought I killed these guys." Dixon sighed he controlled his tetrapath to counter attack.

The ship lurched and gravity very suddenly went sideways. Talia clung onto the control panel and Scott managed to cling onto a nearby catwalk. Dixon fell and landed hard on his back.

"Dixon!" Talia shouted.

The ship continued to roll, and gravity was now pointing at the ceiling. Dixon barely caught onto a railing before he fell again. The ship rotated another ninety degrees and they were almost normal again.

Water now flooded the portal closest to the control panel. But there was another one up on the catwalk Scott was on. She tuned that one to Cantera Bay.

"Dixon! Are you okay?" Talia shouted as she turned around to get a good look at him.

Three tetrapath monsters were flying at her. She dropped to the next railing down to avoid their attacks. Scott, who was above her now, set Clarity down and jumped onto the tetrapath from above.

He slammed it onto a pipe and blood splattered everywhere. They converged on him, just as Dixon's tetrapath leaped out and impaled the roaming tetrapath in the back. A tumbled mess of monster fell, slamming into a large pipe. Blood splattered all along the pipe, and the monsters fell into the water below.

"I'm not sure they're dead," Dixon said. "We need to get out of here."

"There's an open portal up on the catwalk Scott was on," Talia said, pointing above them. "We'll have to climb."

[Talia? Scott? Dixon?]

The voice all at once sent chills and disbelief and joy through her body.

[Miranda? You're alive?] Scott was the first able to give a response.

[Yes, sorry. I had to take a portal to Earth! I was knocked unconscious for a little while, but I'm up and running now! But I can't get back.]

[That's ok. We're coming to you!] Talia climbed her way back to the control panel. [What part of Earth?]

[Uh, A something. America? Africa? Albania?]

[Which one?]

[America... Try America.]

Talia programmed the portal for America, Too happy to care that her sister wasn't being specific.

[I can't believe you're alive, sis. I thought I lost you!]

[It was clo-]

Talia didn't hear another word from her sister. The room shook violently. Half of the wall ripped apart as the wall split open on a jagged underwater mountain.

Talia was knocked in the air, tumbling uncontrollably. She landed hard on her head, and then a large pipe fell on top of her, pinning her legs to the ground. A new tetrapath landed right next to her, limp and lifeless.

Water splashed around her ears. She looked up at the massive holes in the ceiling carved out by the rocky bottom of the ocean. Water was gushing though at an alarming rate. She took a deep breath as the water rose over her.

She looked to her side. Dixon was holding his head and slowly getting up as the water filled up past his legs. He was up and floating in seconds.

He saw her and swam over to try to lift the pipe.

[It's too heavy Dixon. Swim to the portal.]

[I'm not leaving you.]

The tetrapath floated and bumped into her.

[Scott, do you still have the cure?]

[I think so... Yes. I have it right here. Why?]

[Hold onto it. I'm going to try something.]

It was a desperate plan. One she knew that had little hope of working. But it was better than drowning. The plan hinged on a big if. If Scott's powers could amplify with the infection, maybe hers could too.

She reached into the mouth of the tetrapath and punctured her hand on its teeth. Her body convulsed instantly. Her blood thickened. She screamed uncontrollably, losing all of her air.

[Talia!] Dixon called out in her mind. [What are you doing?]

It was too late. She was halfway to being a monster. But it worked. He portals came into being. With a mighty swipe of her arm, she teleported Scott, Dixon and Clarity to the catwalk right in front of the portal. And then she brought her mist back to teleport herself up to the catwalk.

The mists washed right over her. In panic, and with no air left in her lungs, she tried again. And again. This time, with her other portal. It would not take her away.

Desperate, she tried to teleport the pipe wedging her down. It would not budge. And then Donovan's words rang in her head, taunting her.

"New feature. Your mists wash right over them."

The tetrapath were portal proof, and now she was one of them. She was portal proof. The pipe above her was covered in tetrapath blood. It too, was portal proof.

She looked up, the water level was nearly twenty feet above her now.

[Talia?] Dixon called out. [What's happening?]

[The tetrapath are portal proof. No time to save me now. Go after Miranda.]

Dixon dived into the water, but Talia teleported him back to the catwalk.

"No!" he shouted.

Talia could hear his anguished cry through her portals. She spread a thick mist over the water to prevent him from diving in, and another to teleport him back to the catwalk.

Her lungs ached for air, and her vision was growing spotty. The monster within her thrashed and tried to free itself. But not even the new strength could lift the pipe.

With her last ounce of energy she groped around in her cloak pocket. There, was her mother's diary and the ancestral branch. A green orb seeped into a page of the diary, and it floated out of her hands. The world grew dark as her death memory floated up to the surface.

CHAPTER 30: PAVARTI'S LEGACY

[20 minutes ago]

Kiandoli's head was spinning as the lights in the cryo-lab flickered in and out. She took in a deep breath, bracing for any more turbulence. To her right, strapped to a bed as she was, the two scribes let out a soft moan.

"I think we've landed." She said, feebly grabbing the woman in the black dress by the hand. "See if you can undo the straps."

In seconds, she was in the woman's mind, manipulating and changing events. She found out all about her. This was Rein, a sad girl who could make others sad.

They weren't the most secure. Reina was free and halfway through freeing Kiandoli when a purple fog appeared in the middle of the room. A small girl in a baggy space suit materialized.

"Reina!" Kiandoli snapped. "The teleporting girl. Get her!"

Reina put a hand on Talia's exposed shoulder.

Across the room, strapped to another bed was one of her old subjects. Older now, as she was. The woman with over a dozen life memories stuck in her. The woman did not stir. Still, better to be safe.

She placed a hand on her face and put the woman into a deep memory trance. Sure that there would be no disturbances, Kiandoli walked to the middle of the cryo-lab and knelt down next to the teleporting girl.

"This is perfect." Kiandoli said as she opened the girl's helmet, and placed her hand on her head.

"I think the ship is sinking." Reina said, kneeling beside her.

"And her friends are here too! That is the only reason she would come back here." The details of the last few hours rushed through her mind as she prepared to alter the girl's memories. "Oh, her sister is dead! And the others are coming. This will be handy."

Small details of the girl's life fit into place and then Kiandoli used them to her advantage. The hidden memory vision, the knowledge of Pavarti's portal system, everything.

"I hate to be a pest while you're working, but how do we plan on getting out of here?" Reina asked.

"This little girl will help us. I'm motivating her right now to turn on the portals. And from there, we can make our way back to whatever is left of Naprea. Go and drag that other woman, Clarity to lay down right next to Talia here."

They finished up and made their way back to the beds. Just as they crouched out of sight, Scott and Dixon came rushing in to help Talia.

They talked for a while, arguing about how to get out of the sinking ship. The girl was playing her programmed part. Claiming her portals were out of use, and the portals killed Clarity, and slowly coming to the realization that she needed to activate the portals on the ship.

After a few minutes, the girl shouted. "Broken panel by the stairs."

Kiandoli got a good look at where the girl was focusing. After a few more exchanges, the three of them left the room.

"Oh, perfect!" Kiandoli shouted as she got up from her hiding place.

Just under the stairs that lead to the second level of cryo chambers there was a broken panel. She pried on it and on the other side was a red velvet box.

"What are you doing?" Reina almost shouted behind her. "We have to get out of here! Don't you hear that grinding noise? We're sinking to the bottom of the ocean!"

"I thought I programmed you to be more patient." Kiandoli turned around, holding the box.

Reina gave her a confused look, but Kiandoli just darted around her and began checking on the frozen people stuck in the cryo-chamber sleep.

The first three were confirmed dead, the next few showed signs of life, but possible brain damage. She kept checking. Dead, sick, dead, injured, dead.

A sickening crack echoed down the chamber, and water rushed in through open doors. Reina let out a scream, and Kiandoli ascended the stairs to the second level of the cryo-lab.

At last, she found one with all the right vital signs. She started pushing the buttons and reawakening the subject.

"Are you trying the save them?" Reina almost spat her last word. "You need to stop this!"

Reina grabbed her arm, and that was all she needed to invade her mind.

"I'm sorry, but you're not cleared to see this," Kiandoli said as she rewrote her mind again.

Reina crumpled to the floor like she was paralyzed from head to toe. She shook her head in panic, and Kiandoli calmly pushed her over the railings into the water. She stayed absolutely still, convinced that she was paralyzed from birth. She could not overcome the lack of connection to her muscles, and she sank to the bottom of the room and drowned

The man in the cryo-chamber coughed loudly and sat up in his seat. A thin red laser shot him in the head and be began to convulse.

Kiandoli opened the box and pulled out the object. A small, black book with gold letters inscribed on it. *Holy Bible.* She didn't know what to make of it, but she placed it firmly in the man's hands and the shaking stopped.

After a few seconds, he looked down at his hands. He patted around the body, feeling the skin, the hair. He stretched his neck, licked his teeth, and patted his slightly plump stomach.

"This body is pretty old. Couldn't you find a younger one?"

"Not in the time that I had, Doctor Pavarti." Kiandoli bowed as she said the word, and made a sweeping gesture to the flooding room.

"I see." Pavarti looked around. "Do you have a mirror, at least?"

Kiandoli shivered for a second. "Uh, Doctor, shouldn't we be trying to find a way out of here?"

"We either have a way out, or we don't." Pavarti said calmly. "Now, do you have a mirror?"

"There is the glass from the cryo-chamber." Kiandoli pointed.

Pavarti moved his head close to the glass, and strained his eyes. "And the portals?"

"Being activated by the enemy."

"Where do we stand, as a whole?"

"They have invaded Earth, Doctor Pavarti." Kiandoli said. "And Naprea has fallen."

"Just the ship, or the town as well?"

"I can only assume the town has fallen. We are at the bottom of the ocean. I don't know how."

"Oh, no. Not this body. I can't believe we kept this one here." Pavarti grabbed at the loose strands of hair at the front of his head. "Are you sure this is the only one available?"

"Yes Doctor. I checked all of the chambers. They were sick or dead."

"Very well." Pavarti opened a latch behind the cryo-chamber and a small hidden room was revealed. It was a dome, full of control panels that looked high tech and archaic at the same time. "We need to get things running then."

"What is this place?" Kiandoli walked through the opening behind Pavarti and rubbed her fingers across a control panel that was as foreign to her as anything she had ever seen.

"No, no, no!" He shouted as slammed one of the panels.

"What is it, doctor?"

"Everything is down." Pavarti picked up the Bible, looked at it and then chucked it across the room. "This is the last body. My links to key moments in Earth's past are severed. And my life memory has almost faded from overuse. This is my last chance to save humanity."

"Humanity, sir?" Kiandoli asked as she finally reached him.

"Yes, professor." Pavarti flipped a switch and a portal to their left appeared. It looked like some sort of dark portal. Different than the red she was used to. "We're all humans. And this was all to save us. Back on Earth... Something happened. A long time ago for us. And now I only have one shot to do it."

"Do what?" Kiandoli asked.

"Save us all." Pavarti walked to the dark portal. "I still have one safe house I can get to from here. If you would do me one more favor?"

"Anything." Kiandoli said.

"Press the big red button that just appeared on the screen after I've gone through this portal."

"What will it do?"

"Stop anybody else from mucking this up. At least for a little while." He walked through the dark portal and was gone.

Kiandoli pressed the red button. A timer activated, starting from ten. The timer reached zero and the room got intensely white.

End of book two.

The series isn't over! Want info on when the next installment comes out? Head over to Landerallen.com and sign up for the email list. You'll also receive bonus content like deleted scenes.

Copyright

Acknowledgements:

First of all, big thanks to my wife again, for putting up with my incessant drive to write. I wouldn't have accomplished any of this without you.

I also wanted to thank my beta readers for making this book the best it could possibly be!

Lisa Brazie
Meg Cousins
Rachell Zell
Jared Johnson
Kristen More
Rachel Zell
Brittany Gevas
Steve Allen

About the author
Lander is a writer (hence the novel in your hands) who lives with his wife and 3 children. He grew up on the northern coast of California, and now resides in the mountains of Utah.
Please visit me online at:
www.landerallen.com
facebook.com/thelanderallen
twitter.com/generallando